THE LIES
BOYS TELL

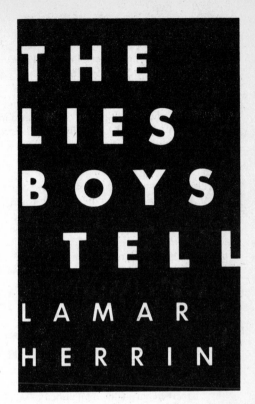

a novel

THE LIES BOYS TELL

LAMAR HERRIN

![HarperPerennial logo] **HarperPerennial**
A Division of HarperCollins*Publishers*

A hardcover edition of this book was published in
1991 by W. W. Norton & Company, Inc. It is here
reprinted by arrangement with W. W. Norton &
Company, Inc.

HarperCollins books may be purchased for
educational, business, or sales promotional use.
For information please write: Special Markets
Department, HarperCollins Publishers, Inc., 10 East
53rd Street, New York, NY 10022.

First HarperPerennial edition published 1992.

Designed by Margaret M. Wagner

Library of Congress Cataloging-in-Publication Data

Herrin, Lamar.
    The lies boys tell / Lamar Herrin. — 1st
HarperPerennial ed.
        p.   cm.
    ISBN 0-06-097506-7 (pbk.)
    I. Title.
    [PS3558.E754L5   1992]
813'.54—dc20   92-52635

92 93 94 95 96 RRD 10 9 8 7 6 5 4 3 2 1

In memory of my father,

Claud W. Herrin,

as promised

THIS book is the winner of the Associated Writing Programs Award for the Novel, 1990. AWP is a national nonprofit organization dedicated to serving American letters, writers, and programs of writing. AWP's headquarters are at Old Dominion University, Norfolk, Virginia.

———————

THE author wishes to thank the National Endowment for the Arts for its generous support during the writing of this novel.

PART ONE

THAT August afternoon Ed Reece dreamed that his older son, Larry, had already returned and stood on the front lawn taking practice swings with his father's driver. Pale and unsteady, Ed stood behind the living-room picture window, his navy-blue terry-cloth bathrobe hanging open. Then he found himself standing outside on the small exposed front porch. He saw that the whole bagful of his golf clubs was scattered on the lawn, and that Larry's swing, once so fluid and promising, had with the years of inactivity, of abandonment, of outright repudiation, grown stiff. He said, Don't take them if you're not going to play with them, but the sternness he may have intended in his voice turned to mush as his throat filled. Gently, as though he were laying his brittle-boned father to rest, Larry placed the driver on the grass. It was then as his son strode toward him that Ed became aware of neighbors parading past in their cars. Gil Conners, a frequent visitor and rummy partner during this period of convalescence, offered a smile of such fond fervor that it broadcast the extent of Ed's sentimental need to everyone on the street. Grimacing, Ed tried to wave Conners away, but the uplifted arm beckoned to Larry instead, who stepped up onto the porch and embraced his father. When Ed tried to force the two of them inside the house, Larry pulled back and kissed his father on the mouth, and for an instant, in spite of the parading cars, Ed was kissing his son as a very small boy, back when his upper lip was bare. Then he felt the hair, prickly and unclean around the mouth and chin, and over his son's shoulder he saw the discarded driver on the grass. It occurred to him that he had no one to leave his clubs to, and there at the dream's deepest penetration the thought of a once-prized set of golf clubs put anonymously up for sale seemed too poignant to bear. He believed he sobbed. Blocking his vision, disproportionately large, his son's face looked down on him full of ineffectual concern. Neither bare nor hairy, Larry's upper lip seemed cast now in an indeterminate shadow, and Ed moved to return his son's kiss only to be stopped by a succession of sobs. Take my clubs, take my clubs, he tried to whisper into his son's ear, but the sobs claimed his voice too.

It was then that he woke, gasping for breath.

He kept his eyes off his flaccid calves and his sunken ankles as he sat up on the edge of the bed. A pale green carpet extended from his bedroom down the hall to the bathroom door. In the bathroom he would have rugs as plush as fields of clover to stand on as he visited the lavatory and commode. But he remained where he was and, following doctor's directions, tried to blow a Ping-Pong ball to the top of a clear plastic tube, emptying his lungs so that he might enlarge them. Some days it seemed to work, and he felt as if he were stretching his lungs out to a dizzying sort of transparency—the residue of fifty years of cigarette smoking vanished in the act—but other days he saw the cloudiness in his x-rays clouding in behind each breath he blew and thought of a man losing ground to the hole he dug. The wrong image, he knew. He didn't need his wife, Sylvia, to tell him that. Or to add: If you can't make your mind work for you, for God's sake, don't let it work against you. He didn't need Sylvia to tell him what to do with his mind. He cleared it, and fighting eyestrain concentrated on that small fluttering ball, whose weight as he blew against it seemed the equal of the Titleists he played with.

Then, winded, he sat there, his spine bent, and with a desolate sort of honesty cleared his mind of golf too. Except for a few great shots and a few memorable rounds . . . but chips off bedrock were worse than no bedrock at all, and he got rid of those few great shots and memorable rounds too.

He tried to.

The fear of a complete evacuation caused him with a shame-faced smile to hold some things back. Then the smile vanished. In shame he tried to empty out. But the things he retained and those he managed to reject all seemed to obey some tidal rhythm of their own, and once more as the tide flowed full he'd feel full of the inessential, the jetsam and flotsam of his life. He'd carry this comfortable, overlarge, red-brick home inside himself then, carry his automobiles and his houseboat and his electric golf cart, carry his wholesale paper and janitorial supply business, carry his membership in the country club and various civic organizations and his rotating deaconship in the church, carry it all, all his worldly possessions and titles, as if in spite of his age and modest prosperity he still had to caddy for himself. Then when he had no room to draw another breath it would all flow out of him, sluggishly at first, but so quickly at the end that he'd experience a clean stab of fear that could be the onset of an unexperienced terror—and he'd seek to hold something back. Whatever it was—and it *might* be a simple golf shot, a long iron dead on the pin, or something peaceful and removed from his days on the road—would act to reverse the flow and he'd get it all back again.

It seemed that way.

He stood now in front of the bathroom mirror, smiling, even though the picture he saw there was composed of elongating bone and ashy, dead-skinned hollow. In spite of the chemotherapy treatments he still had most of his hair, but the wavy black had turned completely gray—the impersonal and ephemeral gray of mold. All the vigor of his hair had gone to the eyebrows—wild, visor-shaped tufts—but the eyes themselves showed the colorless smear of old steel. The color in his leanly cut cheeks had also vanished; he looked as if someone had dipped him in a dustbin. Even the pink of his tongue was coated. It fascinated him, this transformation he'd undergone, and in those moments of his emptying-out, as in those rarer moments of his musing detachment, he regarded his face in the mirror as a grotesque ghost, but comic, pathetic really if its intention was to scare, a Halloween mask left over from a previous year, domesticated by its year in a closet or at the bottom of a drawer.

A spray-softened jet of cold water fell into a gilded lavatory. He splashed his face, again and again, until the first sharp impression gave way to a numbing familiarity. With a monogrammed hand towel he dried off. Unlike his father, William Reece, victim first of the Depression and then of a heart attack at the age of sixty-five, Ed Reece had provided. The fruits of his industry were there to be seen—electric toothbrushes and gum massagers, electric hair rollers and dryers, curling irons, sunlamps, vibrators, a hip-belt contraption for Sylvia to lose weight, a showerhead with as many settings as a microwave oven. He stood over the commode, whose bowl was full of a deodorizing, disinfecting liquid, the doctored blue you see on some postcards, and peed into it. He'd provided so much that his breath came short when he thought of it—so there was a tissue dispenser built into the wall beside the commode for him to pluck tissues from to spit into. When he'd regained his breath he bent to use the flush—and even that, as an elegant option, he assumed he'd provided, the discreet murmur of water circulating through underground caverns—and started back down the hall to his bedroom. His wife, timing his passage perfectly, stood on the landing below the head of the stairs waiting for him, where he somehow knew she would be.

"Don't go back to bed, Ed," she said in the tone she seemed to have settled on as the one to see her through her husband's illness—firm and concerned, patient and slightly impersonal and unimploring, always ominous with some undivulged bit of wisdom.

He stopped and looked down at her. She wore coffee-colored slacks which bulged, a yellow blouse with a flower pattern in browns and orange. Her hair was cut short and the gray frosted. Of medium height, she seemed shorter, both because of the weight she'd put on in the last fifteen years and because the assertive stance she customarily took gave her the impression of being built close to the ground. With the weight had gone the last traces of the girl he'd married, and the face had assumed a matronly breadth. He thought of her as a well-adjusted woman—what the blue eyes had lost in vivacity they had gained in knowledgeable depth. And he loved and admired her—after all, she had never been seriously sick a day in her life.

"Why don't you get dressed and come down for a game of gin," she suggested pleasantly. "It's cool on the porch."

"It's cool in here," he reminded her. The central air conditioning too he had provided.

She shook her head. "There's a nice breeze. You'll like it."

"Sylvia . . ." He fixed her with a defiance he didn't feel, which went soft on him, threatened to trap him in guilt. "Looks like you'd want to take a break. Can't be much fun for you . . ."

"Don't talk like that, Ed," she warned him in a stern and supplicating whisper.

"I meant you *deserved* a break, that's all."

"Stop it, Ed."

"Yes, I will."

"Shall I help you get dressed?"

This time he looked at her humbly, gratefully, although that wasn't the way he felt either.

"But you don't need any help, do you, dear?"

"No," he said to please her. "I'll be down in a while." Then he continued on to his room.

She called after him, "Take your breathing pills at three."

He sat down again on the edge of his bed. The room had originally been Larry's, but they had long since papered over the cowboys with their spread lariats and the gamboling cows. Later the pennants had come down, high school class pictures and photos of proms. A framed citation from the Woodsmen of the World for excellence in American history had been removed. All the other academic awards Larry had been on the verge of winning until the Vietnam War had come along to unsettle his mind had, of course, never materialized, so Ed and Sylvia had been spared the decision of what to do with those unwon plaques, scrolls, and letters of praise. No, Ed did not want to get back into bed either. Another dream like the one he'd just had and he'd be in no condition to meet his son in the flesh—if flesh was what he came in, if he bothered to come at all.

The wire had read: "I am dying. It's a fact. It's all right. I have a favor to ask. Please come home." He'd recited the words in a nerveless voice, free of self-pity, to an operator who to match him had gone professionally cold. He pictured the Mexican Western Union messengers mounted on burros, bringing his son to bay beneath a towering cactus.

At three o'clock when Sylvia called a reminder up the stairway—"Ed?"—he was still seated on the edge of the bed. He took his pill.

MORE than ever now Russ resembled their mother. He stood with a tilt to the right in his shoulders, matching the inclination in the way he held his head, parted his hair, and the effect was of a boxer who over the years had gravitated toward the crouch he fought from. But his eyes were a clear candid hazel. The resemblance to their mother came from the spread of middle-aged flesh across the face, which gave to the small nose a beleaguered boyish quality, just as it gave to his mother's an expression of gamesmanship and distrust. With his gray slacks and assortment of pens in his shirt pocket and the thickness around the waist, he looked accounted for now, and settled in, this younger brother by thirteen months for whom Larry Reece had always stepped aside.

They managed an uncertain half-embrace.

Larry said, "He sent me a wire. He said he was dying."

"He is."

"I'm so goddamned sorry. So much of the shit between us seems pointless now. You get older."

"You don't show it. The hair maybe, but you always kept thin. Larry, you won't recognize him."

"Christ! Will they tell you how long?"

"The more they learn about cancer the less any two people seem to agree. If you listen to Mother he'll bury us all."

"She's . . .?"

"Equal to the task."

"And Nell? She was his baby."

"It's been hard on her. She comes when she can."

It was near noon. The air, smelling of Greyhound exhaust, stood motionless in a heavy white glare. Nevertheless, Larry breathed deeply and said, "I'd rather see Mother before I see him."

Russ drove him. At the Reece Paper and Janitorial Supply Company he telephoned his mother while Larry waited outside in the company pickup. During high school he and Russ had spelled each other in loading the big truck from the dock around at the side and delivering paper and cleaning supplies to most of the restaurants, motels, markets, dry cleaners, beauty parlors, and gas stations in the area. When they'd delivered together it had been Russ who'd had to wrestle the heaviest box out of the truck, Russ who'd had to unclip the invoice from the board for the customer to sign, and Larry who'd let him. Then for the first couple of years in college the competition between them seemed to have stopped. They'd had different majors, enthusiasms, spheres of influence marked out. It was Vietnam their last couple of years in college that forced them into opposing camps and that gave deeper resonance, greater dimensions, to their quarrels. What resonance, what dimensions? Everybody was looking for a fight then; luckily, Larry and Russ had each other. The Movement kept the Pentagon from invading North Vietnam, perhaps, but when the Americans withdrew it didn't keep the North Vietnamese from slaughtering the Cambodians and the Pentagon from turning its attention elsewhere and a whole host of cowardly accommodations from being made. He could make a fucking list. He didn't want to. He didn't want to find himself on it. Russ slid back into the pickup.

"I'll go stay with Dad and you and Mother can talk outside. She's surprised. She didn't expect Dad to wire you. She's afraid it means he's given up."

"Why didn't *you* wire me, Russ? Or Mother? Why did it have to be him?"

"I can't speak for her, although she'd probably say she didn't think it was time. For my part I was afraid I'd wire and you wouldn't come and . . ." Hesitating, he gave himself something to do, pulled out of the parking lot and up to the bypass around town, where he obeyed a four-way stop. It had been six years since they'd seen each other—actually longer than that, since during the brief and disastrous trip Larry had made from St. Louis to inform his parents about the separation, Russ had been away. His father had used the occasion, for the last time, and almost as a taunt, to offer his older son the other half of the business.

Face flushed, Russ now turned to his brother. ". . . and that would have been the end between us, Larry," he said.

He let Russ take him to his mother. The bypass was the artery which fed the town's motels, its fast-food franchises, its mini-malls, its more opulent car dealerships, and he barely observed it, aware that any change there would only mean a more slovenly sort of glitter. It had once divided the old part of town from the new, but the new had now come to resemble the old as younger generations had built in concentric semicircles around it. The limestone of the area had given way to stucco and brick and that to rough-planed, chicly weathered wood; his parents' spacious two-story home was made of brick. It was the house of his boyhood if not of his birth. It sat on a corner lot shaded by elms to the front and a high honey locust to the side, and was so deeply nestled in billowing green bush and door-side cedars that he thought of a house-encircling wreath, and would have thought so whether someone inside had been dying or not. Russ got out of the pickup and entered the house through a screened porch at the side. Larry remained seated, his suitcase like cargo behind him in the pickup's bed. He was being delivered. Would anyone accept delivery, would anyone sign?

Why should anyone?

There was, he realized then, a profound stillness about the house, about the street, and traveling back in concentric semicircles himself, a profound stillness, the second he'd gotten down from the bus and exposed himself to it, about the town.

When his mother slid in beside him she looked as though she had a list of items she wanted to negotiate. Then without a word, pulled back against the door like a disillusioned young date, she cried.

He knew nothing about comforting her. He could not remember having seen her cry. Her face converted into angry fissures where the tears squeezed out, and finally he took her by the plump upper arm.

She was older, he felt it in her flesh. "Mother, I don't know what to say," he said.

Tears continued to fall, but her voice was incongruously remote and dry. "There were so many happy times when you could have come." Then she looked up at him and her tone stiffened. "Or didn't you think we could be happy without you?"

"I assumed you were happy. I hoped you were."

"We *were*. Ed had almost retired. Did you know?"

"No . . . I don't know. I knew he was thinking about it. I knew it was time."

"You were so contemptuous, Larry. Of everything under the sun."

"It's true." He sighed, let himself sink against the door. "Don't put me in the position of having to defend myself. I'm too tired."

"If you started in Mexico you've come a long way. You *look* tired. You look older," she said, and the softening, the sympathy he heard at the bottom of her voice, stayed there. She turned the lid on it, closed the door.

Her wounded pride—when he was a boy there'd been times when the house had practically keened with it. She'd been a finer-featured woman then. As a presence she'd been able to enter a room and raise everything in it to a pitch of nervous expectancy while she remained outwardly calm. He could remember weeks, it seemed, when the tension in the house had been determined precisely by the degree to which she thought herself wronged.

But he couldn't trust his memory. The memory sat in judgment and bottom-heavy with the years might never get up and walk around an issue. She was a woman caring for a dying man, a woman who kept up, like a second job, a life of her own.

"I didn't know a thing," he said, "until he sent the wire. I'm not blaming you. If anything I'm blaming myself. Exactly what do the doctors say?"

"The good lung, the one they did not operate on, has emphysema—"

"I didn't know he'd had an operation."

"They cut out a lobe. For almost a year the cancer was in remission. Then last month they discovered it had come back. The oncologist says there's no use repeating the chemotherapy."

"Radiation?"

"We'd have to go to Nashville every day for twenty days, or stay there in a motel. Ed doesn't want to."

"Why?"

"I don't know. I don't know what he wants, maybe he'll tell you. The oncologist is against it anyway. With emphysema in the other lung it might make it impossible for him to breathe."

"Is he on oxygen?"

"He doesn't want that either."

"I see."

"The cancer's also spread into his lymph system, Larry."

"A year you say this has been going on?"

"They misdiagnosed an x-ray and told him he had walking pneumonia and to cut down on the smoking. Then they diagnosed it correctly and told him to quit smoking altogether. That's been a year next month."

"The time I've been in Mexico. Do you know how this makes me feel?"

"I don't want to know, not now. I want to take care of Ed. Later, if it's still important to you, you can tell me. You try to do things one at a time, one day at a time." She raised her open hand to the side of his face. She touched a beard of three days. Her hand smelled of a morning lotion, but its feel on his face was light and dry. It was the most provisional touch he'd ever known. "If he wired you it's because he wants to see you," she allowed. "Don't be shocked."

He left his mother and walked through the midday stillness up to the front porch. Entering the house he seemed to push out ahead of him a whole host of memories—just the times he had

turned that doorknob, for instance, stepped through that door—
and when the brief foyer offered him the living room to his right,
the dining room to his left, and the stairs straight ahead, nothing
of the life he'd lived here came any closer than the distant, measured presence of his mother's hand against his face. He moved to
the stairs and let Russell come down—smiling solemnly, a flat-
footedness in his gait, whispering that he'd be back, something
about Larry's suitcase but nothing about the man upstairs—
before he went up. There were two landings, and he paused at
each. A picture that had hung at the second—two blue-black
grackles feeding on a berry branch—was missing, and he felt the
pain of its removal as sharply as he would a toothache. Then the
pain was gone, gone so utterly he couldn't be sure what had
caused it or if he'd felt it in an instant's dreaming interlude or in
fact. He was exhausted. In the upstairs hall, for whatever reason—
and he would have a reason, the question most certainly an answer—he walked to his old room first. The door was ajar and he
didn't knock. As he had on countless occasions—when he'd
wanted to be alone, when he'd wanted to escape his brother and
pestering sister, his mother too, his father, for that matter, and on
his own, fearless and free, to grow up—he opened the door. The
man lying propped against the headboard of his bed didn't make a
move but flew at once to the center of his son's consciousness, his
son's life, where no one, Larry was forced to admit in that shatter-
ing instant, had been in years.

"Come inside," Ed Reece said, so calmly and deliberately he
might have been concluding the wire that had brought him his
son, "and close the door."

AND when Larry left some time later, Ed told himself, he was
tired. He'd been riding trains and buses for three days and could
barely hold his head up. He looked as sick as me. They'd talk when
he got some rest, and that's what he'd told his son, to go to bed, to
come back when he had his wits about him, and then they'd talk.
He'd asked him before he left to take a good look at his father so
that the next time they met he wouldn't be so tongue-tied. He'd

smiled when he'd said it, hoping some levity might bring his son back to life, but once Larry'd gone off with Russ and Sylvia had begun to move around again downstairs, he wondered if well-fed and rested Larry would be the same man. More than just tired, he'd seemed confused and uncertain, and more than that he seemed . . . "powerless" was the word Ed thought of. "Can I get you something?" "Can I bring you something up from down-stairs?" "What can I do?"—and there was something, but he asked the questions as though there were nothing he could do to alleviate his father's condition in the least, as though instead of asking a question he were making a confession, and the sense of powerlessness he gave off then, Ed suspected, was not to be con-fused with the exhaustion of a three-day trip.

The beard and the mustache were gone, but that was not the son he had wanted to call back.

As he recalled it, Russ that afternoon had been off at the bank overseeing the final details on a loan they'd taken out to replace the forklift and one of the trucks. From inside his office Ed had heard May and Henry out at the counter exchange exclamations of surprise, and May say, with that dreamy sweetness with which she anticipated all sentimental occasions, "Won't Ed be pleased to see you." Larry's manner as he entered his father's office was what his father wanted to recall, and precisely, because it was precisely the Larry he'd hoped to see enter his bedroom today. He had not been contrite, tentative, or even subdued. He had, on that afternoon six years ago, been still, and in that stillness there'd been an air of something momentous that had both frightened Ed and held him admiringly to the spot. He'd thought his son in that moment capable of some measured sort of outrage. They'd ex-changed greetings, handshakes, and incidental chatter, but Larry hadn't moved, not really; the blue eyes were full of an electrical intensity, yet they were at the center of that stillness. It seemed anticlimactic now to recall that all Larry had come to announce was his separation from Connie, although at the time it had hurt Ed badly. His daughter-in-law combined charm and strength of character in a way that he had never known before and that made what some people considered her plainness beautiful. He hated to lose her from the family. He worried about his grandchildren, Lisa and Jeff, barely school-age then. Yet there was more to his son's manner—his presence—than that, and whatever it was made the desertion of family, the putting in peril of two young children, seem insignificant compared to what he might be capable of.

Ed had never forgotten that moment. Afterward, of course, they had argued, dully, it seemed, and by rote, before his son had stomped past a stunned and tearful May and out the door. The argument was no more memorable than any number they'd had while Larry was in high school, mostly having to do with Larry's lack of initiative, which Ed came to see more clearly as a sort of exclusiveness and snobbishness, especially when Russell wanted something and went after it. If it was his to give up, Larry did, with an air of superiority Ed disliked, and that made his brother seem like a bullheaded fool. There'd been a girl they'd both dated. A number of the arguments had had to do with the family car, a few with enterprising schemes to make money. They'd gotten over that, though. By the time they'd both gone off to college the air in the house had cleared. And as children they had always been close, so close that in Ed's memory of them now he didn't really bother to tell them apart. He'd return from a week on the road and whether it was Larry there to greet him, or Russ, or both, made little difference, since together they constituted some inexhaustible bounty of sonship, his boys.

They'd lived in central Illinois then. Ed traveled three states selling wholesale to retailers the very paper bags he would include among his own stock when he opened his store. On occasional short two- or three-day trips he'd take either Larry or Russell with him, and the blurring between them was at its height when he'd try to remember who it was he told what on which trip, just who was seated beside him as Galesburg passed by, or Des Moines, or Terre Haute.

There was such a sunny vastness to his thinking then. The land was flat. In those Mississippi and Ohio river basins the soil, like his life then, was too rich to be true. Soybeans and wheat and corn and peaceful towns grew out of it, and he traveled its uncomplicated two-lane roads without a thought to the interstates that would soon rise facelessly above it. He'd fill up his tank every hour or so and stretch his legs. Motels were motor courts then, sometimes cabins scattered out by a pond. At night he'd smell, besides the pininess of the room's woodwork, the fresh fragrant chill of the water, and if the wind was right he'd get the smell of water charged with the animal richness of corn. He'd hear frogs, crickets, cicadas, and depending on the wind, the throaty chorusing of corn, and beside him, in the other bed, on the occasion of one of those two- or three-day trips, the breathing of his son, mild and musically suspended, either Larry's or Russell's, it didn't matter and he didn't know.

So why did he leave the road and go into business on his own? He didn't know that either—although of course he did. He grew up. It was no explanation until he took the time and trouble to make it one, so he could simply say that his sons began to insist on their differences.

He taught Larry to play golf, but Russell surprised him by showing no interest. Instead he wanted to caddy. Later when Russell had to outdo his brother in everything and Larry made an almost stylish practice of allowing himself to be outdone, none of those moments out on the course with Russell content to carry his father's bag and with Larry at work on his swing would have been possible. But for two or three years there Ed had his sons apart in his mind and not yet at war. Russell learned how to mark wild shots in the rough, something about club selection, and where to leave the bags off the green. He became adept at the much more delicate task of keeping his feet out of each putter's path while tending the pin. Gradually, the picture of a boy who would grow into a man with a respect, perhaps even a passion, for a job well done began to form in Ed's mind. When his brother played well Russell seemed particularly pleased, since even then, with a remarkable and unservile canniness of judgment, he understood he'd done his best job when the scores remained low. And it was true, Larry had shot in the seventies while still in junior high. But it wasn't the low scores that kept Larry coming back for more (until with an excoriating self-reproach he would sell his clubs, as if they'd turned verminous in his hands). It was the execution of the individual shot, it was the feel of the long woods flaring up the forearms, the crisp bite of the irons lifting out of the fairway grass, the soaring of the white ball, the arc, the distance—perhaps that's all it was, Ed thought, just the distance you could put between yourself and your next shot so that walking up to it you might for a moment believe that the entire wealth of your life lay out ahead.

It was painful to think of it now—painful because it had about it a gardenlike aura of all things preserved in their loss—but Ed had a memory of his son playing three or four holes out ahead of the foursome he and his caddying son formed a part of. Of his last golfing buddies perhaps only Gil Conners, only Cochise, had been around then—he didn't know, couldn't remember. That was surely because whether waiting on the tee to drive, or on the fairway for his short iron to the green, or on the green for his turn to putt, he'd had his eye out ahead on his son. It was an early summer evening (he suspected he'd doctored the memory, composed perhaps of many memories, but what was to be done?), and as shadows stretched out over the rolling fairways the green grass came alive at its depth. It looked like beautifully molded water then, and upon it walked his son, alone, with the swing Ed had taught him, lifting that ball clean and deep into the evening air. He remembered gasping. But how could he have gasped with somebody like Charley Martin there wisecracking, "Shit, Reece, my back's sore from carrying you around this nine," or maybe that womanizing lush Hank Curry attributing Ed's putting miseries that day to "the touch of a blacksmith"? But he *had* gasped, because even then—and that had to have been twenty-five years ago—he must have known that beauty like that came at a cost he would one day have to pay, and that his son, as he tempted Ed's eye, was lost to him forever, and that finally it wasn't his son he was seeing and living through anyway but himself, that he was watching himself stray like a child out onto the great watery breast of that beauty, and that he was as lost as his son.

He understood then why men chose to play golf in foursomes, and why he should count himself lucky if one of his sons preferred to carry his bag.

"TAKE a look in the kitchen."

Larry did as he was told. A mess of crappie had been thrown down on the counter beside the sink with a few brightly marked bluegill mixed in. The crappie, a fast-paling gray-green, had already been beheaded and cleaned. The fish smell contributed to the queasiness in his stomach, and in his head, like a weather system, an oppressive dullness had settled in. He left the kitchen and walked back into the den. His father, dressed in a blue golfing shirt with an insignia of crossed clubs over the pocket, was playing gin rummy with Gil Conners. The short-sleeved shirt revealed the flaccid forearms and frail wrists. When Larry allowed himself to look closely, there was an astonishing delicacy about his father's flesh, the wrinkles there, over the attenuated muscle, intricately patterned like lace. But he couldn't look long. Turning to Conners, who had a bibulous face, rosy dollops at the cheeks, nose, and chin, he said, "Quite a string."

"Still little," Conners replied, considering his cards and then spreading a run of three spades. "Here about the end of next month the slab crappie be comin' back."

"That it, or you gonna put down those hearts you got and let me go out on you?"

Ed knew Conners held the four, five, and six of hearts, but he held the three and seven, which Conners, or Cochise as they called him on the golf course because of all the skins he took, probably realized, so he would only put his hearts down once he had his other run made.

"Now if I moved this over there . . ." Conners drawled, rearranging his cards for show. Then looking up at Larry he casually spread the rest of his hand on the table and said, "Nice to have you back, son."

Ed began totaling up his lost points. "Can't get me on the golf course," he grumbled, "so he comes over here and barges his way in. Show him your scalping knife, Cochise."

"Used it to clean all those fish with, Slugger. Caught me another one right here."

Then his father's oldest friend stood, and Larry saw the size of the gut that had piled up at the beltless waist of the raspberry-red slacks. Gil Conners he remembered as being almost as lean as his father, who in Conners's company could only look more gaunt and ashen, even if he did play cards with a trace of his old exasperated vigor.

"Here, sit down, son, and take my place."

And when Gil Conners showed himself out and Larry submissively did as he was told, Ed knew that this would have to stop. Ten years ago Larry would have hesitated just enough to alert his father to the subtle defiance in his mood, and then would have lowered himself into the chair with a disdain that would not have shown on his face so much as in the arrogant slant of the shoulders and in the scornful and incidental skill with which he shuffled and dealt the cards. Body language, they called it, and Larry's used to say that Ed and his friends were perfectly content to play gin rummy and golf while Rome burned, or as the case was then, Vietnam.

"Didn't think you liked to play gin," Ed said.

"Sure . . . if you want."

"Me? I'd rather take a walk."

He couldn't decide whether to assist his father as he got out of his chair and walked down the porch steps and out onto the street, where there was no sidewalk since people in this neighborhood preferred to move about in cars, or not, and so did not touch him but held an arm in readiness in case he should falter. In a hazy midmorning heat, Ed Reece walked for almost three blocks, past houses larger and set back on more spacious grounds than his; during this time he worked on his breathing and on concealing the pain in his chest, which Larry noticed by the way his father shied back from it when it hit. It gave to his walk a brittle, hollow-chested appearance, but it didn't stop him until three blocks later when the street swung around a small park. There he sat on a bench.

"You feeling better now? 'D you get some rest?"

The question caught Larry by surprise—it touched and shamed him, to be asked how *he* felt. He'd slept, eaten, and slept again, the guest of his brother and sister-in-law, Jeannie. He'd renewed acquaintances with two nieces and a nephew, different people now. But he'd also drunk three stiff shots of bourbon to his brother's beer and, groggily, had said some things that he might have liked to take back. He mumbled, "Huh?"

"I said—"

"No, I heard you, Dad. Don't waste . . ." He hesitated, realizing he would have to learn how to talk to his father now, learn what would help or hurt him to hear, and he had no idea how long it would take. "I'm all right. How about you?"

"I can go farther than this if I want to."

That sounded like one of his children's boasts, and Larry caught himself grinning paternal encouragement, wondering if this might be one of the ways they would find to communicate. "Anytime you want," he said.

"I'd rather talk," and now, although the voice itself was hoarse and unsteady, its tone was authoritative.

"Okay, Dad."

"I want to ask you a favor . . ."

"You mentioned it in the telegram."

"And I want you to say yes."

His father paused. Under the blue bill of his golfing cap, with that same crossed-club insignia stitched onto the front, the sickly white face and the tarnished eyes made a strong silent appeal.

"Now?" Larry said.

"Now," his father repeated. "I can't ask anyone else."

He nodded. "It's why I came back."

"I want you to take me away from here."

"Yes?" he said, knowing he hadn't heard enough to know what he'd heard.

"I want you to take a check for eleven thousand dollars I'm going to give you," his father said, speaking to him as deliberately as if *he* were addressing a child, "and I want you to walk over to the bypass and cash it in the First National branch office they got over there. It's an account your mother doesn't know about. Then I want you to take that money and walk downtown with it, and at Cushman's Dodge on Sixth Street I want you to buy that green van they got out in the lot. If the green one's gone, buy any color you want. Get it serviced and get it put in your name. Then I want you to drive out of there with it and take it out on the road. Ride out the kinks, son. Can you do that?"

He'd used up his breath and he sat there in the patchy shade of a catalpa tree trying to get it back while Larry puzzled over the instructions he'd been given. He looked puzzled, on alert, a bit breathless himself, but uneasy, somehow embarrassed, and Ed knew he'd seen that look on his son's face before. It was the boy's look in his first brushes with the adult world; it might have been, he realized with sudden tenderness, the expression Larry had worn when his father had first talked to him about sex and brought all the wild surmises in his head into sobering focus.

"Yes, I can do that," Larry declared cautiously. "Take you where, Dad?"

"I already told you—away from here."

"But where . . . is it some clinic, some place like Rochester you've got in mind?"

"Home."

"Home? I don't understand. You are home."

For a long moment Ed Reece regarded his son. Then he shook his head. He shook it slowly, with an air of grievous conviction, his eyes still on his son's. Then his whole body began to shake, and alarmed, Larry reached out for him.

"Dad?"

"I'm countin' on you to know what I mean, Larry," Ed uttered in a hush.

"Okay, Dad." Larry waited until the bone and stringy muscle he held in a steadying grip had gone still, then lowered his hand.

"I'd never mention this to your mother or Russ. It's not the sort of thing I could tell Nell."

Turning away in the direction of a large brick house, Ed worked on his breathing, taking his breaths in short measured pulses, as though he could store them. The house, in the grand style with white columns and shaded sweeping drive, belonged to the Robert Meyerses, friends of theirs for years.

"Tell *me*," Larry quietly volunteered.

Ed intended to, and turning back to his son he let a car go by—from the sound of the pinging valves Marge Caldwell's beloved bug, except that crazy Marge would have stopped and screamed—as though to give them privacy. But he hesitated, and he didn't know why. Larry moved closer on the bench.

"Dad?" he inquired.

A moment later he added, "It's all right."

And in a sort of fear-shaken sigh Ed heard himself answer, "No, it's not all right." Then as he seemed to reach into his extremities for breath, as the sigh threatened to become an evacuation, he heard himself go on. "Something's wrong. I can't tell you much about it, but something's missing. I want you to do me this favor. Your mother and brother can't know anything about it, 'cause the second they do they'll decide I'm crazy and find some way to have me stopped. For *you* to think I'm crazy will take some nerve after all the years you've been running wild."

Larry lowered his head. "Go on," he said.

"It's an idea I've got. I'm not going to try to justify it because it probably can't be done. That's why I wanted you to say yes before you had a chance to say no. I want you to take me away from here. Don't think I don't love your mother, because I do, I love Russ and Nell, and what I've got against Welborne, Kentucky, I could write on the back of a postage stamp. But it hasn't been enough,

Larry, and I can't wait anymore. Matter of fact, I seem to recall you telling me it wouldn't be."

"Me?"

"How many times d'you tell me this wasn't the life—or was that just something you heard somebody say who wanted to burn it all down?"

"That was back then," Larry insisted quietly.

" 'Inciting to riot,' if you got up and said it in front of a bunch of antiwar protesters—wasn't that the charge?"

"One of them."

"I don't want to burn it down. I want . . ." But he stopped when it was clear he wanted to continue. His breath came short. He looked at his son almost fiercely, with sudden color in his face—did his father somehow expect Larry to finish for him? Then Ed finished for himself, in brief propulsive whispers: "I want to go home. D'you understand? I want to die in the house where I was born. I want you to drive me there."

"There? You mean . . ." He'd even forgotten the name.

"Chumleyville, Alabama," his father declared, still whispering.

Larry barely remembered the town. He remembered spots in it clearly where he and his brother had sought some coolness during occasional trips in the dead of summer. A creek they had dammed, a cellar and horse-smelling shed they'd explored the dark back reaches of . . . but not the town. The Reeces had come from there, and his mother's family had passed through long enough to allow Ed and Sylvia to meet and marry, but of the old folks his memory was even more shadowy, perhaps not even the result of his own experience so much as the photographs he'd been shown, the stories he'd been told. At any rate, except for a single aunt they were all gone now. The Reeces were not long-lived.

"You're saying you want the two of us . . ."

"It's the only way I see to make any sense of it. I've got to come back where I started. Someone's got to take me there."

Keenly attentive, but as though at the center of a daze, Larry said, "And you don't want Mother and Russ and Nell to know?"

"Do you think they'd understand?"

"They might."

"And agree to it. Leave here . . . close up the business."

"I don't know."

"Emma's got the bed in Savannah. She's got it stored."

"What bed?"

"I want the bed. I remember when I was a little boy I thought it was as big and high as a boat."

"The bed you were born in? You intend to go to Savannah first, and try to talk Emma into . . ."

"The house is still standing, or it was two years ago. I was born in the front bedroom. If people are living there now we'll have to pay them enough to leave."

"No, I don't think they will."

"They will if we pay them enough."

"I mean I don't think Mother, Russ, and Nell will agree to it."

His father paused, and then with a gentle reluctant rocking motion he shook his head. "It's why I wired you to come back," he said.

Mouthing, not really speaking the words, Larry looked at his father and repeated, "You want to die in the bed in the room in the house where you were born," and only at that moment seemed to understand the comical pathos and the sweetness and despair that underlay the desire, and said, grieving deeply now, as the tears rolled out, "Oh, Dad!"

And Ed watched his son cry, his head bent and the tears falling freely onto his pants leg. The fine blond hair was thinning at the crown, where the pink scalp showed through, and he could imagine the blistering force of the Mexican sun on his son's scalp—but not this. That Larry would seize on the idea, or laugh at it, or even try to improve on it—he had imagined all these possibilities, but not these shaking shoulders and public tears. They embarrassed him. He sat back from them as though from some sort of aberration, and then moved by an impulse of grief and caring as generous as his son's placed his withered hand on Larry's knee. "You're not going to back out on me now, are you, buddy?" he said.

Larry shook his lowered head, then in a voice momentarily

peaceful and purged and somehow impersonal, Ed thought, he said, *"This* is your home now, Dad. These are the people who care for you and will want to be with you when you need them the most. They're here. No one's down there in Chumleyville. We've got no family left there. There may be some high school friends, but put them all together and they don't add up to the friend that Gil Conners has been. That house down there—you haven't been in it since you were a boy. I don't think I've ever seen it. It's really not part of your life anymore. You've lived here, right up that street for . . . how long, Dad?"

"You can count, Larry. More than twenty-five years."

"I'm not sure you can do this to Mother, or to Russ and Nell."

"You're not sure *you* can."

"All right, I'm not sure *I* can. I'm sorry, Dad. I wish I could tell you to forget all I've just said. I have no idea what you're going through. This could be a dream. It's not a joke. It might even be an answer . . ." An unworthy but bitterly plausible thought occurred to him, and since he was speaking his thoughts he said, "It's not some sort of revenge you've concocted to get back at me, is it, Dad?"

With his hand still on his son's knee Ed could feel a jitteriness, like a run of nerves, play out under his touch. He feared Larry was about to enter that state of powerlessness he'd arrived in the day before. These last disjointed utterances were like the feeble bursts of a battery going cold. "If you want to know the truth, I've thought about you a lot these last few years. In your letters I never thought you wrote what you were really doing, so I had to make up what you were too embarrassed to tell. Or, because you were careless or in a hurry, what you just didn't bother to tell. California, New Mexico, Texas—I'd never been out there, but I followed you around. I always enjoyed reading maps and I sort of charted your course. When you got to Mexico I got sick, and the sicker I got the more we seemed to collaborate, until, between the two of us, we came up with the idea for this trip."

"Between the two of us?" Larry's mouth hung open.

"I think you owe me this, son."

"Of course I owe you, I owe you a lot. But I also owe Mother . . ."

"After you settle up with me you can settle up with her."

"Dad, you belong with your family now! Why do you think I came back?"

And he cut his son off, not with sharpness but with a grim, flat croak. "I told you—I can't justify this. It's not even something you can talk about for long. I wanna go back. It's all I can think about anymore. I gotta stop where I started. You can call me crazy if you want to—I don't care about that. Everybody else will. But everybody else isn't dying."

As though he'd received a slap across the face, or a message from a decaying tooth, or a mortal pain in the gut, his son winced.

"I've done what I thought I should. I married the girl I proposed to. I raised you and Russ and Nell, put a roof over your heads and everything in your hands you could find a use for, built up a business that'll keep us going for a while, sooner or later did what I set out to, even had the time to horse around and play my share of golf. All I can say now is that it hasn't been enough."

"Is it ever for anybody?" Larry wondered out loud.

"It's *me* we're talking about," his father upbraided him, a quick congested expulsion for which he knew he would pay the price. It left him gasping. When he'd recovered he tried to wave an arm at the houses out toward his right. That brought the pain ripping into his chest. Through it he said, "You wanna do a survey? Ask Bob Meyers if it's been enough. Next door to him Chuck Wiley will talk your head off. Ask him. I hope it has. I don't wish what I'm going through on anybody. You know what it's like, son? It's like stepping through a false bottom. It's like stepping on water you thought was solid ground. You ever lie at the bottom of a swimming pool and look up at the surface? That's what it's like, except you haven't got anything solid to lie on. You just float. You can see everything that was part of your life up on that surface— you can even see yourself—but none of that's real. It's like a big sheet of tinsel shaking up there. But where are you? That's the real question. You're where you can see up to that shiny surface you stepped through, but the truth is you don't know where you are. That's 'cause you're nowhere, son."

"And you want somewhere to go," Larry said. Out of an intimate, speculative quiet, his voice seemed to take over for his father's.

"Yes."

"You feel stranded."

"Between no place and no place."

"And you want a destination."

"Yes."

"You want a destination so badly it's all that matters, it's all that's real."

"Someplace to be."

"And if you lie down in that bed in that house in Chumleyville you think you might find it?"

"I don't know. It'd be someplace. That's all I can tell you, son."

"I understand."

"And I can count on you?"

"Yes."

"Between the two of us?"

"There's nobody else to tell."

HE felt in the presence of strong forces, none of which originated with him. The green Dodge van, which he test-drove out along the interstate, was one of them. It rode heavy and high and squarish and smooth—he was used to underpowered compact cars. It set him up over the front axle where he could feel the width of the wheels. Behind him he was aware of an emptiness, a sense of exaggerated space, as though he sat with his back to a proscenium stage or the mouth of a cave. The smell of its newness hung there. From around the dash and the vinyl upholstery and the factory-glued ceiling panels came a prickly, sweetish, meretricious odor, but the smell out of the back was deep-lunged and vaster and not always there when he drew a breath. The van had cost just over nine thousand dollars; in his hip pocket he had nearly two thousand dollars in hundred-dollar and fifty-dollar bills—and that was another force.

His father had asked him to ride out the kinks.

He chose the interstate, which once past the exit areas looked onto cornfields and dense squares of trees and choppy, browned pastureland with run-off ponds for cattle in the folds. Then ten miles outside of town he got off the interstate and tested the van on a county road built down in among those twisting folds and up and down those choppy hills. The van held the curves, it accelerated up the hills, and he ran through a checklist of performance points—transmission, brakes, shocks, steering tightness—with his mind somewhere else. He didn't know where. He saw yards full of rusting disabled machines and small clapboard houses, held together by spit. He couldn't understand why someone didn't paint a wall or drive a nail or two, or why anyone would choose to live here—he saw brand-new brick bungalows, the mortar proudly retouched with white paint. There were plaster animals in these yards, waddling ducks, flamingos on stilts. The grass, three sides surrounded by a wilderness of weeds, was cut to the bristly nub. The van took him past crossroad stores covered with outdated tin signs, past plain fundamentalist churches, past weather-grayed barns and sheds that seemed to grow out of the land like outcroppings of rock. The real limestone outcroppings he could barely see—they were overgrown with blackberry bushes—but he knew they were there. The entire area was pitted with sinkholes and honeycombed with caves. As a boy he'd heard stories of cows and horses stepping past that brambly lip and plunging to their deaths. Houses, he'd heard, had fallen through the earth's crust. The murdered and the misunderstood had disappeared. Innumerable and darkly variable, the tales told a town boy of the terrible doings out beyond the last suburb.

There were no kinks. Soon the county road intersected a state road and he took it back toward the interstate. At the interstate underpass he ran into an agglomeration of franchise restaurants and motels. For a moment, running that avenue of towering signs and low-slung sameness, he felt exactly as if he were coming down from an acid trip and that the extraordinary events of the last three hours had reached the moment of their brutal and bloodless impoverishment, *here,* caught between a Ramada Inn and a Bob Evans Down on the Farm. It was the reason he'd long since given up acid and contented himself with pot and an occasional pipe of hashish. Half a mile farther into town and he'd already gotten used to the world as he found it. A stoplight beyond that—the Greenhaven Mall was coming up on the left—and once again he wanted to know why.

And what? What did his father really have in mind? And how? How was he going to help him and still account to the rest of his family? He didn't know. Why didn't he? In defense he could only say he couldn't think clearly. It was as if he'd woken up from a dream (or come down from a high—he'd give himself a likeness, not an explanation) and found himself in another's dream, whose rhythms and internal logic he didn't know but whose motive force made absurdly satisfying sense: to come full circle, the very bed, room, house, and town: the same mothering darkness.

And how the fuck could anyone think *this* was enough?

He touched his full wallet. At the last of the Greenhaven Mall entrances he pulled in and parked the van as close as he could to JC Penney's door. The store took on weight as he moved back through it: from women's lingerie, to children's clothes, to men's shoes and suits, to sporting goods, to hardware and home repairs. In the back he found the beds. The girl who attended him was young, but she wore her hair in the sticky yellow thatch of middle age. "We got a sale on Serta-Sleep. You buy the mattress and save fifty dollars on the box springs." The springs sprang in her loosely tuned drawl, and he said he'd take a Serta-Sleep single-bed mattress by itself. After he'd counted eighty-nine dollars into her outheld hand, she showed him the loading dock in back where he could pick the mattress up. When two snickering high school boys had uncrated it and loaded it in back, the mattress glowed a watery silver-gray in the shadows of the van, and he remembered his father's image for the look of that distance his disease had put between him and everything else in the world, including himself. He had that shimmering surface behind him now as he drove.

At a gas station just out of town he filled the van up, then talked the attendant out of ten dollars' worth of change. From an outside phone booth he called first Savannah, Georgia, information, then the number of his Aunt Emma.

She said, "Larry? Why, Larry! Sakes alive!" and from the

sound of her voice he knew that she had the bed, would never sell it or allow it to come to harm. He might even have known a bit more about why his father wanted to lie down in it.

But he asked her anyway. "Aunt Emma, Dad's been talking to me about the old family bed, he says the bed he was born in."

There was a long pause. With the noise of traffic rushing by outside he wasn't sure she'd heard, or if she heard if she remembered. But she'd been collecting her emotions. Her voice had a rueful, lilting sweetness to it. "Larry, how's he getting along? How is my Ed?"

"He's sick, Emma. You know that. It's hard to say."

"He's the baby. There's no call for him to get sick so soon."

"I know. How are you, Emma?"

"I'm holding my own. If I didn't suffer from this arthritis so, wouldn't nothing in the world stop me from coming up there to see y'all."

"Do you still have that bed, Emma?"

There was another pause, briefer and brighter. "That was Mama and Papa's bed. Ed and I were born in that bed."

"That's what he tells me. Do you have it there in Savannah?"

"Right up in the attic. When Louise died I brought all her things down here, doncha know. It was her bed. She had it after caring for Mama all those years."

"I might come for it for a while—would you mind?"

The pause this time was followed by a wistful exclamation. "Larry, dear Louise passed away in that bed!"

He didn't ask the question again.

He left the van well down the block from his parents' house. Another car—not his mother's Buick—was parked in their drive, and on the screened porch, leafing through one of her mother's *Better Homes and Gardens,* he found his sister, Nell. Age had marked out Russ and his wife, overtaken his mother and transformed his father, and in six years his nephew and two nieces had undergone a rank and weedy growth, but his little sister stood before him now in full possession of her glamour, gold jewelry at the ears, fingers, and wrists, a silk blouse, rose-mallow, parted at the neck. They embraced. He said, "I've missed you, Nell," and it was true, although her years as a woman—she'd married an insurance executive and gone to live among the elite of the state in Lexington—were mostly a blank to him.

"You're thin," she said, feeling him over the back. "This time you've got to stay awhile."

He pulled back to look down at her. Her auburn hair held the body and wave he remembered, and this in spite of the frenetic changes in hair style since he'd seen her. Her makeup had been so skillfully applied that passing over it the tears she'd shed for him had left only the lightest of tracks. "Thanks for coming down," he said.

She gave him a fond, reproving smile. "I thought maybe you'd come to see me first. Even when you couldn't stand the sight of any of us, you and I somehow got along. Didn't we, Larry?"

"He wired, Nell."

"Russ told me."

"But I would have come to see you, you know that. You were the peacemaker. In a family like ours I never understood where you got all that peace."

"By not trying to compete with you and Russ, I guess. I sat still and let things come to me."

"Things have."

"That's not much of a philosophy of life, is it?"

"Compared to whose?"

"I love you, Larry," she reminded him, and it brought to his lips a weak imitation of his big brother's grin, all his sentimental fondness for her bunched up to one side of his mouth.

"Dad?" he said.

"Asleep."

"And mother?"

"She went to the mall. Jeannie's got the kids at the club."

"Kids? Are Alan and Shelley with you?"

"I brought Shelley down. Alan's got a Junior Tennis tournament. Ron'll bring him later this week."

"And how is Ron?"

"Ron's fine. And how are Lisa and Jeff?"

He hesitated, went on to claim that his children too were fine, and in all likelihood they were, but she hadn't bought it. With that same reproving smile she asked him to sit beside her on the glider. She settled herself, crossed a leg. The poise she took on then, although in keeping with the expensive cream-colored traveling suit she wore and the expensive car she drove, seemed alien and vaguely threatening to him.

"Larry, could we talk about something?"

He too crossed a leg.

"This is not an easy thing to say," she warned him. Her reluctance was real and precisely measured—she held a pause. "The doctors don't think that Dad will make it. That's their diagnosis, and we don't have to accept it. They've misdiagnosed his condition before. But we have to take it into consideration. He's sick, Larry."

"I know, Nell."

She studied him, she searched him, eyes a translucent blue over a glinting backdrop of gray. "Maybe nothing's going to work a miracle, but I have to say what I think, Larry. He's always wanted you to come back—you know that, don't you? If he thought you'd come back to stay, it *might* make a difference." He'd already started to turn away—his face was tingling—when she called him back. "Larry, you'd have to mean it. He'd know if you weren't telling the truth."

"He knows already. There's nothing for me to do here, Nell."

"There's a *lot* you could do. You're intelligent." She said it with an air of confirmation, as though a long-rumored state of affairs had just been borne out. "If you didn't want to go in with Russ at the store there are any number of men in this town who would love to have you work for them."

"I'm thirty-nine, Nell."

"That's just what I mean. It's time, Larry. You know it's time. Your kids need to have a place where they can visit their father. They at least need to know where their father is."

"They know where I am," he lied. It had been more than a year since he'd seen them. They knew Mexico.

"They need a man's influence. I can't imagine what Shelley

and Alan would be like without their father. Is Connie living with anybody now?"

"Yes, not a man," he said.

"Oh?"

"A friend."

"Still in St. Louis?"

"More or less . . . close by."

She repositioned herself, crossing the other leg and plucking the stretched fabric free at the knee. The porch caught a bit of breeze, but the combined effect of the overhanging foliage and the screened-off light was soporific. "You've got nowhere to go, Larry, and here at least you *could* do Dad some good. Will you think about it?"

"Find me something to do here that won't have me climbing the walls and tearing down the last bit of morale that Dad has left and, sure, I'll think about it."

"If you'll be patient . . ."

"In Mexico I watched the faithful on Good Friday flagellating themselves from a cross in the desert on into one of the western world's goriest churches. Find me something that won't have me flagellating myself on the streets of Welborne, Kentucky."

"Larry, please don't take it like that. Think of Dad."

"I didn't tell you, Nell. I called Aunt Emma. She's the last one left. I thought she should know how Dad was getting along."

"Did you tell her?"

"I . . ." He felt himself relent. Only it wasn't out of fondness for his sister. It was like letting ten years of soured hopes and ripened disillusions take on weight in him and sink. He gave in and they centered themselves in his gut. He struggled to get out of the glider. "I just told her what she knew, that he was sick. She said she was holding her own."

He stepped over to his sister and leaned in under the wave of her hair, kissing her cheek, which was moist and sweet, the sweetness a commingling of many odors, none of which struck him in that moment as womanly.

"Will you promise to think about it?"

He nodded. "I'll go up now and see Dad."

He found his father awake with no trace of sleep in eyes that though murky and lidded by small drooping folds of flesh seemed extraordinarily alert to him now. "Did you buy it?" he asked.

Larry showed him the keys.

A walk-in closet ran the length of the wall against which the head of the bed rested, and his father motioned him to look. Larry knew where to look—back behind hanging clothes and stored boxes he'd hidden things there as a boy. He'd run through a wire for a pump-lamp he'd made in Industrial Arts and hidden himself. So he knew where to look and he even knew what he would find. He even knew which one—pushing aside clothes and suit bags and stepping back into that closet he was reminded once more that he lived now in another's dream. It gave him a sort of pre-science. He saw the old battered brown Samsonite his father had saved from his days on the road, and smelled in an olfactory mem-ory perhaps keener than the originating moment itself the odor of shaving cream and Vicks VapoRub that always filled the room when his father opened his suitcase on those weekends he re-turned home and presented his sons—the two of them—with small gifts. He'd kept it all this time. Without hefting it Larry understood it was packed.

He stepped out of the closet.

A STREETLIGHT burned at the corner. At two in the morning Ed Reece stood in the shadows of the garage, the suitcase he'd packed and then carried himself down the stairs at his feet. At first the leather handle, after two decades of disuse, had been hard and dry to his touch, but his hand had soon found its familiar fit, and it was part of his lifetime he'd carried down the stairs, managing it without great strain, for those had been the buoyant years. Except for obvious sentimental reasons he had no idea why he had saved that suitcase—or why Sylvia had not thrown it out. He had heard her deep exhausted breathing as he'd made his way down the stairs. His own breath he took cautiously, just as he stood cau-tiously, hands at his side, in hopes that that hot chilling pain—it felt like a piece of dry ice lodged in his chest—would not spread. The night was moonless, but bright with the sound of trilling insects. He heard a dog bark, and four blocks away on the bypass trucks rumbled past and a hot rod ran out its gears; but the night, the neighborhood, lay under an expectant hush that these local noises did little to disturb.

He felt peculiarly lucid, multiply aware of himself, as though he circled rather than occupied his state of mind. He was dying. He stood there hollowed out around his pain, dressed as much for golf as for travel—his checked pants with, he could feel, a tee still in the pockets, a navy-blue cardigan sweater over the light blue golfing shirt, his cap with his country club's insignia on the front. Impersonating whom? An adventurous boy? An ancient madman? A homesick child? A criminal? A thief? What crime had he committed? What had he stolen? Himself—he was about to steal himself. He had made an accomplice of his son. In fact, from a slightly different point of view, he was about to steal his son too. Was either of them worth the bother? The risk? Moving the point of view still farther along that circle, he knew they weren't. Farther still, so that he saw through the community-conscious eyes of his wife and second son, he knew they were. Sylvia and Russ were entitled to his death; if he stole if from them it must be theirs.

Suddenly the circle squeezed tight and his breath came short. For an instant it stopped altogether before with a brief freeing shudder—as though he sucked breath through a membrane that had blocked breath before—he got it back.

He stood still, trembling; then with a minimum of motion he sat on top of his suitcase. Monitoring his pain every inch of the way, he lowered his head between his knees. It was in that position, looking down on the grass, that he saw the silvery sweep of lights as a car turned the corner.

When he realized it wasn't Larry it was too late to rise and move farther back into the shadows of the garage. In his indecision and embarrassment at being caught sitting out on his suitcase in the middle of the night, he tried to scrabble into the shadows and managed only to topple over onto the grass.

He lay there as the uninterested car drove by. The grass had been recently cut, and against the side of his face the stubble felt like a bed of soft nails. Sylvia was a good groundskeeper. Over the years he had watched her evolve from a girl who couldn't be bothered into a woman who bothered to do everything right, and with as much energy and savoir-faire as she'd breezed by things before. If with a seven-iron, say, he took a divot where his head now lay, she'd have it back and plumped for him like a pillow before he could return his club to his bag. Had he thought her girlish free spirit might evolve into something else? It was a question he'd never put to himself in just those words, but had he thought—and secretly hoped—that her girlish free spirit might one day be capable of some genuinely shocking act?

It hadn't happened. That was probably his fault. Four years her senior, he suspected she'd tried to grow up to him, and since he hadn't known his seventy-year old heart at the age of nineteen, twenty, or twenty-one, he couldn't tell her that if that's what he'd wanted he would have married her sister Martha, who was his age and pretty and placid and gracefully slow on her feet. In the company of Martha he had unwittingly stumbled on her kid sister, which as often as he repeated it to himself or his golfing buddies or to Sylvia herself, he knew was a lie. He'd known Sylvia was there all along. When she'd walked up to where he was sitting in a garden chair under the pecan trees behind her family's house, he'd known exactly what was going to happen. It was fall and pecan shells lay like scraps of wrinkled black leather on the ground. She wore some simple peach-colored sundress and no shoes—it was not that warm. Her hair was loose and uncombed and still showed summer streaks of blond—no, it was not that warm.

Then he understood: the heat was coming from within and with her hair loose and her dress airy and ample she was about to become a woman for him there where she stood. But she didn't, not there. She sat beside him in an adjoining garden chair and stretching out her legs winked her scrubby little toes at him, which he couldn't account for until he looked over at her face. Then he understood that the winking toes were the kid's way of saying goodbye and considered alongside the expression she wore might have belonged to another species entirely. Her face was as still as the surging eye of a storm. She said, "Martha had to go with Mama. She's gone." Then he leaned over and kissed her and felt not so much the softness as the depth in those fourteen-year-old lips that he'd only known before cocked into a taunting grin. When he pulled back she seemed to speak to him with the authority of a grave and perilous joy. "You stay with me now. Okay?" He said that he would.

Two years after they'd married he took her to St. Simons Island off the Georgia coast, and only then had he seen her as he imagined she might have been. And she had frightened him. Under the spell of the sea she'd gone a bit crazy. The sand was burning hot and then cool as you neared the surf line, and running over it she seemed to take it as the range of her moods. He didn't know what she was capable of. His strongest impression was that she was ready to conceive, and at night when they made love he inspected the prophylactics carefully.

Had they returned to the sea since then? They had not. Yes, they had, a number of times. No, they hadn't.

"Dad, we can't do this!" I'm taking you back inside."

He hadn't heard his son drive up, or seen the lights, but Larry was picking him up off the grass, lifting him bodily, and it annoyed him to be handled—manhandled—with such ease.

"Put me in the van," he said, assuming it was there.

Then he saw it, glowing green in the dim lights from the corner, a deep-water green, as dark as the markings of a largemouth bass.

"Dad, don't you realize—"

"Goddammit, Larry, I almost went to sleep out here waiting for you. Thought you'd stood me up."

"You're sure?"

"As long as your mother doesn't wake up."

The third of the gable windows belonged to her bedroom, and it was dark.

"Did you leave her a note?"

"What did you expect me to say?"

"I don't know . . . that you're all right."

"I'm not."

"I mean . . ."

"Larry, we need to get something straight. If your mother or Russell finds out where we're going they'll find a way to bring us back. They'll think we're making a fool of them. To be fair I should ask you the same question. Do you think I'm making a fool out of you?"

Freshly shaven, his eyes large and watery in the shadows of the garage, Larry hesitated a moment, and then tried to make up for it by answering emphatically, "No, I don't."

"Shhh."

"Okay, Dad." He nodded.

"You really haven't stopped since you left Mexico, have you, son?"

"Doesn't feel like it."

"Or since you left California or Texas or all the other places you've been?"

Grinning wearily, Larry shook his head.

"Well, let's go then," Ed proposed.

He allowed Larry to carry the suitcase out to the back of the van, but when Larry opened the door and tried to help his father up onto the mattress he'd placed there, Ed would not allow that. Instead, knowing what it would cost him, he pulled himself up into the passenger seat. The pain was intense. "I'll do that until I can't do it anymore," he said. When Larry closed the door and walked around to the driver's seat, the smell of the van's newness went to Ed's head like smelling salts, and through pain he really couldn't make any worse he rolled the passenger window down. There rising past the arching elm branches was the house. It seemed made of solidified shadow, shadow as solid as stone. The sash of the windows, the trim around the porch, shone with a fickle, moon-white impermanence, as did the front door. It had been a home to him only in his health. Sylvia he refused to think about anymore tonight, allowing himself only the concluding thought that she would have the rest of the night to sleep in her house before she discovered him gone.

"Turn on the motor," he told his son, who was slow.

It sounded rich to him, and quiet, discreet really when he remembered it belonged to this van. The transmission was manual with four forward speeds. His son was letting it purr along in neutral.

"It's already warm," Ed said.

As soon as Larry had pulled out into the street, he stopped. "Dad, did you bring your medicine? Those pills I saw up there? Did you bring that contraption you blow into?"

He had, actually, but there was a toughness his solicitous son lacked in this moment that tempted him to say no, that made him want to clarify and reclarify just what they were about to do until he'd fired that soupy regret he saw in his son's face to a hardened resolve.

Ed closed his eyes. "Larry, I want to go."

He didn't open his eyes until they'd reached the bypass light, and then only after reviewing the blocks they had coming before they turned onto the interstate. There was a Holiday Inn, a Howard Johnson's, four other motels, the largest of which was the Town-'n'-Country. Pizza Hut, Burger King and Chef, McDonald's, Wendy's and A&W and a Jerry's, the last two with carports and microphones. Car dealers—Willard's Ford, Cassidy's Buick, Keller's Volks, Rackerman's Pontiac and Toyota. There were three liquor stores, a miniature golf course, a bowling alley, three bars, one—the Royal Palms—a dance hall. There was a string of smaller stores, which he could have listed if he'd wanted to, since sooner or later he'd sold paper and janitorial supplies to every business on this bypass. But Larry was pulling into it now, giving him a taste of the van's full acceleration, and in his enfeebled state, in the broad high seat, Ed felt uplifted, borne.

When he opened his eyes he saw his mistake. He'd reviewed the bypass at the height of its evening blaze, and except for the gasoline signs high on their stilts, the lights were off. He closed his eyes again, and counted the stoplights. When they came to the last and Larry was about to swing up onto the eastbound interstate, Ed said, "I want to go west, Larry."

"West?" his son repeated in a quiet questioning tone, as if he lacked the energy to be stunned. But the van slowed dramatically.

"To the west, please."

"You told me you wanted to go to Chumleyville. You wanted to get the bed—"

"That's right, but first I want to go west."

"How much time—" But Larry cut himself off, swallowing the words.

"Not long, son. Turn to the west," Ed repeated with an apologetic insistence, for he could see that his son was confused, "and I'll try to explain it all."

AFTER half an hour of driving west, Ed Reece told his son to take an intersecting interstate north, and to slow down, they were in no rush. Driving north, they had a late-rising crescent moon hanging in the west, silvering the fields and black-glinting ponds, and when Larry set a cruising speed of fifty miles an hour his father said okay, hold it there, and nothing else. He breathed noisily, but it was a sound, like a rattle in the van, his son quickly got used to. His throat-clearing growls always began with a quiet gathering of forces, so by the time they became actual angry uprisings, sustained at full volume for perhaps three seconds, and repeated, Larry was prepared for them. At the moment of maximum exertion Ed bent stiffly forward at the waist; otherwise he sat back against his seat, his arms laid to rest at his sides.

That silver tint to things turned soot-gray as dawn broke on the streets of Owensboro, Kentucky, a small, mostly unfurbished city on the banks of the Ohio. At the bridge his father waved him across. They had traffic coming toward them from Indiana now, and cars behind them wanting to cross, but up on the ramp Larry hesitated. The mud-laden chill of the water entered through the window, and although low in its channel, enough of the Ohio remained to give the impression that it would not consent to be crossed again and again just to satisfy an old man's whims. At that moment he thought of his mother waking to find her husband of forty-five years gone. "You were going to explain," Larry said.

"I will, son," and Ed's voice, at first try, was a husky, hollow rasp. "Just drive across."

Once in Indiana they had bottomland planted in wheat and barley off to their left, and off to their right the Ohio, whose broad muddy current they drove back against as they followed Route 45 upriver. By the time they reached Rockport the sun, with no rosy interlude, was glancing off the water into their faces. "Watch your signs, Boonville," Ed instructed. He risked raising his arm to pull down his visor and experienced no fresh shoot of pain. "Be a left turn there up ahead. We can stop in Boonville for breakfast."

He saw the turn before his son did, and it carried them—Route 66—out of Rockport before they'd really gotten into it, away from the Ohio and its mud-smelling banks, pilings, and piers, and quickly into the fields. A half a turn of the handle at a time, Ed rolled down his window. The smell of corn poured in—a prickly, procreative odor. A field of bushy-pelted wheat allowed him a vista—of oaks and elms gathered around farmhouses, indistinct in the early-morning haze—before it was replaced by soybeans, abundantly holding their rows. Then, to top it off, a field of alfalfa, like a carpet of lush green foam. He had never farmed, but State Route 66 cut long and straight like the furrow of a plow through this rich river loam, the road's shoulders so narrow that the van actually blew cowlicks in the wheat and corn. The sun had swung around to enter the van on a slant through the two small rear windows, and Larry, of course, noticed it too.

"We're going back west again," he said, a quiet questioning groan.

"*North*west," his father corrected. "Boonville's not far. Take a right on Route 61. There's a good little restaurant this side of town."

And it was still there, still in business, if diminished by the presence of a car wash to one side and a Wilco discount house to the other. Larry had not thought this moment out in advance, but at this busy breakfast hour could not imagine his father seated among Boonville's best appetites competing for the attention of a waitress on the run. What would the sight of his father do to those appetites? As loathsome as they were, McDonald's and Burger King had drive-through service that made discreet good sense to him now. But his father said, "If this was thirty years ago I'd recommend the hotcakes."

It was the beginning of an explanation, and he helped his father inside. There were booths, tables, and at a counter stools where only the broad-backed men in town sat. A couple turned their heads as he and his father walked in, and in their unkind, cow-sullen expressions he could hear the clipped and unkind tone of their voices, but the restaurant was too busy setting the town in motion to pay much attention to Larry and Ed Reece. Luckily, they found a booth off near a corner. The waitress came up scribbling what remained from the preceding order before turning a blank page on theirs, and it was only when his father changed the hotcakes that Larry had ordered for him to eggs and toast that she looked at him. She was a heavyset, middle-aged woman, who nevertheless had a nervous pecking manner about her, and behind bottle-bottom glasses her eyes seemed to peck at his father—until she'd had enough. When she brought their orders she barely gave him a glance. But Larry did, he took another look at his father through the waitress's eyes, and saw that under the fluorescent lighting his face looked gray and exhausted. Not halfway through his eggs his jaw began to fall. Once Larry had him out to the van his father said, "Think I'll crawl up in back, son, and take a snooze."

But he didn't crawl, this time he allowed himself to be lifted, and the sight of his father lying fetally tucked up on that brand-new mattress momentarily paralyzed his son. Boonville, Indiana—a town of grain elevators, pickup trucks, inquisitive and soon-satisfied folk. Where were they, for Christ's sake? Daniel Boone was Kentucky's, he thought. Wasn't it Boone who had called Kentucky that "dark and bloody ground"? Then he snapped out of it, his father without a blanket to cover him or a pillow to cushion his head. He closed the van's back doors and on his way around to the driver's seat strayed far enough out to see that the discount house next door was still closed. It was when he took the step up into the van that he felt his own exhaustion, and he came down into the driver's seat like dead weight—the weight his father appeared to have lost as he lay on the shimmering surface of that mattress, floating like a body of sticks and parchment-dry skin.

"I'll be up in a couple of hours. Just drive around till then."

"Drive around?" Larry asked, dumbfounded. "Where, Dad?"

"Wherever suits you, son. Pretty country out there."

He didn't even have a map. He started back the way they'd come, but soon felt an obscure sense of shame in doing that, and since he didn't want to go back to Boonville either, struck out to his left, up State Route 161, resigned to getting lost. It didn't take long. When he saw a sign pointing him to Lincoln's boyhood home, for a brief moment he thought he was back in Kentucky, the Ohio river taken at a leap, for wasn't Lincoln, like Boone, Kentucky's own? He didn't turn in, but continued on, angling vaguely back to the east, he thought, corn and more corn. Counties—Warrick, Spencer, Perry, and Crawford: it struck him he'd never seen a county named for an Indian. Towns and cities and states, yes, but county seats, power after all, derived from sturdy Anglo-Saxon stock. In case he'd missed the point he came to English, Indiana, where he stopped in a small shopping plaza, which contained among other things a package store and a K-Mart. He sat there a couple of minutes to see if his father would wake up, as his children frequently had, in an ill temper, once he'd stopped the car. When his father didn't he entered the K-mart and from the rust-red, sky-blue, and canary-yellow blankets on sale chose two of the canary-yellows. Sticker slapped on sticker had brought the price of pillows down to $3.99, and he bought two of those. He had money, almost three hundred dollars of their cache in his pockets, and for an instant standing over these bins of discounted goods he felt a silly surge of power. It lasted until the cashier, where he took out his wallet as though it were something shocking or illegal—filthy photos or a bomb—and gave the skinny, lank-haired girl who checked him through a look at all the bills. On the way out he bought a Styrofoam cooler from a display of picnic supplies. In the liquor store he bought ice, a bottle of club soda, and another of Jim Beam bourbon, not beer.

Then he put his purchases aside and drove his still-sleeping father deeper into Indiana, vaguely aware now that he was drifting back west and doing nothing to correct his course. For a while they exchanged the flat farmlands for broken terrain, and he had chicken farms and hog wallows and meat cattle to look at—and smell, for he drove in close, still on the narrow state roads that obeyed the contour of the land. Curiously, the names of the towns changed too: Paoli, French Lick, Orleans. It was a French-settled enclave—he learned the name of the county as he left it, Orange—which provided a sensualist's spur to his imagination, accustomed now to rectitude and corn. Then Lawrence County, the town of Mitchell, and across the White River—a muddy army green—to Bedford.

For purposes of comparison he had only Kentucky towns to draw on, for since he'd left the state fifteen-sixteen years ago he'd lived in cities—if he forgot Villajoyosa, Mexico, that is. Indiana towns seemed quieter, cleaner—they didn't smell of their distilleries or tobacco warehouses, for one thing. They were more open to the sky. Did that make them less distrustful, more accommodating, more enlightened? Did that make their necks less red? He drove through them measuring the obedient, easy-grinning ways of their inhabitants against some of the foul things he knew about the human race, determined not to be disarmed. Bloomington and its university, twenty-six miles due north, where he did not want to go, pushed him out again to the east and he drove 135 into hilly, forested Brown County and towns—Story, Pike's Peak, Gnawbone, Beanblossom—whose curio shops and general stores were so cunningly quaint and Americana-conscious that he roared back again to the west, not really slowing down until he was in flat open country again, rows of soybeans and corn.

What did his father want of him? Was there something he expected his son to gain from all this tacking back and forth up into the heart of Indiana? Or was he simply expected to drive so that his father could sleep, a case of the son rocking the father's cradle? The fact was, he couldn't believe in any of it up to now. He was stopped before a major four-lane highway connecting Indianapolis and points south, and those trucks passing massively by overhead, those RVs, and that endless string of cars and fellow vans seemed considerably more believable to him than he did and his father.

So he got up among them, heading south. He let the flow of the traffic take him, grateful for the rest he could take from shifting gears and negotiating curves, and really wasn't aware of what his father was doing until Ed had managed to crawl from the mattress up into the passenger seat and was sitting beside his son. Then before he could express his surprise or concern, his father said, "See that sign for Martinsville? Get off there."

"Where are we going, Dad?"

"From Martinsville to Franklin. From there to Shelbyville, Rushville, and New Castle. Route 44 will swing you around."

"Swing me around what?"

"Indianapolis. Never liked calling on cities. They offered me the northern half of the territory, but too many big cities up there for me. You got Chicago, then Gary and Milwaukee . . ."

"Dad, is this important to you?"

"Important? I don't know if it's important. Since when did you mind having a little fun?"

He got off at Martinsville, population maybe ten or twelve thousand and except for its gas-station signs and grain elevators nothing really much taller than its trees. Gaunt-faced and still, his father didn't look as if he were having fun. And he wasn't—not yet. It was as if he were very gradually immersing himself in tepid water, water that had yet to declare itself for or against him. Actually, Martinsville looked a bit frayed to him, and caught out of place: he noticed one of the two movie houses had been turned into a furniture store, a small corner department store partitioned off into offices for lawyers; where he'd once gotten his hair cut he could now buy adult books. So when he told Larry, "Take a left at the next light," it didn't surprise him that his son drove them up a street to a small warehouse with a cinder-block office attached that no longer sold paper goods but monuments now, tombstones in fact. He took it as a clumsy irony, and smiled. "We won't be doing that everywhere we go," he said.

But they did it again in Franklin, because crossing the railroad tracks, where the defunct station now housed the Chamber of Commerce and one of the last old-time steam locomotives to run this line had been pulled off and put on display, Larry suddenly exclaimed, "Hey, I remember this!" And he remembered, he claimed, the small rock building—cottage-sized compared to the warehouses of most of Ed's old customers—where his father had paid his calls and brought his son—in this case, Larry—along. The sign was still up—K. R. Turner, Paper Supplies—but the paint was flaking and the wood rotting and Ed suspected the business had long been closed.

It didn't matter. He would never have gone in had rosy, bald-headed Kit Turner been there to welcome him himself. It was the drive between the towns that mattered, when an order had been written and another awaited him down the road. Rather it *was* the towns but only insofar as they produced in him some small incredulous ache that life from one day to the next could never be quite as peaceful as it seemed, and *then* it was the countryside that allowed him to suck the full pleasure from that ache, for *out there* he had no reason to question his eyes. It was like that be-tween-shots moment in golf, that swelling excitement you felt walking up to your next shot, even though the one before you might have hit fat and the one coming up you might shank. Aware that he owed his son an explanation, he thought, yes, that's exactly what it was like.

But Larry was no longer asking questions. Ed suspected he was bored. Then he realized that that stony set to his features was not boredom so much as exhaustion, and that Larry was driving on mechanical skill. Just past a small town called Mays, twenty miles shy of New Castle, he asked him to stop at a Dairy Creme with picnic tables set out beneath willows in back. He waited there while Larry brought him a hot dog with relish, which he wasn't supposed to have, and a strawberry shake, which as a placebo he could have in abundance. Larry drank a large cup of coffee and ate half a hamburger before throwing the rest away. He looked at his father intently, smiling to disguise the real meaning of the look, which was an alien and disbelieving demand: Dairy Creme hot dogs, hamburgers, shakes, out on these tables, in this time and this place, with all the devastating history being made in the world—who would have thought it, who, why?

"You look tired, son," Ed said. "Why don't you crawl in back and let me take the wheel?"

Larry started out of his slump. "In back?"

"You need to sleep."

"I could sit up in front with you if you wanted to try the van out for a few minutes, if that's all you want. . . ."

They stopped and got gas, which Larry pumped, but when they pulled out Ed was behind the wheel. It hurt him to shift gears. Once in fourth, with an open road before him, he tried to relax and enjoy the ride, but the high heaviness of this van—which he too had provided—made him feel his frailty as he never had before. And the front-wheel drive left him no margin for steering error, no time to make an adjustment. With New Castle coming up he expected his son to ask him to pull over. But he didn't. Larry kept his eyes on the road and didn't even seem to notice that his father had taken the bypass around town—and it was a town that Ed liked, with its parks and distinguished old homes it had an air about it of something enshrined—and swung them back out toward the west. He wasn't sure he could handle town traffic, and the sudden swing west, without a stop, as if he'd just rounded a post or pylon, had a brief exhilarating effect. He gathered momentum. His hands on the wheel were those of a corpse, so he kept his eyes off his hands, his mind off his enfeebled arms that seemed to balance the wheel, and hence the van, between them rather than to steer, and let that momentum take him for as long as it lasted. Halfway to Anderson along Route 38 he noticed his son was asleep. And the way that he slept—hanging in the safety belt strapped across his chest, then tossing with the acceleration of the van into his seat—also worked to give Ed back the road. He did not see his ten-year-old son riding beside him, it was nothing like that, and his ten-year-old son did not restore him to the days of his health. The man beside him might have been a stranger, a hitchhiker, but his loose hanging inertness meant that the van and that particular stretch of Indiana highway belonged to Ed Reece now, and that for all practical purposes he was alone.

His son had gotten him this far.

On the strength of that gift he drove maybe thirty miles into the late cooling afternoon. In one measured sweep of the eyes he took in a world of vast yet intimate space: from the Queen Anne's lace and black-eyed Susans growing beside the road, to the tasseled undulations of the fields of corn, to the heat-hazed green of the trees surrounding farmhouses—or gathering in larger numbers around crossroads towns—he knew it, he had once made it his with the propertied excess of a child. For a long moment, measurable in neither minutes nor miles, he had it all again. Then as he knew it must, yet hoped it would not, at least not so quickly, so tracelessly, it began to pale and flow out of him, and with it went his strength or momentum, whatever it was that enabled him to drive this van.

Five miles east of Tipton, some sixty miles north of Indianapolis, he pulled up before a motel he'd stayed in years ago. Then the Baker Hill Motor Court had been something splendid, situated on the only elevation of any sort thereabouts. Now its sign had lost its luster and its rows of gray stucco units were crumbling and pockmarked, as though they'd taken a shelling. Three cars were parked there. He woke his son.

"It's seen its better years, but how 'bout checking us in."

Alarmed that he'd slept and deserted his father, but relieved by how well Ed had managed, Larry did as he was told. Then he drove into Tipton and brought back a box of fried chicken, mashed potatoes, and cole slaw. His father ate an entire breast, two rolls, and a four-ounce paper cup of cole slaw. The potatoes, which tasted of their pot, they threw away. The television, an RCA Victor black-and-white, sat up on a tarnished gold stand and gave back an aged, greenish image: they watched the end of the local news and the weather report from an Indianapolis station. More heat and an afternoon thundershower were forecast, but the weatherman was a babbling boy who probably couldn't be trusted. The national news began with presidential campaign reports, and

Larry was surprised and relieved and somehow put on guard when his father said, "You can turn that off if you want to." Then, rising off the bed, painfully bent but with his voice conversationally clear, he added, "Think I'll take a shower," and Larry, seated in a thinly padded armchair by the window, let him. He got out of the chair to turn off the TV, though, worried that if his father fell in the shower he might not hear him. I should be there, he thought. When his father stepped out of the shower and his breath had a shallow, shivery sound to it, he thought, I should be there to dry him off. He was aware that he didn't want to see his father naked, that an operation on a lung would have to leave a horrible scar. But that wasn't the real reason he sat there. He was curious: How far could his father go without him? What would he try next?

He came out of the bathroom with his blue pajamas already on and got into bed. Add that to the miles he'd driven to get them here, the meal he'd eaten, and the shower he'd taken, and Larry had to admit that Ed Reece had had a remarkable day.

After he'd settled his head in the pillow, Ed said, "I wanna rest now, Larry. Why don't you go out and take a look around. Enjoy yourself."

Enjoy himself? Where? Tipton, Indiana? He took his look around by sitting in a flaking garden chair in the grassy oval of the motel's courtyard—where in more prosperous times a swimming pool might have gone—and by letting his eyes wander. It was nearly dusk. A chill—harbinger of autumn—passed by him, come and gone like the silent shadowing flight of a bird. Real birds, split-tail swallows, filled the air overhead, on their way from field to field. He followed a flock until the motel rooms cut off his view, but the best way out for his eyes was the way they'd come in, up the curving drive from the highway, beside which filling stations and repair garages and the usual complement of nondescript businesses were camped. There at the mouth of the drive stood the telephone booth, already lit, just where he'd seen it when he'd gone out to get the chicken.

Sometime later—the booth was sharply lit now—he got up and, good at it, talked the motel clerk out of another ten dollars' worth of change. The phone booth was warm, but its surfaces were cool, and $2.25 for the first three minutes got them started. His mother's voice sounded anxious and angry, spent and tonelessly cold, and the first thing he thought of when he heard that mix of emotions was: ten dollars won't be enough.

"I have him, Mother. He's all right. He's had a very strong day." Then without pausing, "That's all I can tell you. It's not my place to say any more than that. I'm only doing what I've been asked to."

"Larry," she stated flatly, a preliminary identification.

"Yes."

"Where are you? What does this mean?"

"I can't tell you that, Mother. I can't even tell you why I can't. I'm calling because I don't want you to worry any more than you have to."

"Worry? Where are you, Larry? What does this mean?"

"It's something I've promised Dad."

"Larry, your father may be dying. What does this mean?"

"Yes, I think he is, Mother. That's why I made the promise."

"What did you promise, Larry?" Before he could answer she broke out in an angry demanding sob: "Larry, I want to see Ed! I want to see him! I want to see him, do you understand?"

He tried to calm her. As soon as Ed asked him to, he assured her, he would bring him back. In the meantime he promised to take care of him, to do everything . . . but his mother would not be calmed, reassured, won over by a promise. He had betrayed her. How could he take care of his dying father when he couldn't take care of himself? She forced him to give ground until she forced him to dig in his heels. "He drove seventy-five miles today," he threw back at her. "You wanted him out of bed, didn't you? Well, now you've got him out!"

He felt the heat of the booth in that moment and leaned his forehead against the cool Plexiglas. Beyond it, two teenage girls were walking by in jeans and glo-bright T-shirts, off the farm and on their way into town, almost certainly to drink beer, smoke pot, and get laid. It would all come to pass. He thought of his ex-wife, a farm-reared debauchée herself at the age of fourteen. The cuter of the two girls walking past hardened her face at him. He actually saw, in a neat practiced grimace, her nostrils flare. Then his mother broke down.

"Don't do this to me, Larry! Don't do this to me! Where is he? Let me speak to my Ed! He can't get along without me! I have to take care of him, Larry! Just let me speak to him, please!"

He told her that Ed wasn't there, that he was resting. Without committing himself he said he would do what he could, that he just wanted her to know . . .

She waited for him to stop, then in a long swooning cry that seemed to start from a distance and to finish filling his head, she said, "Oh, Larry, Larry . . . Larry . . ."

Gently he tried to let her down, as if with his reassuring voice he could hold her hand and see her off to bed. Then he cradled the receiver. The phone rang at once and he almost bolted from the booth. But it was only the operator wanting another $1.65, which he deposited with fingers gone uncooperatively cold.

Later with a second drink in his hand he sat on the edge of the bed watching his father sleep. He had the bourbon to thank, he knew, and his own fatigue. They held him in a sort of suspension and allowed him to sit there studying a face whose fine flinching tremors never gave his father a moment's rest—the eyelids, the temples, the nostrils, the corners of the mouth, the entire forehead, dry and chalky-white after the freshening effects of the shower had worn off. He was watching the onset of the final shaking—he knew that too. How long? If forced to predict—a gun to his head and his back to the wall—how much time would he give this man? Time enough to see him through this trip? He suddenly doubted it. The ear he saw looked dead already, vestigial, like something unshucked, covered with an uneven growth of white hair. His father hadn't shaved, and the white stubble too seemed to be growing with alarming fecundity. If his father died, he realized, while still in his care he might have to shave that beard, and to get it all, would have to mold the cool lifeless flesh to meet the razor's edge. His mother had insisted that she and not he was the one to care for him—had that been what she'd meant?

By midnight he managed to get some sleep, although he had the bourbon to thank for that too.

The next day they tacked slowly west—Frankfort, Lafayette, and then, following the bends of the Wabash, to Williamsport. Ed had started strongly, but an hour after breakfast had had to lie down in back for a rest. He'd slept lightly, not unpleasantly, dreaming of a particular store always good for an order which from the start he understood they were not meant to find. When he awoke, Larry had pulled off on the shoulder of the road. Before them a large blue sign with luminous white lettering welcomed them to the state of Illinois—the state all his children had been born in. When Ed had ducked up into the passenger seat—only straightening his back after he'd sat, to hold off the pain—his son asked, "What do we do now, Dad?"

"Drive on," Ed said.

In a patient but sadly foregone manner Larry hypothesized for his father. "You want to come here before we head south. First you want to go back to Baldwinsville, and see it, and then you want to go back to the town where you were born. That's it, isn't it, Dad?"

"I hadn't thought about it," Ed said. "Would you like to go to Baldwinsville?"

"Me?"

"It's where *you* were born. Actually, I drove your mother into Peoria."

"Dad, we're out here because you . . ." But his son trailed off.

"Drive on, then," Ed said.

Between Danville, Illinois, and Urbana, passing through a string of villages that showed a post office to the highway, a one-truck fire department, a pickup grocery, and a large slumping house or two deeply shaded by oaks, Ed said, "If your mother'd had her way you'd have been born in Chumleyville too. She wanted to get pregnant on our wedding night. You have me to thank you're still a young man."

Larry glanced over at his father, who was looking out the window, more solemn-faced than he would have expected.

"Took me that long," Ed went on, "to picture myself as father material. D'you ever get the feeling you're about ten years behind every one else your age?"

"Times," Larry said.

" 'Course, I was the baby in my family. The second I opened my eyes I was already ten years behind. You were the oldest. Not that that has a helluva lot to do with it. Look at Russ. He was born with more business sense than he ever learned in college."

"He has the head for it s'all," Larry said.

Ed continued gazing at the countryside. It was a day of low-flying clouds and cloud shadows passing over the fields, then sudden and precise effulgences of sunlight.

"I rounded it off at ten years," Ed said. "When I was forty, say, I had the intelligence of a man of thirty—I mean, that's about how much I understood of my fellow human beings. Which isn't bad. A man of thirty can get the job done. In fact, it wasn't until I went in business for myself that this began to bother me. Then there's a difference between a thirty- and a forty-year-old man. You open a business and you gotta know something about the world."

For a long while his father didn't say any more. Thanks to the racing clouds the light blinked on and off and for a few moments the fields—oats now, Larry thought, denser, more pendulous than the feather-tipped wheat—took a sort of watery respite from the sun. "And you didn't learn it out here?" he asked.

Slowly Ed shook his head. "Anything I learned selling paper bags to one customer I'd forget by the time I got to the next. Real salesmen belonged to another breed than me. I came out here because I loved to drive these roads. A Plymouth Savoy didn't have the greatest suspension system in the world, but that's what I drove and for four- or five-day stretches I never touched the ground. I liked all this corn and all this sky and these towns where they roll up the sidewalk at half past eight. I got a screw loose, son? A card or two missing from my deck?"

"It's . . . peaceful out here," Larry conceded.

"I *learned* when I got home, I guess, and had to deal with you and your mother, Russ, and Nell. Those could be pretty hectic weekends. If I didn't want to fall more than ten years behind myself, I had to learn a lot fast. . . . I guess it must have been something like that." He stopped. Larry heard a congested exhalation. It had been, he realized an instant later, a particularly weary sigh. "I have to make it make sense, Larry," his father confessed to him. "I have to find a way to explain it all."

Larry said, "I know."

"So I ask myself—I been asking myself for almost a year now: what is it I really like about all this corn and prairie and sky and these straight flat roads? It's not just corn and asphalt, is it? It's not just a handsome ear of corn and a white line down a particular stretch of road, is it? You see what I mean? And I think I got it figured out. Out here's where I *didn't* do all that catching up I *had* to do when I got home those weekends, and when I came off the road and we opened the business. And it's all that catching up I had to do then that's caught up with me now. I guess that means I should hate all this, doesn't it—but I don't."

They were passing through a small town now called Ogden, really just a wide place in the road, and out beside them, a wider road, an expressway, would let them catch up on lost time and speed into Urbana if they chose, but Larry stayed down on Route 150. More and more of those fast-sailing clouds were breaking off from the horizon now, some trimmed and bellied-out in gray. There was less wind down in the corn, whose long leaves seemed affected only by local gusts, and almost none on the ground among the bushy rows of soybeans. No, not the bean itself, not the ear of corn, not Route 150. He broke into his father's solemn reverie. "Yet you took us with you . . . you took Russ and me."

"I've been thinking about that too, and I've decided the reason I liked taking you and Russ when you were kids was because it didn't change a thing. I mean, you didn't learn anything from those trips with your old man, did you, Larry? They didn't make you into a shrewder radical or anything like that?"

His father was smiling, about a once-humorless matter, and quietly Larry laughed.

The smile faded a bit, took on a slightly rueful weight. "I did make love to a woman out here once, but that didn't work," Ed said.

"You what?" The question both asked for clarification, in case he hadn't heard correctly, and expressed amazement, in case he had.

"She owned a restaurant in a little town outside of Davenport, a town I never did business in, but I stopped off to eat there once. Her name was Peggy. She made chicken pot pies worth going back for. So I did and after a while we became friends. She was older than I was and heavy but still a good-looking woman, and she had a good-humored way of exercising her authority. I liked that. I liked how casual she could be and still be the boss. And I thought that since we were friends . . . but it didn't work. Well, it 'worked,' but I couldn't feel the same about being out on the road for a couple of weeks after that. The next night I remember I bought a bottle of whiskey and put myself to sleep. Then the next time through . . . well, the truth is I made love with her again, just to make sure. So that's twice. I'll be honest with you, son. I wish it had worked. She was *that* kind of woman. But it didn't. It put a weight on everything. It felt like I was pulling a trailer, driving these roads."

"What happened to her?"

"Peggy? She probably made enough to retire and go to Florida. We lost touch. I quit stopping for her chicken pies. She's the only woman other than your mother I've made love with. What have I missed?"

Clarification and amazement—again he asked, "What?"

"I thought you could tell me."

"What you have missed?" He forced a grin to the side of his face. It wasn't just that talking about sex with his father embarrassed him. It was the fact that the question came from a dying man, and that realization—each time it was born in him and tore him away from the lulling effect of the road—changed everything: it suddenly made these farmlands golden for him, it suffused the monotonous world of these farmlands and farmtowns with a golden glow. Death was like a solution, then, that brought

every speck of beauty out in the world around you, but that would
not let you breathe, let you be. "I don't know how to say it," he
said.

"S'up to you."

"When it hasn't been an obligation or a test of your manhood
or when it hasn't self-consciously had anything to do with your
'style,' then . . . then it's been wonderful," he said.

After a long pause, his father unbegrudgingly replied, "I'm
glad."

"It hasn't been that way lately." And not so much to spare him
the pain, or to lessen his loss, but more as though he could honor
his father's honesty with some of his own, Larry went on: "Mexico was probably bad for me, or maybe I just don't know how to
handle coming up on forty years old. I got involved with two
women at the same time down there, and when I couldn't take
the tension of running back and forth between them there were
three or four others I saw once or twice. I don't recommend the
mathematics of that. It wasn't the deceit that bothered me so
much as the franticness, what it told me about myself, how stu-
pidly committed I could become to a single course of action. I
mean I thought if I f—" He stopped, stumbling on the word.

"You were going to say 'fuck,' " his father said.

"Yes."

"S'all right."

"I thought if I fucked myself sick I could fuck myself well," he
concluded.

"I suppose I thought something of the same that second time
with Peggy," his father said. "What were the women like?"

"The women?"

"Those two."

"You said you had to make it make sense, Dad. Remember? I
can make Suellen and Pepa make sense too. Put them together
and they were one woman. Suellen was from California. She had a
boyfriend or ex-husband who sent her money and she took a lot of
drugs. The only time she'd tell me anything about herself was
when we made love. Then she'd talk about growing up in Encina,
not so much about her teenage lovelife as when she was a little

girl. Things like pets she'd had. I remember her going on one time about kissing gourami, her favorite tropical fish—it's crazy, that's the only time she'd feel like talking. Pepa, of course, never shut up. She thought of herself as one of Mexico's first liberated women—she'd had a marriage annulled in Mexico City and an abortion, I believe. She owned her own boutique. I used to tell her the earrings she wore would make great bass lures. The only thing wrong with her looks was a slight bend to her nose, which she'd ask me about constantly. I'd always lie, I'd tell her she had a gorgeous nose, and she'd always pretend to believe me. Then to show her gratitude she could set by her liberated status and treat me like royalty—all in good conscience, you understand. After she'd served me supper we'd make love. I never really believed in all the rapturous sounds she made, but that's because I never really believed in her, I guess."

"Too bad," his father said. "She sounds made to order."

"I told you: it's a way to explain it, a way to make it make sense. Put them together and they become a complete woman. But, of course, they don't. I don't know who they really were. I wasn't getting much beyond myself at the time." He went back to his driving, studying the road, checking the rearview mirror, his right hand dropping to the gearshift as though he had reason to shift down to third—a car to pass. But the road was clear. "It was Mexico, Dad," he reflected grimly. "It's a hard, hot place and things seem to burn out at twice the speed. You see a rosy-cheeked girl one day and the next day she looks like a drudge. It gets you going that way, and unless you've got a lot more resist-ance than I had it won't let you stop. It's nothing like this."

He signaled the fields, their perfect flatness permitting his fa-ther to follow the gesture to the horizon if he wanted to, banked in clouds. Or he could follow a long curving corn row, whatever at a glance would tell him that a sense of order and proportion reigned. No, nothing alike. Only in the sense that a dying man would see that which survived him. In that sense, Mexico and the American midwest were the same. "Do you miss Connie at all, son?" Ed asked him.

And he watched his son flinch. It had not been his intention to

cause him pain or to force him to recall that argument of six years
ago when he had spoken—had crowed—about new pursuits for
himself, about self-realization, but he suspected that that was
what had happened. He'd just wondered about Connie. If de-
feated by the mathematics of Mexico his son had given a thought
to her. "I try not to," Larry admitted with a weak laugh.

"But you do," Ed said.

Straight-faced his son said, "You want to get to the point where
you quit measuring every woman you meet off of the same
woman—that's what I mean."

"Because they don't measure up?"

"If they didn't have to they'd probably measure up very well.
Does that make any sense to you?"

"Makes enough. Why's she your measuring stick, son?"

Larry glanced over at him. He wore that weary, imploring look
that Ed had seen a number of times since he'd been back—but
that he could not remember having seen before. It was as if somebody had kicked the props out in his face. The pale eyes especially
sagged. "Dad, I haven't faced this yet, okay?" he said.

Ed suspected he had—faced it again and again and gotten
nowhere. "I'll take a guess," he went unheedingly on. "She's
smarter than the rest, and sweeter. She's a helluva lot healthier.
She's got more lasting power. She's got more horse sense."

"Connie? Horse sense? C'mon, Dad . . ." His son's voice trailed
off.

Ed didn't bother to call him back. He was on the point of
expostulating that after he was gone Larry might spend the rest of
his life not "facing it," but didn't, for as he sat there his fickle
strength suddenly began to drain out of him. It felt like that—like
a complete blood transfusion, perhaps, and the blood he got back
seemed given a paler cast. In the exchange he lost the vigor and
conviction of his thoughts. He remembered too much. "Okay,
son," he said.

Moments later, he spoke his mind. "A man might make three
or four mistakes in his life, and if he makes them in the company
of his wife she never forgets them. The woman doesn't have to be
cruel and spiteful, and it doesn't much matter whether she's your

Connie or my Sylvia or Russ's Jeannie. A man can take one look at his wife's face and see that she remembers every childish and shameful thing he's ever done. I'd like to know why that is. I don't think it's the other way around."

Larry didn't know why, although he did his father the courtesy of considering the question.

"It's something I've learned. It may be one of the few things I've learned riding around out here. Think about it the next time you want to face things with your wife. Women don't get in the doghouse, son, only the men."

"Now some women do," Larry objected, but without much conviction.

Ed left it at that. The weakness he felt gave a sense of hovering remoteness to the towns they drove through, to the fields and the farms. Outside of Urbana he asked his son to stop at a Wendy's to pick up something to eat. This time he did not get out of the van. He sat in the parking lot and after so much space felt the presence of the flanking cars and the red and yellow Wendy's wall before him as a particularly menial sort of confinement. Halfway through the hamburger, the mayonnaise and tomato began to drip so badly he knew if he tried to eat to the end he would make a horrible mess. He fitted the rest of the hamburger back into its Styrofoam shell. He had no appetite. That hovering remoteness to things was not going to be overcome with a Wendy's hamburger and strawberry shake, which he continued to dutifully suck up his straw as if he were blowing that Ping-Pong ball to the top of its tube. He had not blown into that tube or taken his pills for the last two days. He told himself if the disease was consuming his body he wanted to know at any given moment how much of himself he had left. At home they'd strung him up in a web of benevolent lies. Here if he began to float at least he was floating free. That was what he told himself. He would float free and come at last to rest in that bed. The alternative was to die strung up in that web, each strand of which, he dimly understood, was not so much a treachery as a misrepresentation of some sort, yes, a benevolent lie.

When he couldn't hold it off any longer, he allowed his wife's face to appear in his mind's eye, and to the three or four others he saw there bravely added the look of this last mistake. It gave a somber, deeply offended cast to what up to now had been an amused if disapproving frown. He looked until he couldn't be accused of flinching, then crawled onto the mattress in back. He told his son to bypass Urbana and take 45 south to 16. He named the towns: Tuscola, Mattoon, Taylorville.

Still without a map, Larry trusted his father's memory and drove in a southwesterly curve along routes 45 and 16, as far as Taylorville. There he parked before the county courthouse, almost in the cannon's mouth. When his father woke up he announced, "We're in Taylorville, Dad. I don't want to go to St. Louis. I'd just as soon not go through Baldwinsville either."

The voice that came out of the back of that van sounded cold and cavernous to him. He had not turned around. "Take 104 west to Jacksonville. Get on 67 and go north to Beardstown, Macomb, and Galesburg."

He'd gotten almost to Beardstown before his father climbed up beside him. When he helped him down into a filling-station restroom, he could feel an added brittleness in his step. Late afternoon outside of Galesburg they stopped again, and before Larry could check them into the motel, leave, and come back with Long John Silver Fish 'n' Chips, his father had gone to sleep. He found the pills in a side pouch of his Samsonite suitcase, a place his fingers remembered well, for there among balled socks he'd sometimes been allowed to fish out the gifts his father had brought after a week on the road. He read the labels carefully, then without quite understanding why copied out the contents onto the back of a card advertising the Meadowgrove Motel, where they stayed. "Theo-Dur—take one tablet every 8 hours for breathing." "Dilaudid—take one tablet every 3–4 hours as needed for pain." "Lasix—take one tablet every 12 hours as needed for swelling."

Since Ed was sleeping so soundly he decided to wait until the next morning before insisting he take his pills. The next morning he awoke just as his father was stepping out of the shower and up to the lavatory mirror to shave. The operation on his left lung had left a long sickle scar that reminded Larry of a shoulder harness; it stretched from the back of the shoulder, under the armpit, midway out across his chest. It was as wide as a narrow belt; water still glistened there, although once dry it would have a dull cartilaginous meatiness to it, he knew. Ironically—and this was the realization that brought him fully awake—the scar was the healthiest-looking thing about his father, for the rest of him was stringy, bent, fishy-pale, the flesh defining the bone as it fell away from it, the thinnest of flab.

Yet Ed claimed he felt better than he had in days, and for that morning and the first part of the afternoon he had them circling among towns in northwestern Illinois—Kewanee, Spring Valley, a place called Prophetstown, quiet in a chaff-filled heat—before directing them on to a crossing of the Mississippi at Rock Island. They had to drive down a bluff to get to it, and there would be a bluff to climb on the other side, and going down before they went back up Larry came within sight of his senses. The Mississippi, as dirty as it was, split this urban unsightliness of Rock Island–Davenport right down the middle; it split the continent too. In spite of its bridges and wharves and tour boats, it looked utterly inhospitable, and unforgiving, as alien as some sort of molten ore. He slowed the van. "You sure you want to go over there, Dad?" he asked, aware he sounded like an impressionable child.

It was something to be impressed by, for as many times as Ed had crossed it he'd never shaken the fear that by the time he came back its bridges and the ferries he'd frequently used would have all been swept away. "It was my territory, son," he said.

They crossed. They climbed the bluff and with a faintly forbidden sort of momentum found themselves coasting along Route 130 out over the Iowa prairie. They swung north of Iowa City through Tipton; south of Cedar Rapids through Mt. Vernon, Fairfax, Belle Plaine. By the time they reached Marshalltown, Larry felt as if they'd been shouldered up onto the center of the state, where nothing looked quite as flat and fertile and rectilinearly arranged as it had in Indiana and Illinois, but where the land stood higher, broken up by occasional ridges and cliffs. They seemed to hang up there, letting a drift west that the prairie encouraged take them on to Webster City and Fort Dodge. He thought it was his father's best day. It was as if they'd found an air he could breathe, for his throat remained relatively clear, and he had only gone to the mattress once, and not from exhaustion, Larry sensed, but as though he had rediscovered something in his swing through the state that he could best savor lying down. Peggy? Had they driven by her restaurant? Was it the taste of her flesh or chicken pot pies that had come back to him? He wondered but did not ask.

That night while his father slept Larry stepped into another phone booth with another ten dollars in change and decided only after dialing the area code that it was his brother he wanted to talk to, and not his mother. He wanted to pick up at a point in a conversation they'd had.

"You said no two people could agree on how to treat his disease. If the doctors can't make up their minds then maybe the patient has to take his cure into his own hands. I don't know anything about it, but *this* might make a difference. I see him getting stronger."

"*What* might? Where've you taken him, Larry?"

"I told Mother I can't tell you that."

"You can tell *me.*"

"Look, he's all right. I'm calling to tell you he seems stronger and since no two people can agree, this might, I said *might,* make a difference."

"Let me guess, Larry. You've got him in Mexico at one of those laetrile clinics."

"We're not in Mexico. You're gonna have to accept this, Russ. You think I came back here to get involved in all this because I wanted to? *He* asked me to. It's a secret he asked me to keep."

"You wanna know what I think?"

It was a question asked quietly, even smilingly, but with the effect of a snarl.

"If it makes you feel better," Larry said.

"I think that bourbon you drank the other night wasn't enough. I think you've gone back on drugs—if you ever got off."

"That's a relief, Russ. For a minute I was afraid you were going to say we were keeping score again and I was trying to go one up on you."

"I have another theory about that. Since you couldn't love Dad while he was well you want him all to yourself now that he's dying. Am I right, brother?"

"You can really be a smug and arrogant son of a bitch when you try," Larry said.

"Sure I'm right."

"When have you ever been wrong, Russ?"

"I'm right because since we were kids all you ever really gave a damn about was yourself. You can drive away from here with a dying man because you don't have an idea what family loyalty is all about. Family loyalty—I guess that's too reactionary a term for you. Where'd you get the car, Larry? Steal it?"

"He'd been saving the money. It was something he must have been planning for months. Can't you see I didn't have anything to do with it?"

He knew he'd made a mistake. If Russ wanted to he could now go to the car dealers in town and eventually discover the license number and the make of the van.

"You agreed to do it—whatever it is. I'd say you had something to do with it—plenty, in fact."

"You would have done the same thing, Russ," Larry heard himself plead, "if he'd put it to you the way he put it to me."

It was a question Russ must have already asked himself, for he answered it without hesitation. "No, I wouldn't have. I would have thought what it would have done to Mother and the rest of us."

Of course, that's exactly what he would have done. His father had made it clear; that was the reason Larry had been called back. It was a fundamental difference in character, a fact, which as he now accepted as such widened between them like an abyss. He had to shout over it to make himself heard, and he resented it, since he was certain his brother was perfectly content to remain on the other side.

"You've been in the business world too long, Russ. You still take inventory down at the paper company, don't you? Twice a year you still go through the place counting every roll of butcher paper and box of cups and sack of dust absorber on the premises, don't you? Your problem is you think you can do the same thing with yourself. Twice a year you can count your contents and be done with it. You're two cars, five bedrooms, two and a half baths, a couple of TVs, a microwave oven, a wife, three kids, a backyard, a deck, a half-drunk bottle of bourbon, it's all there, you know your way around, in the dark night of your soul you know who you are and where you are and how much you're worth, so that you won't give it a moment's thought when your father asks you to take him—"

He had almost blurted it out. He had stopped speaking so suddenly that the telephone booth was hot and close with the sound of his voice—it made him want to drop to the floor where fresh Iowa air entered through the small vents.

Colorless and impersonal now, like a police interrogator, Russ asked, "Where are you, Larry?"

"Somewhere you've never been, Russ," Larry said. "It won't look anything like your world."

"Are you taking drugs?"

"No."

"Are you drunk?"

"No."

"Do you know what you're doing to Mother?"

"I don't 'know.' I can imagine."

"Bring him back."

"I will the second he asks me to. He's got a right to decide how he wants to die, and because he's willing to assume that right and to risk hurting some people he loves, it might mean he can go on living."

"That's bullshit, Larry."

"Don't be too sure, Russ. Not *too* sure." And he hung up.

The operator wanted almost seven dollars for this call, and he couldn't understand why until he remembered that western Iowa was a lot farther from home than Indiana had been.

The next morning Ed woke him groaning. It was more of a

spoken sound, a despairing croon, and before he went to his father Larry went to the suitcase for the pills. His father's eyes were shut and there was a concentrated, inward-looking expression on his face of great intentness but not much pain. The crooning groan seemed too pure and musical to be the voice of pain, yet it was the Dilaudid he asked for. After he'd taken the pill with half a glass of water Ed tried to lower his head slowly back into the pillow but reached a point where he had to let it drop—and then Larry heard the pain. He imagined it closing like a small clawed hand inside his father's chest. "Ow!" Ed exclaimed in protest and surprise, then "Whoa . . . whoa . . . whoa" in that sorrowful, lilting croon.

Larry asked, "What should I do, Dad?" and Ed delayed awhile in answering, unwilling, it seemed, to interrupt himself. Then he said, "Go back to bed. Let's rest some more," in a small voice, located somewhere off to the side of where his real interest lay.

When Ed woke again it was almost noon. He sat up in bed, then stood, brittly bent in his pale blue pajamas. He said, "Maybe yesterday we went too far. I feel better now." Instead of shower- ing and shaving he walked to his suitcase across which he'd spread his clothes and began pulling his checked trousers on over his pajama pants. Uncertain, not knowing how to interpret these signs, Larry said, "Why don't we stay the rest of the day here," and while he carefully worked the trouser's zipper over a protrud- ing fold of the pajamas, Ed proposed, as a slightly preferable alter- native, "We might as well drive around."

They never got out of Iowa. The day was overcast. The sky, mottled in yellowing and leaden bands of gray, hung over them like an enormous lid, and they drove the prairie beneath it as though through a vacuum. Past momentum, the momentum of preceding days, eventually brought them to the Missouri River, which they did not cross. They actually shied back from it, but at a distance of some miles seemed to be following its course south as they took Route 275 through open farmland and more cattle ranges than they'd seen before to Sidney, a town in the southwest corner of the state. Ed said that that had been enough, that that had been fine. It was a town he knew, although not one he'd sold bags in. Like many, then, it was a town in danger of being forgotten, which his father tried not to forget. They drove through it—its grain elevators and stockyards on its northern edge, a grove of schoolyard cottonwoods on the south, and in the center, open to the sky, its courthouse and banks—on past a small shopping plaza, the Fremont, to a motel with a restaurant, the Carousel, although neither of them at the moment wanted to eat.

They'd caught the town at the evening hour. It smelled of its fried suppers and its ripening fields and the ripening stink of its stockyard. Its youth were back on the streets, and it also smelled of the fumes from their oil-burning cars. Nothing about it seemed any more venerable than the six-pack, fast-food trash thrown in its ditches, yet it had taken its bite in the land and would remain. Larry mixed himself a bourbon and soda. Across the room his father gave the impression of sitting precariously balanced on the bed, yet when he asked to be included Larry mixed him a weak bourbon and soda too. Why, he wanted to ask him, had that been enough? Why had that afternoon drive through western Iowa, which had come to a close in the town of Sidney, been fine?

But in a rush of fondness he said, "How are you, Dad? Are you feeling any pain?"

Ed raised his face to his son. It was ashen. The eyes hung in it like scummed pools. On the wall to his right there were two framed photographs: one of a western mountain range and the other of a Germanic-looking local church. To his left, the tiles in the bathroom were a cold dull green. In this room his father looked like something someone passing through had gone off and left, an object simply not worth the bother to haul on to the next town. Whoever it was had stuck a plastic glassful of weak bourbon consolingly in his hand.

"I'm afraid," Ed said.

"You're afraid," Larry echoed quietly.

"It's not the dying. Dying might be the one good thing that everybody's got coming . . . once I lie down in that bed."

For a long moment his father did not speak. Then he sighed, a rattly release of breath, and sank farther over onto his knees. From that position he brought his drink to his lips. "There's not much bourbon in this glass," he complained.

Larry held the bottle out to him. "Have some more, Dad," he said.

"This was as far as I got, son. This was the end of my territory." He looked up at Larry, not at the bottle. "If I'd taken the northern territory I could've done half my business on the phone. More money in Chicago than in the whole state of Iowa. But I wanted to come out here."

Ed's eyes drifted off, and Larry lowered the bottle of Jim Beam bourbon to the bed. He waited, wondering how long his father wanted to be alone with his thoughts, if it was good for him, or if his son's company was. The bourbon he knew would be poison. "What are you afraid of, Dad?" he finally asked.

"Afraid I didn't go far enough," his father answered immediately, but at a toneless remove.

"What do you mean?"

"S'because my territory stopped here, but every week I set out from home I had it in me to go a lot farther than this. It hurts now that I'm out here again, at the end of my territory, that's all." He paused until he had Larry's eye. "What have I missed?" he said.

"What have you missed?"

"If I can believe those postmarks on your letters you got a lot farther than this. What have I missed?"

"Nothing," his son said.

"You sure?"

For a dutiful fifteen seconds he searched his mind for what it might have meant. For his father's benefit he went through the act of unraveling the miles. But it *was* an act, and it suddenly shamed him. Bitterly honest with himself, he said, "It was just the motion, Dad."

"How 'bout when you stopped?"

Larry grinned emptily. "It was just gettin' the hell outta town."

"That day you got outta Welborne you convinced me you had something in mind. There was a lot more to it than just leaving Connie and your kids. You wanted to *do* something. You were so pent-up with energy you had me half believing it would take a country this size to do it in. What happened?"

"Nothing happened. I ran out of steam. I got older. I don't

know. I saw a lot of people running around with a lot of pent-up energy just like me, and we weren't very good for each other. I lived in a commune in the Sierra Nevadas for a while with a bunch of eastern mystics of every persuasion, but I didn't like goat's milk or tofu or puja bells, or them. In fact, I can't recall many people I *did* like. Most kids I met didn't have a thought in their heads past the next rock concert. Friends I had known from the Vietnam years acted as if eating a saltless, meatless meal from an organic garden in your backyard was an act of political protest, and I wore out my welcome with them. I guess I thought there was a place and if I kept moving long enough the country would meet me halfway, and it didn't. I got ten years older."

"Six," his father said, "since that day you turned down half of the business."

"I would have run amok in Welborne, you know that."

"No place you liked better?"

"A little village outside of Santa Fe called Cerrillos was nice, until all the art-gallery types moved in."

"You worked for an art gallery, didn't you?"

He faced his father's insinuation. "I had to eat, Dad. I'm not a hermit. Until I couldn't take them anymore I had to have some sort of company."

"In Mexico you had your share. . . . Pepa, I like that name, and . . ."

"Suellen. That was different. You're out of your country. Not everything reminds you of something you'd like to forget or blow up. *Later* it begins to, but not at first. With your taste for traveling I'm surprised you never got down there."

"I thought of it, I knew where it was. But in my traveling days this was my territory, and if I'd gone to Mexico what would I have done with Sylvia and you kids?"

They went to sleep with the spaghetti and meatballs that Larry had brought in from the adjoining restaurant half uneaten on the table between them. The next morning the smell of that tomato sauce lay in an oily film on everything in the room. They stayed in bed, Larry with a headache and a torpor in his bones, until late morning, when Ed said he wanted to go. Neither shaved nor showered. Not an hour after they'd started back east Ed went to his mattress, instructing his son to stay on Route 2 all the way across the south of the state; if Ed was still asleep by the time they hit Centerville, Larry was to wake him. By then Larry had stopped twice, once for gas and once at an A&W root beer stand, where his father, both of the pillows under his head and one of the yellow blankets tucked up under his arms, slept through the placing of the order and the twanging response of the girl reading it back on the speaker. For the space of that corn dog and root beer Larry made himself forget that his father was in the van. The sun was out. Those A&W carhops had not changed in thirty years. They were still chubby-faced, blue-eyed, still possessed of a gaudy and guileless smile. Only when his carhop—Sally, her nametag read—removed his tray from the window did he face it: his father wasn't going to make it, something would have to be done. Entering Centerville he did as he'd been told. Past it, Ed asked his son to pull off at the side of the road. After he'd helped his father down from the back of the van he stood back and watched him hold to a fence post as he peed, before him a herd of mildly curious Hereford cattle, and beyond them the curving dome of the vast midwestern sky. There was nothing to be done. Preserve these memories; prepare for the day it all vanished without a trace.

Before they reached Bloomfield his father asked him to take Route 63 south, and at the Iowa-Missouri line when Larry reminded him that Missouri had not been his territory, his father said he knew that and it didn't matter, to drive on. The first town they came to was Lancaster, but before they entered it they had passed, small and set back from the road so that he might have missed it had he not been looking, the Schuyler County Hospital. Lancaster was little more than a depot for the surrounding farms. The only motel they could find was an E-Con Travel, and after Larry had carried in the suitcases and gotten his father seated before a television whose oranges and greens spread out fierily over the screen, he announced he was going back out to see about food. He went to the desk clerk instead, a man in his early thirties, whose hair was excessively oiled and the set of whose bones—

square and frank and handsomely whole—told Larry he was a believer of some sort. In case he wasn't back in an hour Larry wondered if the desk clerk would be so kind as to look in on the man in room 23, who wasn't feeling well.

Then he drove to the hospital he'd seen, where he was told not only was an oncologist not on duty, but there wasn't one in the entire county, and where he settled—promising not to take up much of his time—for a radiologist. He was not about to bring his father here. In such a short time, then, all he could do was describe his father's condition and show the radiologist the card, on one side of which was written "Meadowgrove Motel—Nothing Fancy, Just a Good Night's Rest," and on the other side the names and doses of the pills. The radiologist was younger than the motel clerk, most likely doing his internship here out of the state university medical school. He was pale and beard-shadowed. He had adopted a professional manner which allowed for only the thinnest of smiles and no small talk, but he'd yet to perfect it and on two occasions interrupted himself to express surprise, even incredulity: "Traveling around where?" "Eating what?" One of the medications—Lasix, the pills for swelling—he admitted he wasn't familiar with, but deferred to the oncologist who had prescribed them. Without seeing the man, of course, he could prescribe nothing else, recommend nothing else. Bring him in and he would x-ray his chest and send the results to the hospital in Kirkwood, where, yes, he would find an oncologist. At the end he was at his best—clipped and decided and coolly indignant: the patient should be under the care of his doctors in . . . Galesburg, Illinois, he turned the card over and read.

Driving back, Larry stopped off in a 7-Eleven for anything— aspirin—and $10 more of change. The booth this time was located between a package store, that looked like a concrete bunker hung with beer signs, and a small restaurant, whose plain bill of fare would not exceed cutlets and fries. He badly needed to hear his sister's voice, but—remembering his unkept promise to her—not as she would harden it against him. He deposited enough for the first three minutes and said, "Be calm, Mother, don't scream. Listen quietly to what I have to say," and was deeply relieved, as though that were all he'd hoped to accomplish, when she said, "Yes, Larry, I will."

He said he was in a bind. He said he wasn't irresponsible, thoughtless, cruel. He said he was taking care of his father as best he could, and that he was no worse than when they had left, but that he worried constantly about what *they* might be going through. It was no use trying to talk Dad out of this . . . this thing he wanted to do, because he'd already tried. It seemed best for all of them if he, Larry, the unfortunate one chosen for the role, went along. All he could really ask of them, then, was that they trust him . . . and here his mouth began to go dry so quickly he wasn't sure he'd make it to the end . . . and think of him as somehow representing all of them in their dealings with . . . this dear dying man. Couldn't she see things in this light?

He marveled at her control as, still quiet, her voice seemed to pool out to him, and to take some of the dryness out of *his* mouth. He wondered if she was under sedation. He assumed she was. "Larry, it's all been explained to me. When patients reach Ed's stage in their illness they frequently become the victims of fantasies they can't do anything about. They get ideas, son—they have strange desires. Sometimes they even sound funny. They told me about one case of a man who had to drive a locomotive before he died . . . you know, be the engineer in a real steam locomotive. The doctors couldn't convince that poor man that none of those even existed nowadays. Patients with fantasies like those behave like children sometimes, and it's perfectly normal, the doctors said, as long as you take it as part of the disease. All we can do is help nurse them back to reality, they said."

"Did they mention what *that* was?"

"Reality?"

"Yes."

"It's us, son. It's the people who love him and have lived with him for all these years. It's his friends and his family. It's the town where he's made his reputation for being an honest, upstanding man. I don't know what he's talked you into doing, but it can't be as important as all that." She paused a moment. "Can it?"

"No . . . I don't know," he mumbled.

"Ask yourself, Larry: which is 'realer,' whatever it is you're doing or what's waiting for him here?" She saved him another mumbled reply by going on at once, her voice brisker now, as though its pooling edge had pulled back to show him firm sand or bottom mud hardening at once in the sun. "Do you remember Dr. McManus, the psychiatrist? He remembers you. As soon as you bring Ed back he'll explain to him what's wrong."

"No, I don't remember him."

"When you bring him back we'll all sit down together. He's a very intelligent man."

As cooperatively, as unaggressively, as he knew how, he said, "I'm not sure I can do that, Mother. I'll have to talk to Dad."

"It won't do any good for *you* to try and talk Ed out of it. That's Dr. McManus's job."

"I'll ask him, Mother."

"Larry, stop being difficult. You aren't listening to me. You say you want us to trust you. We've trusted you with Ed up to now. It's time for you both to come to your senses. Bring him home."

"Mother," he said wearily, "none of us is having an easy time of it, *none* of us is."

"Don't begin to feel sorry for yourself."

"You and I haven't had much in common the last few years, and one of the hardest things about all this is that something we do have in common is coming between us now. D'you know what I mean?"

She waited, intractable and composed. "No, I don't," she said.

"We both love Dad," Larry said. "Isn't that what's causing the problem?"

She waited again, then said, "Does that give you the right to kidnap him from me?"

He snagged on the word. "What?" he said.

"That's really what this is, isn't it, Larry? A case of the son kidnapping the father from the mother. You always liked to complicate things, but the plain truth is you're the son and you're kidnapping your father from me."

"Is that something Dr. McManus said?"

"I said it. Either you promise to bring Ed back right now, or it's what I intend to charge you with to the police."

"The police? Mother, just because Dad doesn't want to stay there in Welborne doesn't mean you can call in the police."

"It does if he's incompetent to make rational decisions. It does if he's under the influence of an irrational fantasy, as Dr. McManus has explained. It does if someone else takes advantage of his condition—and *aggravates* it."

"I'm not aggravating anything! Stop it now—please!"

She'd provoked him into an outburst so that coolly once more she could play off of it.

"Do you remember Douglas Bridges, the lawyer?"

He didn't. He realized he'd probably managed to blank most of Welborne's stellar citizens out.

"Well, he remembers you. A lot of people do, Larry. And given your record as a protester and radical he thinks I'd have a strong case if I wanted to press charges. He says he might not be able to convict you in a court of law, but once you cross state lines it's like you're extending the crime and then it's a much more serious offense. Have you crossed state lines, Larry?"

"Mother, stop. Okay? Just stop."

"Russell feels the same way."

"What about Nell?"

"Nell doesn't want to hear the sound of your name."

"And with that kind of welcoming committee you expect me to disregard Dad's wishes and bring him back?"

She held a long silence. He had time to look around, even to slip into a wishful fantasy of his own: that out beyond those pickup groceries and farm machinery displays and ragged bars, out into all that pastureland, wheat, and corn, there might be a patch of ground where a man could live in peace with his neighbors, even though they were only cows and hogs. Then in a tone that tensed affection off of resentment, acceptance off of distrust, and that made it impossible for him to come close, his mother said, "I don't know if you know this, Larry, but we've always forgiven you for everything you've done before. I think I can speak for Russell and Nell—"

He'd had enough. "My father is a sick man," he said, "but he is *not* crazy. If he comes back there it will be because he wants to. And you can tell that to Police Chief . . . who, mother?"

"Police Chief Bradley. He'll remember you too."

"Tell him. Tell him to go arrest a judge or two on the take, or the mayor for all the bootlegging, land-finagling money he must have made, or a few members of his own force for shooting up niggertown when they're bored. Tell him to leave us alone."

Quickly, but with a sharp desolate regret, he hung up the phone. He paid the extra $5.60 the operator asked for gladly, as though that could somehow salve his conscience, and drove to the other side of Lancaster, Missouri, and the motel where his father was waiting with a shored-up sense of purpose that barely lasted the opening of the door. Larry was clearly coming apart, and the way he sat down on the bed reminded Ed of that first day they'd talked, that state of powerlessness he'd arrived in that seemed to trail behind it an enormous amount of futilely spent energy. To give him something to do, Ed asked him to get up and turn off the television and a baseball game from St. Louis he'd watched the monotonous middle innings of. Then he noticed that Larry, who'd gone out for food, had come back empty-handed, and took his guess.

"Did you call them?" he asked.

He had to repeat the question. He had to coax an answer out of his son.

"I called Mother," Larry finally admitted.

"Anybody else?"

"A couple of days ago I talked to Russ. And Mother once before that. I couldn't let them think you'd just disappeared."

"What did you tell them?"

"Not where we were—or where we were going." He responded as if he were fending off blows. He sat slumped over on his knees, dressed in a wash-faded shirt and jeans scrubbed blue-white, the work, Ed guessed, of a Mexican maid, who would have given his son's clothes a pounding over stone. He pictured a nut-brown woman with enormous arms, but realized he was only conjuring up the image of a Mexican woman as a way of asking himself about the strength of his son, whose arms had always been thin but capable of remarkable feats: he remembered Larry lifting hundred-pound boxes and drums up onto trucks; he remembered, as though he'd hit them himself and felt the currentlike contact from the tips of his fingers to the tips of his toes, some near-three-hundred-yard drives. He noticed a fleshiness in Larry's triceps now, not much but enough so that the underbelly of the arm hung; freckles had taken root there in mildewlike clusters. The neck just beneath the ear had begun to loosen and sag. Larry had his father's lanky, angular build—Russell would stay close to the ground like Sylvia—but when men of Larry's build started to show their age a sadness came over their skin, Ed thought, it seemed for a moment—a period, a year—as though the skin wanted to paper out smooth and reverse the process that had coarsened and cured it—before the final withering began. It only made it that much worse. Heavy men just got heavier. But men like his son had to undergo a change in kind, a transformation—and then Ed knew he was thinking about himself.

Larry was on his feet now, to get the bourbon and soda and ice. And the very worst of it, Ed realized, was that in forcing his company on his son he was probably also forcing him to route his thoughts through a dying man, just as he, a dying man, had been routing his thoughts through his son. It gave him a brief and not very trustworthy understanding of why Larry in his presence might suffer these periods of powerlessness and why he, Ed, might feel a flickering buildup of strength. For he did feel stronger—strong enough so that he didn't have to kid himself about what it meant.

"I may as well tell you,"—his son was pacing before him now, rattling the ice in his plastic glass—"that mother has threatened to get the police after us. She thinks she's found a way to have me charged with illegally taking you away."

Even strong enough to ask, without clouding his mind, "How is she, Larry? How does she sound?"

"Today she sounded calm and controlled. Too calm. I don't know. I'm not even sure the woman I talked to was Mother."

"A steel trap just before it crushes your leg might be the calmest thing in the world." He grinned at his son, just to let him know the analogy was unfair. "I'll be honest with you, I guess I thought you'd call her every so often. I can't be sure of it but I guess that's why I didn't leave her a note—just so you would."

"But not tell her where we were?" Larry had stopped before him. He was in such an undecided, disbelieving state his presence seemed to be scattered around the room. It may have been the effect of the rattling ice.

"I didn't think you'd tell her that."

"I'm glad you trust me. She doesn't. It's hard to defend yourself if you can't explain."

"In this case it'd be harder if you did."

Larry stood mutely off by the closed door now, blank except for a small sign announcing checkout time and house rules. Beside the door, the frayed rust-brown curtains were also closed. Ed said, "You know, I slept through most of the day. What's it like outside? Nice evening?"

"It's a beautiful evening. It goes on and on. Dad, you'd better explain it to me again too," Larry said.

There was a spark there, a hint of something rattled and irreverent that might kick up a small storm. Ed waited, very much as if he were studying the weather off on the horizon.

"I mean," Larry went on, "that first time you told me about it it made a beautiful, sad, crazy sort of sense. There was a minute there when it might have made the only sense I've heard made on the matter—in this country, at least. I mean, there's so much of this that's meaningless, that's *extraneous*, that in the end if you can just hold on to what's yours and take it back to where you began you can beat them at their own game. So we were going to go get that bed and home in on Chumleyville. Forgive me, Dad, you were desperate and scared, but that was the way you made it sound. It was an adventure. But now we're out here driving in big lazy circles in the midwest as if the first fast-talker that came along could have us for a song. You'll have to forgive me again, and I'd

put it any other way if I could, but *this isn't what I signed on for.*
You see my predicament, Dad? You see how hard it is for me to
justify myself when I talk to Mother and Russ?"

For a moment then he had it overhead, a cloud that couldn't
quite bring itself to pour down, but rumbled, groaned, leaked a
little exasperated moisture, flashed forbiddingly to itself. It was
something. It managed to collect most of what Larry had left
scattered around the room; somehow it got between Ed and his
fear. "Hand me that box of tissues," he said, "and pour yourself
another drink."

Then he worked at clearing his throat, aware that there was
more phlegm to get up each day and a little less breath to do it
with, but accepting the fact, and what it meant, and with the
breath he had left getting up what he could. Leaning up on his
chair he tossed the wadded tissue the rest of the way into the trash
basket. By then Larry had freshened his drink and moved back to
that open space before the door. Ed said, "I never traveled in
circles, son, even when I was sitting back and letting the car take
the road. Sooner or later I always paid my calls."

He paused again, to give his son's jitteriness time to subside,
and the jittery rattling of the ice. "You were right," he continued.
"Missouri wasn't part of my territory, but that doesn't mean I
don't know my roads. Route 63 will take us through Kirksville,
Macon, Moberly, and on into Columbia. Thirty-five miles past
Columbia it goes right through Jefferson City. We'll have to go
about twenty-five of those miles before we pay our call."

It took his son so long to figure it out because he was thinking
St. Louis, St. Louis, Ed was sure, and forgetting Connie and the
kids had moved in May to a house in the country where, she had
written, they could have animals, for a start maybe chickens and
ducks and goats. When Larry did remember, the sprawling midwest suddenly became very small. Ed could see it in his face, his
shoulders and his knees: starting, the whole of him seemed to
come to a point. Then he shook his head, and as his thoughts, his
objections, began to multiply he shook it more vigorously. Ed let
him finish, then said, "I know, son, you didn't sign on for that
either."

Finally, in a heavily measured voice, Larry replied, "No, Dad. I don't want to see them now. Now is not the time."

"How long's it been?"

"Before I left for Mexico. I got a ride up from Santa Fe."

Ed said, "I'll be honest with you," although he wasn't going to be, not entirely. "I wasn't thinking of you. I was thinking of myself. I want to see my daughter-in-law again, and my grandchildren."

He heard the ice start to rattle again, at a more agitated pitch. Larry jerked away from him, then finding nowhere to go, jerked back, bringing with him that bad weather, that turbulent yet turned-in cloud. "Dad, things have changed! You don't know what you're getting into! Connie's not the same. There's a whole world out there you haven't got the least idea about, and that's the world Connie's in."

"You were going to tell me about it," Ed reminded him, "but you didn't, did you? Where my territory ended and yours began. What's out there, son?"

Then it was as though Larry had swallowed all that furious energy and were measuring out, coldly, his reply. "For a year now, maybe longer, Connie's been living with another woman. They used to call it a lesbian relationship. As a matter of fact, they still do."

He wasn't shocked. Instead he seemed to go on a state of alert that allowed a small but lively part of himself to feel curious, then strangely pleased, then even more strangely thrilled—and that, on a delayed basis, did shock him.

"What's it done to her?" he asked.

"Done to her?" his son repeated, flustered. "It's played hell with her heterosexual sex life, for one thing!"

"I understand that, but . . ." And then he asked a question that made perfect sense, but a sense he was not accustomed to making. "Do you like her better or worse since then?"

Larry stood there shaking his head. "Dad, I tell you, you step outside of Welborne, Kentucky, and other Welborne Kentuckys, and it's a whole different world. Questions like that don't make any sense."

"I'll ask another one then. Which do you like best?"

"Which . . . world?"

"Yes. Welborne's, or the one 'out there'?"

Larry began to shake his head again. Then he did the honest thing and stopped, and Ed watched an expression of impotent anger take control of his son's face. The anger became a wrenching of self-disgust. Larry was a man who'd somehow been taught it was unmanly to show compassion to himself. Had he, Ed Reece, taught him that? "Neither one," his son declared bitterly. "If you want to know the truth, I don't much care for either one."

PART TWO

IV

SHE sat still and listened to the wind. She heard it nearby in the forest of second-growth oak and ash next to their property, where it made a musical shiver, and she heard it in the leaves of the tulip tree in their front yard, where it made a coarse quiet clatter. Out over the fields, in the middle distance, she could hear it rattling the cornstalks and in the thinnest and cleanest of whispers parting the long grasses. More than a mile away at the limit of her hearing, it combined with the sound of passing semis on the expressway between Jefferson City and Columbia to give her the impression of an institutional sort of restlessness, penitential and dull. She sat before an open window looking onto the front porch, a glass of burgundy in her hand. It was late, past midnight, and when she'd been a girl on a farm outside of Marion, Ohio—hating it, of course, hating the remoteness, hating the list of deprivations it had caused her to suffer—she had never enjoyed listening to the night. It came with age, she supposed, and a willingness to sit quietly by in one of the world's dark corners while everyone else crowded out onto the brightly lit stage. In college she'd played guitar and sung folk songs while studying to be an actress. Now she wanted to take care of animals and could best imagine that world continuing on without her when she listened to it at night.

A cicada that had been cutting on and off in long ringing pulses started up again, obliterating the softer-voiced peepers and crickets. When it stopped she could hear restive stirrings from the henhouse out back, followed by a flurry of crotchety clucks as one of the hens started on her nest. Then Mike, their Labrador, barely muttering a bark, ticked across the bare boards of the back porch to lap water from his bowl. That gave her the sound of the burgundy passing down her throat. Which brought it momentarily home.

Of all the people in her house her daughter, Lisa, was the only one not making a sound, and that may have been because she had not had to give up her bed. Or energy-wise beyond her years, she may have been conserving her forces for all the tiring and tiresome demands she would make during the day. Jeff, who during the day good-naturedly ran his head off, she'd had to move in with his sister, and she heard him now talking in his sleep, a tonelessly sustained string of pleas, commands, and matter-of-fact observations she no longer worried about or tried to chart into the future. His last utterance hung unconcluded in the air, its urgency lost, and in behind it she heard Jan in her room still at work, her pencil scratching across her long yellow pad, occasionally the crumpling of an unsatisfactory sheet or a crackling noise as she impatiently turned the pages of her large legal books.

Jan had not given up her room either. She'd wanted to take the children and go to a motel until this senseless visit had ended, and the children had volunteered to sleep elsewhere—Jeff in a hammock they'd strung up out back and Lisa, uninvited, at the house of one of her recently made friends. But Connie had wanted them all here—she wasn't sure why. Perhaps she just wanted to see if she could make the room, really, how much room she could make in herself.

On another swallow of wine she settled more deeply into the easy chair. She wore a gray sweatshirt with pouch pockets in front; she wore sandals and jeans and her pale red hair cut short. It was how they'd found her that afternoon, hoeing around the tomatoes in her garden, her face streaked with sweat, and she hadn't washed or changed since then. They would have noticed she'd put on weight. It hung off her eyes and wrapped a puffy scarf around her throat and thickened her thighs, but short of jogging three or four miles a day or burning the sort of self-consuming fuel that kept Jan thin, she didn't see what she could do. Larry, for once in his life, looked speechless, speechless to the bone, and Ed . . . well, he looked horrible, of course, very frail, but putting startling first impressions aside she could tell he was happy and relieved to be there.

After a moment's disbelief she realized she'd been expecting him. Last spring when he'd written asking her to notify him at once of any change of address, she'd suspected that something was wrong. She'd written right back, and while she was at it had written Larry in Mexico to tell him where he could now find his kids, but in the busyness of the move from St. Louis and in the setting up of the goat pen and henhouse she'd put by her concern. But this afternoon when she'd looked up from her hoeing and seen the green van pulling up the drive, it was as though she'd tracked them down off the expressway herself and directed them through the three turns it took to get back to their house. She knew what she would see. It even seemed fitting that Ed Reece, a man she had liked, perhaps even more so when Larry had dismissed him as an establishment stooge, should pay her a dying call. Jan had called it madness, medically, morally, and yes, perhaps legally. But Connie had leaned her hoe up against the side of the house and met them at the head of the drive. She'd been there to help Ed down from his seat. The mystery was that there'd been no mystery—that it had been clear at once. Larry had whispered to her that it was what Ed had wanted, that Ed had insisted, and who was he to tell him no? Or, for that matter, who was she? She'd helped him in and given him her bed. Later, from her garden, she'd fixed them a summer supper of beans, tomatoes, and beets. Much later, deserving it, she'd gone to her easy chair with a glass of burgundy, where as all the night sounds found a home in her she listened to *them,* and realized that even though the wind had sung to her, the crickets and the cicada, the hens and dog and her own tone-deaf son, she'd been listening to them all along: the weak growling groans of a human engine running down as her ex-father-in-law tried to clear his throat, and the frightened whispered avowals of his son, her ex-husband, that it was okay, that everything would be all right.

Earlier in the evening there'd been a moment when Larry had explained to her what his father had persuaded him to do. She understood that he'd been caught in the middle, almost been shanghied into driving that van, and yes, could appreciate the irony behind the fact that his father had chosen to reject a place, a way of life, just as he, Larry, was trying to come to terms with it—and had sympathized. Then she'd told him something she'd been thinking about during her months back in the country, and a conclusion she'd come to. There was so much in our lives we could talk our way out of or reason our way around that when we came up against something we couldn't, we considered it crazy and absurd. But finally it was only those crazy, absurd and inescapable things that mattered.

She'd been thinking about Larry's incredible trek around the country with a dying father, maybe just about the incredible fact of death itself, but as example she gave him what was going on in their daughter Lisa's life. He knew the story of *her* life, of Connie Williams's, and didn't have to have it repeated now. How until the age of fifteen she'd been imprisoned on a failing farm in the center of Ohio. How then she'd been sent to Cincinnati to live with her Uncle Hal and Aunt Ellen, where she'd had a wide selection of boyfriends to chose from and where her belief in Romance could flourish and where virginity would quickly come to seem like a phony distinction, a little gold star they pasted up beside your name because you couldn't get the real thing. And how her Uncle Hal had smiled on her free-spiritedness, given her a key to the house and no lectures, and when the time came had sent her off to study acting, since no one else had believed in her theatrical aspirations. Larry didn't need to hear all that. Only that Lisa now, at fourteen, was already chafing at this isolation in the country, and as boy-crazy as her mother ever had been would surely find some way to leave it, substituting St. Louis for Cincinnati, leaving behind a brother two years younger, just as Connie had left behind her brother, Sam. That her life would repeat itself in this way seemed crazy and absurd to her, and that nothing could be done, unjust. But all that she'd learned until now told her that she was facing one of life's inescapable moments.

Had she expected sympathy in return? Support of some sort? After all, Lisa was his daughter too. But tortoiselike, Larry had pulled down within himself, sticking his head out just long enough to remark that there were too many differences for her to worry about history repeating itself. She and her friend Jan weren't your typical mid-Ohio farming couple, for one thing. For another, Lisa in St. Louis would have no Uncle Hal.

"You don't care?" she had asked.

"Of course I care!" he had answered, momentarily aroused. Then he'd spun sharply down to a sympathizing abjectness. "I know I haven't given you any support with her. I'm sorry, Connie. I'm not an utterly ungrateful shit. And I'm not accusing you of anything—remember that."

"Very generous of you," she'd replied.

"I mean it."

And she'd persisted, for no good reason she could name. "And if you didn't mean it, what would you have to accuse me of?"

"Nothing."

"The example I set?"

"Lisa'll be all right. . . . I can't get into this with you now. I've got Dad to worry about."

"It's a good example. Show me an Ohio farming couple who set a better one. We're the salt of the earth. We pull our weight out here."

"What can I say?"

"A good year? Did you enjoy yourself in Mexico?"

"No."

"I'm sorry. You may not believe me, but I've made a point of wishing you good years. When the children have asked, I've said, 'Let's hope he's happy.' "

"I wish you wouldn't," he'd muttered morosely.

"Your poor father," she'd said. "That poor dear man."

He'd looked at her then, full of his abjectness, the taste of it intolerable in his mouth. And she'd said, "Go to bed, Larry."

She wanted to take care of animals. She wanted to be in their midst, for even when animals were sick, she believed they were at peace. She knew they could panic—from her years on the farm she still remembered a look of unsocketed frenzy in a mare's eye when a king snake had slithered through her stall—but it was a peaceful panic, a panic that had as its substratum that deep animal peace. She simply wanted to do what she could to make their suffering brief. With that in mind she'd driven over to the State University in Columbia early in the summer and inquired what additional undergraduate courses she would have to take to apply for admission to the vet school. She'd been told that a degree in theater arts hadn't provided much of a base, and given a list of classes. In the fall she would take Chemistry 101 and Physiology as a part-time student. If she lasted that long she would take Organic Chemistry and Microbiology in the spring.

If someone had told her the day she'd left the farm for Cincinnati that twenty-three years later she would in effect be working her way back she wouldn't have bothered to laugh. Or that her brother, Sam, after taking all his beer-drinking aggressiveness to Vietnam, would be farming the acres their father had let go to seed when Hal had gotten him that job in Procter & Gamble and he and her mother had moved to Cincinnati too. But she'd seen it for herself. Last summer she'd accepted an invitation to revisit the farm for the first time, and her sense of things was that Sam had now both himself and his land fit for inspection. He grew soybeans and oats; also he raised some hogs and a few dairy cattle. She hadn't cared much for his new wife, Carol, who seemed anxious and tight-lipped around the kids, but she'd liked Sam—out on his land, down in his barn, mixing feed, fixing his motors, milking his cows. She thought he looked like a wise and resourceful big brother now, although he was her junior. She remembered a talk that they had had, not so much what they'd said as the fact that Sam had stood the entire time with his hand absently outstretched onto a cow's back, and she'd heard that quiet, firm, four-footed peace she sought in the rhythms of his voice.

On their return to St. Louis they'd stopped in Cincinnati, where her father's drinking and arthritis and her mother's gossipy litany of complaints had kept their visit short. Anyway, she had always felt less their daughter and more Uncle Hal's niece. As was their custom each time they met, she sat down with her uncle and brought him up to date on her life, and since Hal had never bothered to censure her for anything she'd done, she omitted very little. It was also a way of updating herself. This time, what characterized the woman who began to emerge through her words was, above all, her power of accommodation, the ease with which she'd been able to move from one employer to the next, from job to job, man to man. To see it laid out like this over the last few years shocked her a bit and aroused her suspicion, but there she was. After she and Larry had separated she'd taken a job with an acquaintance of her uncle's, a real estate agent and speculator named Frank Wilson, and her first lover had been the architect Wilson had hired to help develop a list of inner-city properties. When Wilson's faith in the rehabilitation of inner-city shells had lapsed, she'd taken a job with the architect himself, and when their affair had reached a natural rounding-off point she'd been able to stop it before the recriminations started. It had gone on like that.

She'd learned enough about the profits and pitfalls of downtown gentrification to find work when she needed it. Of her other affairs, the longest had lasted two months, and in each case she discovered a capacity for not clinging that she'd been able to pass on to the men and that made not just the sensible parting but the whole thing fine. Not clinging could also be interpreted as not sticking, not taking hold, not making a thing last, she knew; she'd preferred not to interpret. She told her uncle she was content, although the fact was after she'd made enough money to buy half of an old brick duplex on Lafayette Square she'd begun to lose interest in her work. One of her last sales had been to a young lawyer, Jan McKenney, who'd bought the other half of the duplex she lived in and with whom—quietly, unmomentously—she'd entered into her first lesbian affair.

Had it really been like that? So quiet and unmomentous? Rather, hadn't it felt like a fundamental split in herself, a chasm back over which she now had to gaze? Perhaps it was supposed to

feel like that—perhaps she even wished that it had—but it
hadn't. She was the same person, there in St. Louis and here
reciting a necessarily abridged but not really expurgated version of
her life for the pleasure and approval of her Uncle Hal.

He was a one-man sunset. Cloudy white hair and ruddy red
face, he gave the impression of sinking down to his rest. But his
eye was alive, a shade of hazel running brown over green, as the
muddy waters of his beloved Ohio ran brightly over the reflections
of riverside bushes and trees. He didn't ask her about Jan. He
grinned at her admiringly and asked if she remembered the last
time they'd talked, when she and the rest of the family had come
back through town. He'd taken her aside then and as much as it
had hurt him had told her she'd be wise to start thinking about
making her own living. Larry he'd sized up as a professional graduate student who would stand pat on his first dime, provided he
ever made one. Yes, she remembered, although she hadn't really
believed he'd been hurt, only aware of those occasions when other
men would be. He'd gone on to make a few suggestions, give her a
couple of names, one of whose had been Frank Wilson's. She'd
been grateful—and still was. So she assured him that in spite of
the years that had gone by she remembered their last talk very
well, and the wink he gave her in return was somehow meant to
span the years, keeping both their intimacy and his mockery of it
alive. That was his style. She'd quit trying to figure him out,
admitted to a strange sort of attraction for probably what was least
trustworthy about him. He slipped into a folksy role. Like the fella
said, she'd done him proud. Then he gave her a longer-lasting
wink, one with more weight. Although it certainly was sad what
had become of her ex-husband. What had?

She'd gone back to Jan. Even before they'd become lovers Jan
had offered to have Larry run down and made to pay the child
support Connie had never collected a penny of. Afterward, when
they'd knocked out a door on the back stairwell to join the two
apartments and this curious and almost indolent sort of intimacy
had entered their lives, Jan threatened to take matters into her
own hands, outraged every time she saw Connie drive the kids to
school because neither the streets nor the school bus was safe.

And Connie would calm her. Not just about Larry—more frequently it was the male hegemony in the courthouse that vexed her, or the laxity in enforcing environmental laws—but whatever the cause of Jan's unrest Connie would calm her, and it was then as that battle-quick body gave up its intensity and regained in the act a languorous warmth and suppleness of skin that Connie felt desire for her. It was like an act of creation. She had this demiurgic power, and once she had used it and effected this change, it excited her—pleased her deeply.

They'd become lovers only after they'd become friends and confidantes, and although Jan had had experience of this sort before it was Connie, when the moment came, who took the initiative. She hadn't planned it. She simply knew in that moment that she could do it. No, with that first touch to Jan's trembling neck she knew that *it could be done.* There was, in addition to the affection and the very immediate thrill in that touch, a subtle sense of impersonality, as though then and there they had made contact with a power or presence that exceeded them. With a man her passion had always built in a rush, clouding her mind and confusing her senses, but right from the start she had had with Jan this outlet which was also, paradoxically, a fund from which she could draw. So maybe it wasn't a passion at all, but a state of contentment, which instead of intensifying clarified until it became pure. She couldn't say. All she knew was that holding Jan, coaxing her closer, kissing her neck, her lips, which tightened and pressed loyally back against hers, she was not entirely herself and that something was working through her. Her act of faith was to believe that the same thing was working through Jan, or could be made to, and that given over to it entirely they might reach a point where not so much as a quiver of their old uncertain selves remained.

But she didn't know. Peace was what she wanted—peace as it presented itself to her in Jan's untensed body, peace as she observed it in the elemental ease of animals—and when she returned from her brother's farm and her visit to her Uncle Hal thinking of animals, and when two months later Jan raised the idea of moving to the state capital, Jefferson City, where more environmental cases were tried, she agreed as long as they could live in the country where raising chickens was not in defiance of zoning laws. And where they could have a dog and goats and work up to cows. And where they would make an example of their own little plot of land, forgetting in the process the boy-crazed Lisa and the adventure-mad Jeff. . . .

"Connie."

Jan had stepped into the living room. This time she wasn't mad, that had been earlier, and she'd gotten over it by herself while Connie had been seeing to their guests. Their first guests, it occurred to her then.

"Come have some wine. Bring a glass."

"You going to stay up long?"

"Long enough for one more glass."

Jan brought the wine in from the kitchen and filled their glasses. The furniture in the room was ill-matched, some pieces new, such as the spare, clean-angled sofa from Scandinavia where Jan sat, and the lamps, made of blocks of wood and stainless-steel tubes, and some Connie had brought with her from her marriage with Larry, most of which they'd gotten at garage sales or goodwill stores. This easy chair, for instance, with its collapsing springs and high-riding armrests. The house, a simple yellow-painted ranch with some stone facing, made no stylistic demands, accepted it all.

Jan said, "He's obviously a dying man. I just don't think it's fair to you or the children, that's all."

"I don't think it's 'fair' either. Larry didn't want to bring him here, you know."

"Then Larry should have found a way to stop it." They were speaking in low voices, full whispers. Beyond the window the insects trilled at an inhuman pace and the large leaves of the tulip tree made a soughing noise. Jan checked herself and sighed. "I'm sorry. You may not believe it, but I have a compassionate nature."

"Of course I believe it. You just get angry, sweetie."

"Not at the men who are dying. Only at the ones doing the killing."

"He's a friend, Jan," Connie said. "I really don't think of him as my ex-father-in-law. Maybe that's because he and Larry could never get along. . . . He'd call me sometimes fairly late at night. This was after Larry had left. He'd always call from his office, and I got the impression he was lonely and had gone down there where we could talk in private. It felt like that."

Jan nodded and drank from her wine. Connie drank from hers. At the other end of the house Jeff began to mumble something more in his sleep, and Lisa, half awake now, in a dull seething undertone cursed her brother, who didn't belong in her bed. They did not hear Ed Reece.

"It was like we had to become friends on the sly."

"It wouldn't have done to offend Larry by actually liking his father," Jan replied. "Not out in the open."

"No."

"He seems a decent sort of man . . ."

"He is."

". . . but this is not a decent thing he has done."

Jan rose and walked to the window. With her arms crossed beneath her breasts she stood there staring into the night; or perhaps, from her angle of vision, it was their van she stared at. It was impossible to tell. The night shone marmoreal on her pale face and neck, the pale pink of her shirt. The one time Connie had watched her try a case Jan had managed for herself a measured and almost impassive demeanor, her wide-set brown eyes, in a face as slender as hers, seemingly possessed of flanking powers, able to size up a witness or see both sides of an issue at once. Even though Connie knew that Jan's indignation had run deep inside. *Because* her indignation had run deep inside.

"Come here," Connie said.

"I know how you are."

"I'm *glad* he came. He's come to say goodbye . . . to me and his grandchildren. It's sad, is all."

"He could have spared you the sadness."

"Please?"

Jan turned and took Connie's outstretched hand. To reach her mouth she had to straddle the outstretched legs, and then to lean in on the armrests. They exchanged a kiss of perhaps five seconds, which still seemed terse and charged with questioning implications. Then Jan pushed up off of the chair's large bristly arms.

"Don't worry—okay?" Connie said. "Promise?"

Jan nodded, but that was for Connie's benefit. Connie held her wineglass up to Jan's to seal the promise, as if with that one high silvery note they could cleanse the night of its impurities. But that was Connie too. She sat there taking small gusts of the breeze in her face. She heard her ex-father-in-law once more, some muttered give-and-take—unintelligible and barely human—from her daughter and son.

Then Jan said, "He's not the way I thought he would be."

"Ed?"

"Larry. I thought he would be an egomaniac. But he seems tired, and cynical about himself."

"Tired of carrying all that ego around?"

"I don't know. I don't know him. I don't like him any better this way than the way I'd imagined him. Maybe tired of unloading that ego on others, as if he expected all of us to carry some of it for him. His first look at me said: Why aren't you doing something? Can't you see I'm falling under my own weight?"

"I know that look," Connie smiled.

"It would be an act of mercy if someone went ahead and let him fall."

"To see if he could get back up?"

Jan shook her head. "I've got nothing against him—except the years of misery and aggravation he caused you."

"Don't make it worse than it was."

"It was bad. What makes you think it has stopped?"

Jan had turned then, and a directness that was almost peremptory had entered her voice. It caused Connie to sit back in her chair. "He may be changing," she said, defensive whether she felt that way or not. "I don't think he knows what this is doing to him."

"Or what it will do to you—the least of his concerns. . . . I miss you, Connie"—it was a statement of fact, a declaration, but Jan's voice went quickly small—"and it's only been a few hours . . . how long?"

"A few hours is all."

"Are you coming soon?"

"In a minute."

"Do you want to come in with me?"

She said it quietly and she said it once—about *that* Jan would never insist. Nevertheless, Connie admitted to a certain irritation. She'd taken care of them. She'd found them all rooms and gotten them settled. If they could just stay put for one night—and she included herself—then something would have been accomplished. She said, "Not tonight," her tone heartfelt and appreciative, for Jan's sake she made sure. "Tonight, I'll take Jeff's room. Tomorrow we'll be back where we belong."

SHE woke not to the morning sun but to the smell of her son's breath in her face. It had a sweet, slightly meaty flavor to it, which meant that he had just woken up himself. Naturally, he'd come straight to his bed.

"How long's Dad gonna be here, Mom? If he stays for like a week you know where I can sleep? Out on that mattress they got in the van. No way I'm gonna stay in there with Lisa again. *She likes to cause pain!* D'you ever look and see how sharp her elbows are? Mom?"

She held him off humming.

"What's the matter with Granddad? Why can't he cough all that crap up? It's easy. Why can't he do this?"

He made a digging, revving sound deep in his throat, and she placed a hand over his mouth. When he'd stopped she removed her hand and opened her eyes. Her son wore his familiar apologetic grin. He was blond like his father and broad-faced like her, but his manner was all his own. He won affection by creating little scandals, committing little outrages, for which he was sure to be forgiven. She tucked his head down on her shoulder.

"He's very sick, honey," she said. "It's hard for him to clear his throat because he barely has enough air to breathe."

"He's dying then," Jeff deduced quietly.

"I hope not," she answered, then paused. She drew a long breath. "But I'm afraid so."

Jeff lay heavy and still.

When it had lasted as long as it should she roused him. "I want to make him a nice breakfast. Why don't you go out to the hen-house and find us some eggs?"

He took his sluggish time about it and she thumped him once in the gut, what he'd been fishing for, she knew. On his feet, he said, "And what about Dad, Mom?"

"Please go get the eggs."

In the bathroom, before taking a shower, she checked through the clear glass in the top half of the window to make sure Jan's car was gone. The van was where Larry had left it yesterday, half on the crushed gravel and half on the yard. She spent a moment looking at it, its deep metallic green dulled by ground haze and layers of travel dust.

Then she spent another moment looking at her face in the lavatory mirror, the puffing at the cheekbones and chin, the splotchy weathering, that makeup would obscure, of the wind and sun. She hadn't worn makeup all summer. Her gums around the canines and bicuspids had begun to recede and she hadn't consulted a periodontist either, contenting herself with the strong straight incisors, unyellowed still.

She could look at herself without flinching, which was all she asked of the mirror. Halfway through her shower she went ahead and washed her hair, rubbing it dry with a towel.

While dressing in Jeff's room—clean jeans for dirty ones, a red-and-gray checked shirt for the sweatshirt—she heard Lisa dash into the bathroom and slam the door. Once Lisa had consented to unlock it Connie stuck her head through and without ever having to really look at her daughter told her to hurry because they had guests. When she knocked on the door to her own room the voices inside ceased, and after a pause of perhaps five seconds Larry answered.

She told them she was going to make breakfast if they wanted to eat.

Jeff had left three small brown eggs on the kitchen table. She assumed she'd find two or three more under the Rhode Island Red down at the end of the row, where, Jeff didn't like to admit, he was afraid to stick his hand since he hadn't *really* been pecked, only squawked at. But she combined these three with seven others from the fridge and made a platter of scrambled eggs. Keeping toast in and out of the toaster she fried another platter of bacon and sausage. It was Lisa who came in first, indignant that she'd been run out of the bathroom only to find breakfast still not made. After she'd sat down hard at the table Connie stood her up and told her to set it.

"Well, how many are we anyway? Would you mind telling me that?"

Lately, she'd gotten into the habit of saving her first look of the day for her daughter until the moment it counted, and she gave it to her now. Though rushed, Lisa had gotten the eyeliner and lilac eye shadow on right, and she'd brushed the long auburn hair she was threatening to savage and dye three or four of the latest punk shades, but she'd applied the oily pink lipstick badly, smearing it over her underlip. She wore a yellow T-shirt too small to tuck in so it gave the impression of hanging from her budding breasts. She stood with an insolent cock in her hip.

And Connie forced herself to remember what she'd been like at the age of fourteen. It was another habit she'd gotten into. Dutifully, she recalled her own sullen uncooperativeness around the house. Then she measured out a warning: "There're five of us. One, your grandfather, is a sick man. Either be sweet today or expect nothing from me for a long time to come."

"God! I'd better be good! Think of all I'd be giving up!"

Still, by the time Larry and his father came in, Lisa had the table set, and she suddenly became sweet and inquiring—how was her grandfather feeling? had he slept well? could she put some jelly on his toast? For a moment Connie could recall her as an impressionable and kind-natured child. Then Jeff raced in with another reaction, or perhaps another tactic, and in breathless exclamations posing as questions asked everything he could think of about the van.

She finished squeezing the oranges.

Ed Reece sat bent over his plate, the color of ash. She wanted to help; being perfectly honest with herself she admitted she also wanted to keep this man from her children's sight. Caught between these conflicting desires she had to force a sheltering tone into her voice. "Did you have a hard night, Ed?"

He shook his head, heavily, back and forth. "Afraid I didn't let you folks get much sleep."

"I slept great!" Jeff protested, overdoing it with gestures as though he were speaking to the deaf-and-dumb-and-almost-blind. "Lisa's got the best bed in the house. And I know Mom was sleeping great 'cause I'm the one who woke her!"

"We slept fine, Ed," Connie said.

Even Lisa lied. "Really we did, Granddad."

"I make a lot of noise when I lie down," Ed explained. "My throat fills up. S'better when I'm sitting—like this," and he raised his head and gave each of them what he clearly intended as a good-morning smile.

And she felt *her* throat begin to fill. She busied herself, serving him eggs and bacon and toast, and before it was over had even served Larry, who with feigned and cutting casualness asked, "And Jan?"

"She's already gone to the office," she told him, and wanted to add, "To bring home the bacon," since that was what Larry was munching on so superiorly in that moment, but she checked herself. She would not be drawn into a fight. Out of the corner of her eye she could see that Ed was missing his mouth with most of his eggs, and it was going to be all she could do to keep the kids in line. Lisa, at that age when even the most accomplished of adult activities could gross her out, was pretending not to notice Ed's mess, and Jeff was grinning provocatively at his sister's discomfort. Connie walked coffee around to Larry and his father, pausing over Ed's shoulder to glance threateningly at her son. Jeff played dumb until he couldn't anymore and then lowered his head, rolling it a moment later to look sideways at his sister, who sat in a tall affected queenly pose and with a fixed smile watched Ed lose another forkful of his eggs.

Connie returned to her seat. She told Jeff to take his face out of his plate. Larry could help, but she'd be damned if she'd ask for it.

She was only interested in cheering up Ed. "I don't think I ever really enjoyed breakfast until we came out here," she remarked between bites. "In the city somehow it's not real sun and not real birds you hear. It's like lighting and sound effects for a stage."

She paused. Ed, she got the impression, had gladly put down his fork, and was now smiling at her. There *was* sun, mixing with that morning haze. Above the clucking of the hens, there *were* birds, squeaking sparrows and cardinals piping in long liquid notes. She made her point. "So the food doesn't taste quite real either. You know what I mean?"

"These eggs come from your hens?" Ed asked.

"Jeff brought them in," she said, telling a partial truth.

Ed said, "You can tell the difference."

"After breakfast, if you want, Jeff can show you the henhouse. His favorite is a big Rhode Island Red. She'll probably be sitting on two or three eggs he missed this morning."

She grinned at her son knowingly, forgivingly, then showed the grin to his grandfather. It was then, when her back was turned, that Larry asked Lisa if *she* preferred the country to the city. His actual words were: "Does a country breakfast taste any better to you, Lisa?"

She couldn't be sure but she wondered if Larry was trying to provoke their daughter. Lisa would have understood the argumentative opening the question gave her. For once she showed the good sense to recall her mother's warning before saying a word. During the pause they all looked at her plate, her country breakfast, which except for two bites of toast she had not touched.

It was Connie who could not resist remarking, "Lisa's just begun a diet. If she's anything like her mother, a twenty-one-, twenty-two-, and twenty-three-year diet, at which point she'll say what the hell and stop."

"But I'm not," Lisa answered airily.

"Like your mother."

"I'm not anything like you."

"Maybe just a little bit," Connie hinted, knowing she had gone too far. A child of fourteen, as she well remembered, could savor secret knowledge just so long before she exploded with it, and Lisa had built to that point. It didn't surprise her that Larry had seen it, only that he bothered to intervene.

"Remember the spinach, Lisa?" he asked her.

She was glowering at her mother now, and to get her attention he had to ask the question again. "Remember that spinach we paid you a dollar to eat?"

Connie could see the memory pass across her daughter's face, relaxing for an instant the forehead and the tough little lines at the corners of the eyes and mouth. Then it seemed to pass more slowly and momentarily gave her a whole different expression: she remembered, a happy time.

"*You* remember, don't you, Connie? Did I ever tell you, Dad, about the time Lisa swore she wouldn't be responsible for what happened if she had to eat a plate of spinach. Said she'd read in a doctor's office it could be very dangerous to insist that children eat *every* food, that probably every kid in the world had one food that if under certain conditions they were forced to eat *might be their last.* From previous retchings and seizures and the like, Lisa had figured out that hers was spinach. Never told you that one?"

"Don't think you did," Ed said.

"I don't remember!" Jeff interjected. "You didn't tell *me!*"

"Tell your brother, Lisa, how you proved the doctors wrong and made a dollar to boot."

But Lisa wouldn't—she let out a scornful screech at the suggestion—so Larry did. He told the story of the time Lisa didn't die even though she ate a whole plate of spinach because her father had placed a dollar bill beside her plate and told her if she came through the ordeal alive the dollar was hers. Then he took out a wallet fat with bills—Connie had never seen him with so much money before—and placed a five-dollar bill beside Lisa's untouched plate and another beside Jeff's almost-empty one, the object now, he told them, to make it through breakfast alive.

She glanced first at Ed, who had taken this story of barely averted death well, as entertainment, then back at her children, who were wolfing their food down. And she said to herself: He's bought them. After however long it's been, the *real* object has been to buy his way back into their good graces and to get them out from under the cloud of their bad-tempered mom. Actually, once they'd finished their breakfast, *they* took *him* outside, Lisa and Jeff teaming up for once to show their dad the henhouse and goat pen, and left her with their grandfather, whom, she admitted, they had probably done their best with. So, she conceded, had Larry. So had she.

At a distance Connie and Ed could hear Jeff now in among the squawking hens. She remembered those telephone calls Ed had made to her during the first years of Larry's absence. They'd spoken to each other easily then, with a peculiar a.m. air of intimacy, although the calls had never come quite that late. "I want to tell you something, Ed," she said. "If it matters to you, I don't think what you're doing is crazy. Sooner or later all of us want to go back. It's really what I'm doing living out here."

She poured them coffee. They listened to Jeff and the hens, and now, with the children nearby, to the heavy throaty baaing of the goats. In spite of his deterioration there was an impressive sort of stillness about Ed Reece, and she found herself waiting to hear something wise.

He said, "It's not the same."

She held back a moment, then asked, discreetly, "Why isn't it?"

He'd been looking through a kitchen window out past the screened porch, where Lisa, the backside of Larry, and all of the Labrador Mike, were visible at the henhouse door. Then he looked directly at her, and that stillness was alive, intense. "Because I'm afraid," he said.

She laid her hand on the back of his. She felt the deep grooves between the bones and changed the position of her fingers. "I would be too, Ed," she whispered.

He stared at her, his eyes going small in a scowl. But she had the feeling he was scowling inward, at something unclear in his own mind. Then, with an alerted little leap to his voice, he tried to change the subject. "So you like it out here," he said.

"Yes, Ed."

"And the kids do too?"

"Jeff more than Lisa."

"Lisa's at that age."

She nodded knowingly and sipped from her coffee. But something—not just curiosity, more like an apprehensive sort of faith—told her to make sure. "What age, Ed?"

"When your children start to leave you," he said.

"Ah . . . and when do they come back?"

He shook his head. "Maybe later," he said, "maybe later if you're lucky." He paused, and she could sense him struggling to pin down his thoughts. She wondered if he was on drugs. "If a fellow was smart he wouldn't count on them coming back at all. . . ." His voice trailed off, inviting her, she thought, to finish.

"That way if they did it would be a nice surprise."

She had the feeling she hadn't said the right thing. For a moment he seemed to lose patience with her, and squinting his eyes, peered back outside. She looked with him. The children had released Maisy and Daisy, the two black-and-white-spotted goats, into the backyard, and they were cavorting and curvetting now, Mike, intrigued by their craziness, awkwardly trying to join in. Larry stood motionless among them, a fond and utterly impersonal smile on his face.

Ed caught her with her head turned. "I'll tell you what it is. It's waves, Connie. One wave comes by to fill you up with stuff you don't give a damn about and another comes by and washes it all away. That might be how your children come back, and how they leave again, caught up in all that worthless junk."

She wasn't sure what he was talking about. "Larry?" she said.

"Larry? Sure, Larry, but also Russ and Nell . . . all of them. It's since I've been sick. You get sick and you find out how much you've tried to fit into one lifetime. It won't let you breathe. Then it all starts going away. . . ."

She reached for his hand. This time her touch seemed to have an instantaneous recuperative effect. "You and Larry, you two still can't get along," he said. "Why's that?"

"I know divorced couples with children in the middle who get along a lot worse," she answered.

"Why d'you get the divorce?"

"*He* divorced *us*, Ed. He's been gone six years. That's abandonment. There're common-law divorces just like there're common-law marriages."

"*She* tell you that?"

"You mean Jan? Ed, I got the divorce before I met Jan."

"She take Larry's place?"

She hesitated and would have suggested they change the subject if she hadn't heard behind the investigative tone an echo, a
hollowness, really another tone, she knew, of confusion and loss.
She said, "It's something else. It's a different kind of intimacy. It's
less intense. I'm at a stage in my life when . . ." and she hesitated
again, not wanting to lie to him or to give the impression that she
was wise enough about the stages of her life to know the needs or
kinds of love they called for—when she didn't. Her life was a
mystery to her. What she wanted to tell him was that she'd
learned to live with the mystery, that she no longer felt victimized
or demeaned by a life she couldn't plot to her liking, or even
understand. ". . . when I want to conserve things, I guess. That's
funny, isn't it? I've become a conservative and I'm living with
another woman."

He smiled—and she thought she saw two smiles too, one press-
ing cautiously back against the other.

"Does that shock you, Ed?"

"Not now," he said.

"Jan's . . . committed. She's a fighter for her causes."

He surprised her. "Larry was too when you met him."

And that mystery of her life turned another of its facets momentarily to view. She had never thought about what Larry and
Jan had in common, not really, not at any depth. Their differences
had seemed so apparent. "That's true," she said.

With his head he motioned toward the backyard. One hundred
feet away Larry stood in the same loose-limbed slouch, content
that his children, their goats and dog, gambol and frisk about him.
His father said, "We got another man on our hands now."

She'd had *that* man on her hands too, and was about to tell him
so, when Ed Reece began to gasp, and then gathering his forces,
to grind away at what had risen in his throat. She brought him

water and a box of tissues. She assumed there was some medicine he took but was afraid to leave his side. When his growls began to weaken, she placed a supporting hand on his back, but drew it back in shock—the wall of his body was so thin! The presence of her hand there seemed illicit, as if she could reach through and choke the heart.

As she took that first step toward the porch door to call Larry, Ed grabbed her at the wrist. He did not once look up at her—with his chin tucked tightly down against his chest and his eyes squeezed shut, he appeared to be engaged in strenuous prayer—but he obviously took encouragement from their touch. She stood there faithfully until he had gotten it all up. By then his grip on her wrist had relaxed and she'd taken his hand, whose boniness this time did not surprise her. Actually, she felt a strange sort of fondness for those bones, as though she were handling objects once dear to her childhood. She said, "It's okay, Ed, it's okay," realizing Larry had spent a good part of the night telling him the same thing.

They sat there for a moment in silence. Ed's breath came in light raspy catches now, and from the backyard came barking and baaing and clucking and Jeff's voice, leaping out of his throat. She became aware that Ed was looking at her and that his look was charged with a desperate sort of fixity. For an instant she resented it deeply, this cutting of distances, this seeking her out when before he'd only called.

Finally she looked up at him. Her first impression was that he wasn't there at all, that behind that stricken face and those unseeing eyes he'd made good his escape. Then she realized that that was what fear did to a man.

"He thinks it's some kind of protest . . . an attack on the system."

"Who? Larry?"

"He thinks we're going to beat them at their own game. He said that."

"He would."

"It's not that. I can't explain what it is. I laid there when they cut out my lung and those waves started coming and I thought,

what can I do, what can I do. I felt like an old shoe filling up with
mud, filling up then emptying out, but I couldn't think of anything. Then I began to see the room where I was born. I don't
know whether I was awake or asleep and dreaming, but I began to
see the very room, and then the bed. I didn't even know that I
remembered them. Do you understand?"

"Yes."

"I imagined lying down there."

"Yes."

"Sometimes it's the only picture I have left in my mind."

"And you explained all this to Larry?"

"He thought we could go get the bed and go straight there. He
said it's what he signed on for."

"You couldn't do that."

"I had to go back the way I came. It's the only way I ever
imagined doing it. First I had to drive these roads . . ."

"Ed."

"I know it doesn't make a lick of sense."

"Yes, it does."

"You understand?"

"I believe so."

"He doesn't," he said sadly, and although he added, "It's not
his fault, Connie," she knew he had gone as far as he could go. He
sounded beaten and bereft, he sounded *stranded,* and suddenly—
it was a quiet precise realization, combining tenderness and a
freezing point of disbelief—she knew what he was really saying,
and really why he was here.

She got up and walked to the door. The haze threw a dull
ragged curtain over the tree line to her right. There were clearings
in that forest and paths in and out, but clarity of mind, which was
all she could hope for were she to locate the most secluded of
those clearings, would be of no help to her now. Her mind was
already clear. She saw things with a startling degree of clarity, the
truth in high relief. There was a law of self-preservation, good for
every being on this earth. It applied to Ed and it applied to her,
and if she could only invoke it, it would apply to her as she sought
protection *and* preservation from him. Failure to invoke it did not

mean you forfeited the right to it later on. No, at any moment of your life you might declare: I invoke the right to preserve myself, and you were preserved.

She walked back to the table and laid her hand across his. "You want me to go with you, don't you, Ed?" she said.

Turning away, he whispered, "Please."

And why in that did she distrust him? Why, turned away, did he seem devious and sly? Out in the backyard Jeff had somehow persuaded the goats and the dog to chase him, while Lisa was both trying to trip her brother and keep her distance—if Connie went with Ed she would have to do something with them. Lisa would be the most trouble to leave behind, but even more trouble on a trip. Besides, Lisa had already set out, irretrievably, on her course. That was only a phantom Lisa she saw in the backyard. And the man there, bemused, blankly self-absorbed, in some ways more helpless than his father. Ed's request made sense—*she* made sense! Then she reproached herself for her presumption and the mean-heartedness of her suspicions: how could anyone be devious and sly about the fact of his dying? Still, she somehow felt outmaneuvered, and in her tone managed to put it off on the children, what it would do to them. "I'll have to bring Jeff," she said doubtfully.

Then she added, "And Larry will have to agree."

Suddenly his eyes were back on hers, and she could not distrust naked need, only try to hide from it. As she turned away his hand rose under hers and awkwardly, childishly, clung to the ends of her fingers. "Talk to him!" he pleaded with her. "You talk to him!"

Just the prospect exhausted her. Through a pure act of will she avoided thinking what a trip with her ex-husband might be like. She said it wouldn't be easy but—gently disengaging her fingers—she said she would try.

SHE talked to Larry in her bedroom, where they could close the door. When she explained what she was going to do, he used Jan's word, "madness," and reasoned that the more people involved in this, the madder it would get. She told him what he had first told her: that it had been his father's idea. How did he propose she turn the dying man down? They fought, attacking each other in heavy whispers. It wasn't the same, Larry insisted. He could afford to indulge his father, she with two children to take care of couldn't. It was then that she told him they were bringing Jeff along. Bringing Jeff? A twelve-year-old boy? And doing what with Lisa? Not leaving her alone? Not leaving her alone with that . . . and he'd bitten down so sharply she could hear his jaw pop.

"With that dyke?" she wondered.

"You said it, I didn't."

"Yes, alone with Jan."

Facing her across the bed—until last night a man had not been in this room—Larry asked her to remember that this was not a crazy joyride they were on. He asked her if she'd looked at his father squarely. She said she had. Did he want her to tell him what she'd seen? Was that it? He turned away from her and bitterly predicted his father would be dead within a week, as though she had driven him to it.

An hour later, as she packed the suitcases, she was arguing with Jan over the same bed, behind the same closed door. Jan had come home early for lunch. She never ate lunch early and she almost never ate it at home. Actually, she was through for the day—and Connie knew that to be a lie too since Jan worked twice the hours of anybody else. Dioxin-contaminated oil had been dumped over various towns in Missouri and somebody had to remind the EPA, RCRA, and state SWAT teams that they hadn't found it all. Well, two phone calls and she could be through. She made them from the phone in her room, then returned to watch Connie fold Jeff's underwear and T-shirts into his suitcase and the darkest thing she had into hers, a navy-blue suit she hadn't worn since she'd given up selling rehabilitated shells. Jan said she didn't begrudge Ed Reece whatever comfort Connie could give him. It was the way they'd come for her, it was that blind male presumption that anything she might be doing couldn't possibly compare with their need of her at the time. She was sorry to have to put it like that, the man was sick. But when they wanted her they could always come get her—wasn't that so?

It was then that Jeff charged in, having just been told by his grandfather that he was going with them on a trip and by his father that he'd better talk with his mother first; but having also been promised by his grandfather that since they didn't even have a radio in the van they could at least get a tape deck put in before they left. So what he really wanted to know were two things: was he going to go with them and where could they get a tape deck installed quick?

She sent him to his room and told him to stay there. When she turned back she saw that Jan's cheeks were wet with tears. It was the first time she'd seen Jan cry. On other occasions when she might have cried, when women had been battered or neighborhoods poisoned in the name of a fast buck, she had gotten tough and effective instead. These tears seemed horribly misplaced to Connie now.

She tried to hold her, but Jan pulled away. Dropping her arms to her sides, Connie stood there, waiting, until Jan stepped forward and placed her arms around Connie's neck. With her lips near Connie's ear she had begun to renew her plea, when, with a familiar, self-reproving start, she stopped. Connie stroked, then, from the small of Jan's back up to her shoulders, coaxing the tension out and bringing a long calming flow back to her breath. She thanked her for not saying any more, for recognizing that there was nothing more to say. There were two favors she'd like to ask: that Jan keep an eye on Lisa during their absence and an eye on Ed while she and Larry went to get the tape deck installed for Jeff.

They would not have to cross the Missouri River to do it. Six miles in on the expressway, where 63 intersected 56, she got Larry off in an area of shopping plazas and car dealers and directed him on to a cinder-block building where stereos and tape decks were installed, auto audio systems as they were known. Without going into detail Larry stressed the unusual circumstances behind the request and agreed to pay the young man with the handlebar mustache and the fleshy, bar-hopping face an extra ten dollars if he would install the deck and four speakers while they waited. It occurred to Connie that this young man would be rigging up the van with one thing in mind, the farthest thing from the truth. His business smelled of cars, of their vinyl upholstery and floor matting, of radios, decks, and speaker fabric, for her, always, a dispiriting smell that left the air electronically parched. They sat in a small waiting room on aluminum-framed director's chairs, beside a table stacked with dealer's catalogues, and agreed the best thing they could do now would be to call a truce to their own particular battle, and give all their attention to Ed. She asked Larry to tell her exactly what Ed had.

And he told her. He recounted for her that year of his father's illness that he'd been in Mexico and his mother, brother, and sister had had him under their care. He said that although he didn't remember the two of them ever talking about it, he had always believed a man had the right to decide how he wanted to die. This was the first time that belief had been tested, and now, of course, he wasn't sure.

She could tell him a thing or two about beliefs, the kind that were supposed to stretch out over a life. Instead she said, "I was born in a hospital in Marion, Ohio, and you were born in a hospital where?"

"Peoria, Illinois. What do you make of that?"

"Only that they're not the same, hospital rooms and a bed in a room in a house. I can't imagine Jeff or Lisa taking a sentimental trip back to Barnes Hospital in St. Louis. Can you?"

He couldn't, but it took a long moment before he actually shook his head.

When the work was done they had two speakers mounted in the ceiling at the rear of the van, and two more under the right and left extremes of the dash. The deck was a four-track cassette format, with built-in auto-reverse and fader control, their audio-system specialist explained. As he went on with his instructional spiel, she realized that although she might not believe a word he said about anything else she believed him when he talked about resonant peaks and flutter readings and azimuth alignments. He relaxed then, the small crouched-back eyes widened, and she could hear relief breathing through his voice. Then he demonstrated the system, filling the van with the heavy metal of a group appropriately called the Van Halen. On the way back home when Larry stopped for gas and then stepped into a phone booth with a handful of change, she thought of that audio-systems specialist again, because he'd been a man in his element and Larry, as he made his voiceless gestures and grimaces to the person on the other end of the line, seemed like a man so out of his. She didn't know who he was talking to, but it was as close as she'd come in the last three or four years to feeling sorry for him. She was reminded of dreams she used to have of finding herself alone on a stage with absolutely nothing to say.

When he climbed back up into the van she asked if he'd been talking to his family.

Not really, he told her in that anxious evasive way that had so much to do with his pride.

He was slow getting out of the van, and she left him there, walking through the house before she found Ed on the back porch. He was sitting in a white wicker chair with his hand on the head of their Labrador, Mike, and facing the backyard, whose bumpy lawn was mowed past the henhouse and goat pen as far as the field of ragweed, which extended waist-high out to the corn. The fading afternoon was as still as Ed and Mike, actually stiller, since Mike quivered with a questioning animal expectancy and Ed with his shallow panting breaths.

She took the other white wicker chair. Then Larry joined them, his weight settling on the creaking boards as he half-crouched before his father.

He confessed that before they'd left Welborne he had called his Aunt Emma to make sure she still had the bed. And for some reason he had mentioned the call to Nell. He had just spoken to Emma again, and to relieve her anxiety had told her that Ed was with them. She had told him that Nell had called and discovered his interest in the bed. Now Larry was afraid that they would all converge on Savannah, or—if his mother had been sincere in her threats—maybe just the four of them and the law, and urged . . . he didn't know what to urge, when they'd set out there'd been a compelling sort of clarity to it all. . . .

Jeff had materialized on the back porch and Mike had slipped out from under Ed's hand. In the kitchen Jan was running water into the coffeepot, Jan, whom Connie had asked to keep an eye on Ed, and who, she realized in that moment, *was* the law in this house. When Ed failed to respond to Larry's concern, Jeff moved in beside his father. Does that mean the cops are going to be after us, Granddad? Does it? Then he glanced at his father, expecting the affectionate rebuke he was used to getting at this point. But Larry ignored him. He looked at her, his mother, and she saw how impatient he could become with these mysterious adult games. It sure sounds that way, he muttered petulantly.

She looked off between him and his father toward the fields. The corn had grown tall and tawny-yellow. It always seemed impenetrably dense to her without a breeze tó move it. In that nimble-and-clumsy sidestepping way they had, the goats were jostling each other at the gate to their pen. At the henhouse, three white Leghorns pecked feed off the ground while the rooster strutted past stretching his neck.

Then Ed answered Larry. The police had better things to do, he said. Sylvia did too. She had that house to run and that business to keep an eye on. What did any of them care about a worthless old bed?

Ed asked about that tape deck. She closed her eyes. When she opened them Larry and Jeff had gone off to try out a tape, Mike trotting after them. Before their music reached her from the van she listened to the heavy white hushing sound of the late afternoon, a sound like the quietest and most wide-spreading of waterfalls, accompanied by Ed's short measured pants. She didn't look at him, only at his hand as it lay on the armrest, the veins in high bruise-colored relief feeding the bones. She had wanted to take care of animals, but there was a limit to her powers of accommodation, there had to be. She visualized an amoebalike creature reforming itself around everything that swam within her ken. There were a limited number of times a person could do that. She had those classes she wanted to take. Jeff, for that matter, had to be back in school in a couple of weeks. And there was Lisa. Where was Lisa? But she knew, and with a self-mocking grin glanced off to the forest of second-growth oak and ash. Following in her mother's footsteps—only it was not funny. It was absurd and unfair, and even if in the long run it brought Lisa back here, to such a seat on such a porch in such a remote spot in the center of a country as large and other-occupied as theirs, she would stop it if she could. But she couldn't. As far as she could tell, that would take powers nobody had.

PART
THREE

V

THE second he awoke he thought, We're going across. He couldn't smell the water, not with *his* nose, and with so many heat-emitting semis accompanying them he never caught a trace of its chill. Plus the fact he lay now with his head toward the rear of the van and the distance he felt from the front and the three people sitting there was enormous. Still, he knew they were crossing the Mississippi. The van began to rise, its tire pitch to sharpen, there was an instant's release, and then it was as if they had begun a long suspended leap between halves of a continent. That was how it felt to him. He weighed nothing. His weight came back to him only if he moved. But motionless, unaffected by gravity and undiscovered by his pain, he felt they might sail on like this forever.

He thought he'd earned it. For years—at Winfield and at Canton and at Wittenberg—he'd had to cross the Mississippi on a ferry, and what he remembered best from those frequently predawn crossings was not the chill of the water, rank and fierce enough to take off the top of your head, or the broad glistening back of the river itself, but the weight, the incredible sense of weight of those ferries loaded with trucks and cars, and their slow plodding progress toward a light on the far shore. This was in payment for that—if he lay still. Then not even lying still did any good. With a feverish start his pain returned. The van touched down bumpily on the Illinois shore. He came fully awake then, and realized he did not know where they were, whether they'd crossed at Chester or Cape Giradeau or farther south at Cairo.

He opened his eyes. Jeff sat between his mother and father, the bright blond of his hair turning from one to the other like a beacon. Ed had wanted to be able to see them—it was the reason he'd turned himself around on the mattress, which Connie had now provided with a form-fitting sheet, plus slips for the pillows. But he hadn't wanted to hear them, to *overhear* them, and he couldn't make out what Jeff was saying now. He was obviously excited, and in his presence his parents were subdued. Even if Ed hadn't known their histories he would have had to judge them a family forced into place. Instead of propping an elbow on the window Larry drove with both hands squarely on the wheel, at intervals flexing the tension out of his neck. Connie was turned slightly inward in her seat, and gave the impression of not having spoken for some time. Her hair looked healthy only in patches— or perhaps it had been poorly cut—and Larry's was thinning not only on the crown but down the back. Age seemed to be overtaking them as they sat there. Jeff saw it too and swiveled back and forth between his mother and father as if he were watching people harden into statues before his eyes. And it was true, age did that. He could have told them: from now on till the end of your life, every day will be a race between the age that hardens you in your isolated ways and your love. But he didn't. He'd feel like a hypocrite talking about love, and hypocrisy was not good for his pain. Nor was shame. Still . . . he loved his wife, his younger son and daughter, he loved his older son and his loving ex-daughter-in-law, his grandson, all his grandchildren, it was like a spiral with an ever-widening reach, his love, but there at the funneled-down point he was a champion of his isolated ways, and he was afraid. . . .

Of what? He didn't know. He couldn't say. It was as if he were thinking in pictures. That spiral he saw was like a radio signal we transmit into the night, like the bell of a great horn. We might blow out with a full expanse of lungs, we might send out our signal all the days of our life, for there was nothing out there to impede us. Sooner or later, though, we would reach a point when our breath failed us and that great spiraling transmission began to wind back on itself. We might marvel then at how far and wide our love had ranged. We might applaud our capacity for love, never remembering it was fear that had powered us on. Fear, we might choose to forget, was sometimes responsible for superhuman feats. But we couldn't deceive ourselves forever. The winding down would wind us back to knowledge: we loved because we were afraid, and we were afraid because we were alone, and the greatest lovers were those with the most terrible fear of their loneliness. But even as we learned the truth about ourselves that spiral continued to unwind, until we were back where we started, alone again with no breath left in our fear.

He was not used to visions or illuminations of this sort, and as this one was given to him it was taken away, leaving him with the sight of his estranged son and ex-daughter-in-law at the other end of the van, their son dividing his attention between them. He'd been told at the start that he couldn't play his tapes while his grandfather was asleep, and afraid now that Jeff would turn back and find him awake, Ed closed his eyes. He had no one then. But, he asked himself, isn't that where we all started, alone in the dark? And as we reached out in our lonely need to find people to love, did we ever really open our eyes? And didn't we *create* people instead, blind to who they might otherwise become? Larry, for instance. He loved Larry both as a father and husband created in his own image, and as a homebreaker, an outcast, a rebel, a vagrant, a bum. Connie he'd wanted to give back to Larry for his son's own good, but he thought he saw now that he was putting his work off on her. Everything was coming in glimpses, he couldn't be sure. And the logic he followed was as tenuous as the afterimage of his vision. But as long as it held he realized that this son he'd fathered—fathered twice, once in physical fact and again as a misbegotten object of his love—he'd left unfinished, and maybe that was the real reason he had asked Larry to come out on this trip, so that he could finish with him while there was still time.

He came to a stop and a blurring-out there. How could he

finish anything in the state he was in? And if Larry was a creation of his who begged to be recreated, what did he need to fix in himself first before he tried again? And what was he talking about anyway? He was a dying man, there was nothing to fix because everything was coming apart. And anyway, anyway, wasn't he going crazy? A moment ago didn't he think he was flying?

And there were others to consider. Did he really believe he could clear his mind of everybody else he had lovingly installed out on the whorls of that spiral while he dedicated his last breath and ounce of strength to Larry? They wouldn't stay away. On the influx that always followed that efflux he could already feel them pouring back in. And how many of them, when he looked closely, might also be unfinished, incomplete?

He lay still, either awake or half asleep and dreaming, and in a succession of luminous scenes the others began to appear to him. Some he hadn't thought about in years. There was Harry Conklin, a childhood playmate he'd smoked his first cigarette with at the age of ten; Will Farley, a man he'd regularly joined for morning coffee until his son had been killed in Vietnam; old Ralph Lickerson, a deacon in the church like him, with whom he'd passed the collection plate; Mabel Stuart and her husband Carl, but mainly Mabel, who on a giddy New Year's Eve had told him solemnly she'd go to Alaska with him if he wasn't already married to her best friend; the long sallow-faced girl, whose name was gone, to whom he'd lost his virginity on a Tuesday night because that was the day written on the slip of paper he'd picked out of Kip Mobley's hat; golfing buddies, foursomes passing by him like small migrating herds attended by their caddies, Skeet and Bob Barley and Hawk Larkin and the Rabbi and Jimmy Paul Willard and Raymer and Cochise, a mixture of ages and places and handicaps, men of a swaggering sort of banter he had not really gotten to know; Pete Richie, his caddy, a quiet boy whom Ed had given a job delivering orders until he'd had to fire him for petty theft; his father, his mother, his brother, Randell, and his sisters, Louise and Emma; and then in a consanguineous rush that seemed to crowd the remaining air out of his lungs, his other son, his daughter, and his wife.

They came to mourn him, and behind the mask of that mourn-
ing to take him to task. Nell was sweet about it; while Sylvia and
Russ exchanged cold words under their breath, Nell whispered,
Daddy . . . Daddy, in a beseeching tone that evoked for him a
moment in the woods across from their house, until Chris Sim-
mons had bought the property and built on it. She was asking him
to go back there with her again, just as she'd chosen him before to
console her. When her little Missie had died of distemper Nell
had picked out the burial site and sworn him to secrecy: *he* was to
hold her hand, tell her about dog heaven, assure her that Missie
would always be waiting for her there—*he,* and no one else. From
scrap lumber in the garage he'd built a small coffin, and she in
misshapen letters had painted "Missie" on top. She'd left the
small pattycake prints of her hands in the mounded dirt over
Missie's grave. He'd grieved for her, a sensation as sad and pleasurable as any he'd ever known. Then he'd forgotten about it. But
she had remembered and was asking him now to take her back,
whispering, "Daddy . . . Daddy," so close to his ear her voice was
like the sound of a conch.

He should have known better. Out of the whorls of that spiraling conch, or out of the whorls of his inner ear, he heard other
voices now, sweet like his daughter's, and accusing like hers,
"Hey, Pop," and still quieter, a summons to memory, "Ed"—and
he tried not to listen. But that was like trying not to feel pain, like
directing your attention elsewhere while pain burned through
your tissues with the finest of flames.

Russ, in his loyal and methodical way, had moments he too
wanted to relive, words of advice he wanted to reconfirm, questions he wanted to ask concerning the business, treacherous
doubts he wanted his father to allay—about the life they had
chosen, about the lastingness of its values, about responsibility
and honor and love, of course, and the chances of staying sane.
What could Ed say? The doubts were real, permanent and deep;
he pictured his second son as a once-solid block of wood and the
doubts as cracks. His fault, he knew—these were cracks *he'd* fathered. Everything he'd once loved he'd fathered, and everybody.
When did it stop? A man fathered, it seemed, the second he

ceased to be a child, and kept on until his breath rattled in his lungs like peas in a gourd. Crawling off to die he'd fathered. A man was a fecundating fool. When did it stop? "Ed," she said, and he'd told her, Let's wait, we're in no hurry, and she said, "Ed," her voice quiet and full with an impersonal sort of resonance, and he'd said, There's no future in this job, let's wait at least till I get something that'll take us from one year to the next, and "Ed," as if that name itself possessed some delectable power for her which if she repeated it long enough would engender the child they'd waited eight years to have. "Ed . . . Ed . . . Ed . . ."

Then he'd gotten the job, they'd made a down payment on a house and moved in, and it was in every corner of that childless house, the sound of his name. When he'd finally given in it was like slipping unsheathed into the oil-rich waters of life, an intoxicating and disorienting immersion, and he'd understood: past the accidents of face and figure, height and width, cheerful or sullen disposition, she was this mothering space and he this fathering muscle, soon to be converted into light. "Ed," she said, an admonishment now, and he turned away from her as though from a mind-deranging dilemma, for hadn't he fathered her too? Fourteen she'd been, not when they'd married but when she'd been born to him—and hadn't he coached her up through the years? Freshman, sophomore, junior, senior, and hadn't she graduated as his bride? Then to father her into motherhood at once, then to somehow grandfather himself and come crawling to death there on their marriage bed—no! It was too much to ask! "Ed." No, he would not do it! "Ed." He would not!

"Ed . . ." she insisted in a long musical moan, and it didn't matter that he distrusted her, that all the wiles in the world found a home in her voice, because he was doing it again, she had somehow enlivened him to it, motored as though by this van he was rising up into that measureless mothering space, he had felt that instant's release and as the tire-pitch sharpened had begun to take that long leap, as though between halves of a continent. . . .

Cold fear seized him then, arresting his leap. I am dying, he said, and opened his eyes. His grandson was staring at him intently, too intent to realize in that first second that his grandfather was now looking back at him. Ed thought, I'm not dying, not yet, we're going back, we're crossing back over the Mississippi. Why's that? Why have they decided to do that?

Ed said, "Why are we going back over the Mississippi, Larry?"

"It's the Ohio, Dad," his son answered, but gently and gravely, as though it were an embarrassing secret they shared.

Then it was Jeff's turn. "You said when Granddad woke up . . ."

THEY let him play his songs. During the first, the bass guitar and the drummer were so loud that the only words they could make out were "Shout . . . shout at the devil!" shouted in a menacing wail. They made him turn it down. Then they made him turn the two back speakers off altogether until his grandfather told him he could turn them back on. Once all that had been settled he went into his position: torso bent forward sharply over his raised knees, which he gripped, head held unnaturally high. But when a state patrolman passed, or when they passed a parked police car, he promptly shut off the music and reported the smokey to his father, and then it was as if he'd never been pummeled by heavy metal or had his wits rerouted by space-age synthesizers in his life.

Within reasonable limits they indulged him, and although they shook their heads at his numerous police sightings they got across the southwestern tip of Kentucky quickly, taking 51 south into Tennessee at Fulton. The fact was, a lot of police were out, and it was true, as Jeff reminded them, they were traveling on temporary plates which would one day soon expire—that was the reason they were called temporary. The longest state east of the Mississippi they now had to travel the length of: they could take 54 and 79 across the northwest part until they hit Interstate 24, which would carry them through Nashville and into Chattanooga, or they could avoid the interstates altogether, where it was also true they could easily be spotted, very easily if, as Jeff didn't fail to point out, the police decided to use helicopters. But piecing together two-lane roads across four hundred frequently hilly miles would take the rest of the day and the better part of the next, and what they couldn't forget was that Ed's condition wasn't improving.

With the music turned down his throat-clearing growls and singsong moans rose as if from a fifth speaker and got caught in the steely lines of assault from the guitars.

"Burnin' up, let's go for broke, watch the night go up in smoke," a British-accented rock star yowled, and leaning past Jeff, Larry told Connie, "We can't take any more time. I'm going to swing over to I-24. That'll carry us into Chattanooga. We should talk about the best way to do this, you know. There may be a better way."

"You're really worried he won't make it?" she asked under the sound of the music.

"I'm worried. I'm also worried about him"—he lifted his chin toward his son—"and I'm worried about you and me. You know what it's like? It's like we're contagious, it's like we we're carrying the pest. Driving around the country this way we're contamination on wheels. Your friend Jan—"

She stopped him there. "Do you want me to drive, Larry?" she said.

He told her not yet.

Before they got on I-24 they had a late lunch at a Burger Chef outside of Clarksville, where it occurred to him they were within a hundred miles of Welborne, Kentucky. They might have been closer than that. The muggy heat was Welborne's, so was the grease-sweetened smell of fast food mixing with softening asphalt and lead-heavy exhaust. Burger King for Burger King, Pizza Hut for Pizza Hut, Radio Shack for Radio Shack, Clarksville's and Welborne's bypasses were the same. While Jeff and Connie picked up the orders he helped his father in to pee, then steered him, past incoming and outgoing customers, back to the van. At the door he paused. "We're in Clarksville, Dad," he said and waited for his father to react. When he didn't react, when he stood there feebly folded in on himself, expecting to be helped up into the van, Larry added, "Tennessee."

"I know where Clarksville is," Ed muttered irritably.

Larry tried to put it speculatively, and he tried to let his father know he would share the load. "We could go back," he said.

Ed raised his face to his son. There was an emboldened, a fiercely emboldened look of desolation there, and Larry turned away. "Go back where?"

"We're close. I mean Welborne."

Ed shook his head emphatically.

Larry said, "I'm not backing out on you, Dad."

But his father was trying to pull the door handle down now, wincing from his pain. Larry opened the door and helped him up inside. Through that same door Jeff crawled in a moment later with a toasted cheese sandwich and strawberry shake for his grandfather, and stayed there sitting cross-legged on the mattress to eat his own lunch. From the front seat Larry heard him talking to his grandfather about his music. He liked songs that told a story, he said, and he liked stories that weren't junk, and in a voice that Larry did not recognize as his son's—measured and consequential—he heard him quote the lines: "Billy's got a gun. He's locked inside a room without a door. In a world of black and white he was wrong and they were right." When they pulled onto I-24 he was still back there with his grandfather, and when he finally did crawl back up front, Larry could see through the rearview mirror it was because his grandfather had gone to sleep.

He wanted to thank Jeff, and did. His son gave him a puzzled scowl that changed to a look of considered enthusiasm when he reported that of the three groups he'd played—Scorpion, Mötley Crüe, and Def Leppard—his grandfather's favorite, like his, had been Def Leppard.

"How 'bout Michael Jackson?" Larry tossed in the only current rock star he knew.

"Michael who?"

"Jackson."

"Michael who? C'mon, Dad!"

"Anyway, thanks."

The scowl returned, which he assumed by now must mean "Dads can be dumb." "Smokey at ten o'clock," Jeff reported, "and he's going slow."

He was going exactly fifty-five miles an hour and blocking passing-lane traffic. Only when he had led them through Nashville and past the airport did he get off. They were halfway to Murfreesboro then. On a long diagonal, and high, with an esplanade's view of grazing land, more corn, rusting plots of tobacco, and dense hilly patches of forest, Larry drove them to a mountain fifty miles short of Chattanooga, and stopped. Connie might have taken them farther, but when he'd climbed to the top of that mountain he knew a mile more would be inviting his nerves to snap, and he checked them into a motel called the Monteagle Lodge. The town of Monteagle was strung out along both sides of the railroad, which ran along the mountain's crest. On the far side stood the white-columned homes that the decline in railroad fortunes had caused to become relics; the near side was made up of one motel, restaurant, and gas station after another. He laid his father down and after trying unsuccessfully to get him to take his pain and breathing pills, brought in some vegetable soup and another toasted cheese sandwich from the adjoining restaurant and sat there at his bedside, for the first time now feeding him spoonfuls and bites. They didn't talk much. He wasn't sure his father had forgiven him for the suggestion he'd made that they go back. His eyes had a dull, accusing fixity to them, but the sluggish insistence with which they hung on his as he held the spoon to the withered mouth told him that his father wanted something more. He didn't think he had any more to give. Before his father had signaled he'd had enough, the silence between them had become reproachful. Larry broke it, apologetically.

"It's traveling around with Connie and Jeff, Dad. It's been a while, that's all. I guess I'd gotten used to the two of us."

His father gave him a brusque and distracted nod.

"You know what I mean?"

He nodded twice.

"Or maybe it's just these sudden changes. Last night we're in the flat midwest and tonight on top of a mountain in the south. This country's big, but you can outdrive it."

"I wanna sleep now," his father said.

"You know what I mean about outdriving this country, don't you, as big as it is?"

His father nodded a last time.

That night Larry began to drink bourbon on the rocks in the Monteagle Lodge's bar. It was located across from the coatroom, midway between the lobby and the restaurant, and contained four or five low round tables with barrel-style chairs upholstered in black Naugahyde; the bar itself was padded in black Naugahyde and provided with barrel-style stools. Except for Larry and the bartender, who dried glasses and hung them upside down in an overhead rack, the place was empty. The bartender was dressed in a red vest trimmed in gold at the buttons and over the pockets; the only other decoration was on the walls to Larry's left and rear—rows of gold- or mustard-colored plastic medallions. That made the most sightly object in the room the bourbon itself, whose orange-brown currents streamed languidly among the chunks of ice, and since the bartender was the incommunicative sort, the only thing worth listening to the five or six tumbling taps the ice made against the glass when Larry brought it to his lips.

He thought, This world is not my world, this life my life, wondering where he'd read that before.

Then Connie sat down beside him, still the jeans, the sweatshirt, the sandals, somehow too much of her for the brittle plastic coziness of the place, and he thought, Not hers either.

She said, "How else can we do it, Larry? What did you mean?"

He asked her if she would have something to drink and ordered her a California burgundy. He asked her if Jeff was asleep and told her that for the moment Ed was. He didn't answer her question, entering that state of suspension he'd come to count on when he was tired and had had two or three drinks. Or perhaps what he'd said to his father was true: they *had* outdriven the country and the country *hadn't* caught up. Until it did and a sense of meaningful space reasserted itself, it was as if time, too, lagged behind and he could sit here beside this woman in the wordless ease of an old companionship he had probably not valued enough. It was certainly true he'd had no companion since her with whom he'd felt wordlessly at ease. There had always been, and still was, an air of warmth and tolerance around the blue eyes and the wheat-reddened brows and the softly bridged nose.

"How else can we do it, Larry?"

He asked her to come outside. She worried that they should be there for Ed and he assured her they wouldn't stay long. He got her as far as the railroad tracks separating the two halves of town, where a breeze mixed exhilaratingly with the bourbon he'd drunk, but she didn't want to walk. Then he could feel his exhilaration going in measured pulses, as if he were having his blood pressure read. When it had vanished entirely the endless succession of trucks passing over the mountain at night took his attention, and the dark houses under high-arching trees across the way, and from close by the metal-and-tar staleness of railroad tracks long in disuse.

"We don't all have to go to Savannah to get that bed, that's what I meant."

"I don't understand."

"Just that we're as close now to Chumleyville, Alabama, as we're going to get. If one of us stayed here with him while the other went to Savannah and brought the bed back, then it might be easier for him, and if there was any trouble down there he wouldn't be along."

"What kind of trouble?"

"I don't know. A trap."

"Larry, what are you talking about?"

"That my mother and brother and sister might be waiting for us, that's all. Or their law-enforcing surrogates."

"Do you really believe that?"

He looked up and down the dark tracks. He had a sense of standing upon a great spine in the land, that on each side of them the land fell off, and that his balance depended on his straddling vertebrae—or ties, sleepers, they were called. How could he talk about what he really believed out here?

"C'mon," he said. "Let's go back in."

"Larry, do you really believe that?" She was standing squarely wherever she stood—he could hear it in her voice. "Or are you just looking for a way to go off and leave us?"

She didn't say "again." She didn't have to. She usually didn't, it occurred to him then. When had he ever seen her fighting mad?

When, for that matter, had he ever seen her deeply aggrieved? Time was beginning to catch up to them there on those seldom-used tracks, for he remembered that the middle ground she'd occupied during the last years of their marriage had frequently driven him to the extremes.

"I don't know what I believe! I told you it was madness to begin with and madder yet if you and Jeff came along. I don't know if Dad is going to make it. I don't know any more about cancer and emphysema than anybody else. He may be dead in there now. I don't know what my mother and brother and sister are capable of. They may be anywhere. The only reason I know where we are is that I can still read a map. The cops really may be after us—they always find incredible ways to waste their time! Or maybe it's not a waste of time. Maybe we really are worth a nationwide manhunt, maybe that man in there I could never get along with is the hottest thing on wheels. You see what I mean?"

"If we stayed here and waited for you," she reminded him, "Ed wouldn't see his sister. Isn't she the last member of the family alive?"

"Yes, Emma, but it's not that. It's . . ." He felt his balance going. He'd barely eaten. He wanted another drink. Or maybe—calmly—if he could talk it out with his mother again. He stepped back onto another tie. "I'll tell you what it is. When we started this trip I felt like I had woken up in my father's dream. This idea he had, this obsession—to go back and die in that house, that town—it was like that. It was like a dark illumination. It had a desperate and childish and beautiful sort of logic. It reminded me of some of those happenings back in the sixties—remember Christo trying to wrap up an entire island? It was simple and outrageous like that. But now there's too much going on, I'm running out of steam or faith or something. From one minute to the next I'm sure we're going to wake up and won't be able to live with ourselves . . . if you want to know what it *really* is . . ."

"If that's how you started off—"

"And there's that goddam bed! My father's dying and we're driving over half the country to find a bed stored in an attic somewhere—"

"You want it to make *your* kind of sense, Larry," Connie said, "and it won't."

"And then there's you! Suddenly you're in on it. You're standing here telling me something I already know with that air of first and final authority you've taken on and I don't understand where you came from."

"We were going to discuss the best thing to do with your father, remember?"

"Where did you come from, Connie?"

"It'd be very easy to get in a fight with you, Larry."

"A better question is where you are going to end up. Somehow I don't see you and lawyer Jan rocking out your last days on the farmhouse porch—"

"That's enough," she said sharply.

"You don't seem to like it when I mention your friend Jan."

"No, I don't. And I don't like it either when you pretend to be tougher and more contemptuous than you really are. What bothers you, anyway? The fact that I'm living with a woman or the fact that you aren't bothered enough and really don't care?"

"You want to know? I mean really."

"Yes," she said after a moment's hesitation.

"What bothers me is that I don't see what you get out of it, Connie. To put it bluntly, where's the thrill?"

She stood there for a long disappointed interval, shaking her head.

The sarcasm and the defiance went out of his voice. "I'm afraid I'm serious," he said.

"I'm afraid you are," she said.

"It's not that I worry that what's-her-name—"

"You know her name."

"—that *Jan* 'does it' any better than I do, or that the two are even comparable, because they aren't, are they?"

After another pause, during which she seemed to be summoning her patience or overcoming her disbelief, she said, "Of course they aren't."

"And since they're not comparable, and since I know that sex—I mean heterosexual sex—was not something you were exactly indifferent to, I have to ask myself . . ." He was suddenly very tired. The release, or the reprieve, the bourbon had given him had worn off. Perhaps she was right and he didn't care, and could no longer muster the energy to pretend that he did.

"What, Larry?" she pressed him.

"Nothing. Forget it. Like most men nowadays I was surprised, I guess, and not so surprised."

She moved one tie closer to him on the tracks, and the second he heard her tone, earnest and informed, he stepped a tie back. "You said we had a marriage based on a mutual exchange of weaknesses, remember. You said we'd seen so much of each other at our worst that we really couldn't afford to give it up, not unless we could trust each other to keep our secrets. And we couldn't."

She held a pause until she'd forced him to reply. "All right, I remember."

"You were wrong. You want to know why?"

"Tell me, Connie."

"Because we didn't see 'that much' of each other at all. We only kept seeing the same things over and over—that's what made it look so bad."

He fought the sarcasm rising in his voice, and lost. "You may be right. I didn't see the lesbian in you, did I? And . . . let's hear it, what was it you didn't see in me?"

She simply stared back at him, quietly and fully, her lips barely lifted into a smile.

"Pretty bad, huh?" he said.

But she would not be baited. He thought she was really amazing. Someone else out on these tracks with all those darkened houses to one side and all that depthless glitter to the other might have lost her composure; train tracks were never entirely abandoned, were they? There was always the chance that the ghost of some locomotive might come powering down the line. Maybe that was the reason he'd asked her to come out here, to give her an old-fashioned locomotive-style shaking. It hadn't worked.

"We can't leave Ed here, Larry. Not unless he can't go anymore."

"When will we know that?"

"He'll tell us."

"You're sure?"

"No. But I think he will. He's afraid."

"And you're not?" Her composure had finally gotten the best of him. He found himself flaring up in her face. "Have you ever seen anybody to the grave, Connie? It's not going to be pretty! It's not going to be a last low moo, and that's it. Whatever happens you're not gonna be the same when you go back to Jan and that house in the country. You know that, don't you?"

"Yes."

"One of those trucks you hear going over the mountain is a bus going back the way we came."

"I know that too."

"Then there're the things you don't know . . ."

But she had already started walking back to the motel. He followed along and didn't really catch up to her until she'd stopped before her door, where he watched her squeeze a hand down into her tight jeans pocket and work out the key. Before she closed the door behind her she smiled. Her face had a pale drained look in the fluorescent lighting, and she stood now, as she hadn't on the tracks, with her weight dragging her down. But the smile was amicable and determined and perfectly clear: we will do this thing together, it said, in spite of old grudges and new ones and piques of pride. We will do it for him.

Then Larry walked into a room full of his father's dying—the bilious smell, the shallow panting breaths, those crooning groans, that second-by-second disquiet. He spoke his father's name and got no response. Then he undressed and slipped under the sheet. He slept at once, but not deeply, and not until he heard the train passing and the clicking of its wheels and the settling of its tracks did he believe he'd slept at all. Then he believed.

SHE could not remember falling out of love with him, not as she remembered falling in love. That was in November of 1968 when he reappeared on their college campus, not as its big man or the most charismatic of its antiwar orators, but as an uncertain and

unregistered first-year postgraduate, who appeared to be waiting
for something momentous to happen. Humphrey had just lost the
election to Nixon, and the surge of optimism that had reached its
peak when Johnson had capitulated to McCarthy was now at its
ebb. She saw a brittle, squinting sort of anger in his face; he
moved cautiously, like a man who had recently escaped a stam-
pede. She saw him frequently with his old antiwar crowd, but as
the disillusioning results of the November election became clear,
more and more alone. They had met the previous year at a party
following a demonstration where he had been one of many who
had spoken and where she might have sung. Others had. But her
brother was still in Vietnam and she could not bring herself to
participate actively in a rally which called for the defeat of the
American military forces in Southeast Asia, as the two most in-
flammatory orators had.

Larry spoke for an end to American hypocrisy, and asked those
gathered there to consider whose war it was, theirs or that of the
munition-makers and multinationals who profited most from it.
But his anger had breaks in it, little rifts, when she heard something wistful or even elegiac in his voice that reminded her of the
tone of the songs she most liked to sing, Baez's "There But for
Fortune," for instance, or Dylan's "Blowin' in the Wind." He
was tall and clear-eyed. He did not look sleepless from drugs. The
wind parted and reparted his fine long blond hair, and she had to
remind herself to pay attention to the terrible things he was saying. But she also liked his mouth, gentle really, the mustache
giving a pensive authority to words that otherwise might have
diffused on the air.

That night she talked to him briefly, after the girl she thought
he'd come with had drifted away but before the one he left with
had shown up. She'd wrapped herself up in a silky red shawl with
tassels; her eyelashes were long. She knew she looked theatrical.
Still, they had a serious talk about the war, and before they had
finished she chose to believe that all that clearly focused intensity
in his blue eyes had softened a bit, taken on, momentarily, an
intimate cast. But he'd been drinking paper cups of red wine, and
somebody had passed a joint. A year later, with her brother Sam

safely home, she sat down in front of him in a coffeehouse near campus, and there was no wine, no pot, his SDS friends were not about, his cause was temporarily in eclipse, he was reading a book by Jorge Luis Borges and not by Herbert Marcuse, and there was a look of welcomed relief, she thought, in his blue eyes for whatever intimacy she might offer.

They reminded themselves that they'd met. She fell in love with him that afternoon because she talked herself into believing that by putting what she'd seen of him earlier beside what she saw of him now, she could have him whole—that the parts matched. And she liked the parts. She liked the man who could stand up and command the attention of a crowd, and she liked the man who a year later, less certain, less commanding, had to sit down. She had the uncanny sensation that before she'd ever gone out with him, much less gone to bed, she knew him through and through, and that sensation, that revelation really, she identified as love.

She wore a wheat-colored poncho that November afternoon, her long hair fanned out over it in a ruddy wheat gold. Happily, it was one of those periods in her brief theatrical life when makeup had not ravaged her complexion, and she knew how she looked for him, fresh and full-blown, maybe even glamorous; after so much angry research and so much futile protest, something like a reward. They talked about the season at Guignol that afternoon, not the war or the violent demonstration in Chicago, but about the singing she had given up to devote this last year to the theater and the parts she hoped to play. They made a date to meet the next night in the same coffeehouse, but by chance met again that same night coming out of the university cinema. Except that these things never happened by chance. Unwittingly, they had sat three rows apart and watched Ingmar Bergman's blithesome comedy *Smiles of a Summer Night*. Each had come alone and the movie had left them feeling timelessly and placelessly and apolitically good. It was that night, then, and not the one after, when she could have cleaned the place up a bit and planned things better, that she took him home.

It didn't matter. It didn't even matter that while he was there a boy she'd been seeing stopped by, because by then she had stepped into a different world. It had to do with this intimacy she'd been given, this knowledge, and it left her in an inexpressibly grateful state, and warm, extraordinarily warm. Grateful for his visit, she wished her ex-boyfriend well, and warmly, for the first time, second or third, she wasn't sure which, she and Larry made love. They weren't drunk or stoned. They'd simply reached a point when nothing in their bodies seemed content to remain there, and quietly then, and freely, they overflowed. She could only speak for herself. Once an image occurred to her, that of a river on a warm night rising out of its banks to steal across the land. Larry told her he could feel her coming apart under his weight, or over him as she settled down—so it wasn't something she'd simply dreamed up or after years and years of waiting had talked herself into believing she felt. Anyway she was only twenty-one.

And while everyone else was either smashing or sneering at everything under the sun, she still believed in Romance. She had the living proof. Perhaps she should not have invited him to move in, but she made room and little by little he did. Or perhaps she should have paid more attention to the one leading role she had during her four years in college and in which she gave a mediocre performance—Miss Alma in Tennessee Williams's *Summer and Smoke*. She learned more from the performance—that she didn't have the verve or trickiness or something to be much of an actress—and very little if anything from what the character might have told her about her own life—that great monolithic yearnings prepared the way for great reversals. When summer came and she was about to graduate and neither knew clearly what they were going to do, she mentioned marriage. Not quite the same day, but soon enough so that she got the message, Larry took to the road.

Is that when she began to fall out of love with him? "It ain't no use to wonder why, babe. . . . When the rooster crows . . . look out your window and I'll be gone." She went back to Cincinnati and was playing guitar and singing in a stylish pizzeria made from a fire station when he didn't come "back through town" but actually came looking for her after six months of political despair and hand-to-mouth existence in Boston and New York. A professor of his at the university had teamed up with another at Washington University in St. Louis to arrange a fellowship for him in a sort of interdisciplinary graduate program they'd started there. Would she come with him to St. Louis? This on Vine Street, outside the pizzeria, her guitar case in hand. It was nearly Christmas. No, she had not fallen out of love with him by then. He was less to look at—dirtier and shaggier, with a stained pea jacket, she remembered, and a complexion that reminded her of the blemish-marked pallor of anyone who walked out under stagelights without makeup. But he was the same man she'd sat down with in that coffeehouse—just a hard year older, more in need of a chair.

He consented to a wedding and remained true to his word until April, when the two families could assemble in Uncle Hal's backyard and make the most of a blossoming apple tree, forsythia bushes, and a balmy sun. He was uncomfortable, she knew. The presence of his father and mother, brother and kid sister, seemed to leave him short of breath, gagging on his collar, which he tugged at until his tie was undone. Actually the wedding hadn't meant that much to her. She was more interested in avoiding its opposite, something sordid and quick in the office of a justice of the peace across the river in Newport. So she sympathized with him—she'd take her romance with a dash of defiance in it too—and drank more than normal at the reception and laughed raucously at Uncle Hal's jokes. Ed Reece she remembered that day for his unflagging friendliness and for the furtive looks he gave not to her—who was expecting them, who traditionally was entitled to them—but to his son.

No, there wasn't a time when she said to herself, he's not the man I thought he was, or the man I thought he was is not the man for me, or he's who he is all right, but I now know I want something other, something more. They spent three years that first stay in St. Louis, and the fellowship followed by a teaching assistantship paid them just enough to rent a small one-bedroom apartment in an old brick building that was either too hot or too cold and that smelled of Lysol and supper grease. Before that they'd lived briefly over a grocery on Delmar, and it was the smell of wilted produce dumped out back they'd had to contend with. But she never minded the apartments or the smells, not really, and the meager sum Larry got from the university she could supplement by waitressing and singing, and the fact is she still believed some of the words: "I'll show you a young man with so many reasons why, there but for fortune go you or I."

She did come to mind Larry's benefactor on the graduate faculty, Professor Joe Sellers, whose specialty was eighteenth-century English literature, but it wasn't till later, during their second stay in St. Louis, that she despised him and thought him capable of doing her husband some long-standing harm. In the beginning he was just one of many men she'd met during that time who seemed to change skins overnight, who woke up bearded and beaded in the beds of their students when they'd gone to sleep conventionally groomed in the beds of their wives. A button-nosed man with eyes as sharply active as a fox's, Sellers had gone from the world of the straights to what he must have thought was the sinuously hip, and treated Larry as something of the opposite case, as a radical prematurely worn out. She'd heard him quizzing her husband about the SDS; it seemed he baited him into telling stories of its infighting and ineffectiveness. She got the impression that Sellers liked having a man around to appeal to as a sort of failed or fallen authority, that it gave him an elevated sense of his own importance, and she got the impression that Larry knew this and for the sake of the fellowship or the degree, or just because he was tired and felt overborne by all of Sellers's anxious energy, didn't care. Had it been then?

But there wasn't a day, nothing like a photo to recall in which she'd caught her husband with all her love for him drained out. She'd become a mother in May of 1970, unintentionally, for Larry now had to pick up extra classes to teach and could study less, all but halting progress toward his degree. Jeff's birth, two years later, she at least had planned. She wanted another child; have two together, she argued to Larry, and then take a rest—but secretly she'd wanted Jeff so she could find out if everything she'd felt with Lisa had been real, or a first-only fluke. She'd become absorbed, and not sentimentally. She had taken the feeding and the cleaning and the care and education so actively to heart that she'd gone days, it seemed, without making contact with herself. With her *old* self.

When Jeff was born it had started again, as soon as she'd made that final ecstatic shove and had watched him being placed on the scales, under the warming lights, where he'd rolled his sparsely fuzzed head from side to side as though he were looking for her. He'd been born with his eyes open. When the nurse had given him to her to hold on her breast, she saw a look in those eyes that held *her,* as weak and depleted as she was. It was very bold and very startled at the same time, the color of his eyes a kind of scudding blue-gray. Larry stood at her side, there were two nurses about and the doctor was still at work between her raised knees, but she was barely aware of them. It was as if that look in her son's eyes belonged to a newborn wild thing—to a baby bird, or rabbit, or coon, or freshly dropped calf—and could belong to her, look lovingly on her, only insofar as she tamed him, as with her love she made him feel at home.

Her postpartum depression had to do not so much with the monotony of diaper-changing and formula-mixing as with the depth and lastingness of belief. She no longer believed in Romance, in an all-sustaining love; she had an enormous capacity for belief, she discovered, but it was now taken up with the wonders of being a mother. With Larry she no longer felt fully present. Lovemaking now provided only local excitements—by comparison. And what she compared it to was that image of the whole of her flooding out over the banks of her body at night, to steal across a land that was also herself, an endless sort of dominion. She no longer felt that. She tried to forget it. She kept the blinders on and worked hard for her climaxes. But occasionally she remembered, occasionally a memory or a lingering afterimage of a vastness of vision came over her, and in its wake she suffered a keen depression.

Then her absorption in her motherhood passed, or lessened at least. It may have had something to do with Lisa going off to preschool and Jeff's unendearing behavior during his terrible twos. It may have had something to do with the times: the Vietnam War was over and a stridency she realized she had always dreaded stepping into had vanished—she could go outside again. Out there, she found women talking about self-actualization, about roles other than mother and swooning romantic mate. When Larry ran out his string in St. Louis he took a two-year teaching job in Buffalo, and the second of those years they lived on the outskirts of a town just across the border in Canada, where she met a woman named Renee Clark. Renee had no children and her husband was gone on business for days at a time, yet she kept herself quietly and admirably intact. What was happening to her may have had more than a little to do with Renee. Larry was about to run out his string in Buffalo too, was about to beg Joe Sellers to allow him to come back to St. Louis to finish his degree, and beside the self-possessed Renee appeared at times to belong to another species entirely. Why should she, Connie Reece, despair if her grand beliefs no longer seemed as compelling as they once had, no longer as real? Why not take pride in the fact that she had the capacity to go on? Not everyone could change, could really *be* again and again. She and Renee had these talks. Since then she'd asked herself, of course, if Renee had not been a forerunner of Jan, if at the heart of the admiration she'd felt for her friend she had not also felt physical desire. And she supposed that she had. Renee was a large woman, vaguely Mediterranean, and that air of self-mastery and ease that Connie admired so was inseparable from the flesh that bodied it forth. If Connie wanted it for herself—really wanted it, what Renee was—she would have to take it from the flesh. But she was not yet at that stage.

When Larry asked her to return with him to St. Louis for a last time, she agreed, although with none of his inner raging or sense of shame. Thanks to Renee she found that she was genuinely curious about herself, in essence about the selves she had coming, although she would not have put it that way then. She'd been encouraged, given an example to follow. And she liked the city.

Of course, she'd fallen out of love by then. She sympathized with Larry, felt for him, hated Joe Sellers for the treacherous son of a bitch he'd shown himself to be as he more or less uninvented her husband's interdepartmental degree before his eyes, and she feared that Larry might do harm to Sellers or himself, but she was no longer in love with him. It took them a year to act on the fact. During that time, she mothered her children along and fought off the occasional attack of guilt that somehow this ease that she too was discovering inside her own skin came at the cost of one further twist to the knotted mess her husband carried around inside. They were at opposite poles. Which is why she was astounded when Larry told her that he believed their marriage was based on a mutual exchange of weaknesses. She'd asked him to explain. You see me in all my pathetic nakedness, I see you in yours. It's a bind more powerful than adoration. We cling to each other because we're afraid if we don't, the other will spread the bad word. She'd shaken her head. She said she understood what he was saying but not what he meant. She wondered if his drawn-out dependency on Joe Sellers had done him more damage than she'd assumed. He'd answered her by asking what she thought an intimate life of eight years standing was all about. Then he'd told her: in a nutshell, it was about sharing the unspeakable. It took a moment, but finally she'd laughed. I've never sat down and made a list of your unspeakable qualities, she said. Do other wives do that? He said, You don't have to make a list. It's intimate, ineradicable knowledge. I've got the goods on you and you've got the goods on me. The "goods" and intimate ineradicable knowledge she'd once considered priceless information, the proof and privilege of love. She adopted an investigative tone. Out of curiosity she asked him to tell her just how with all her hideous hungry naked weaknesses exposed she looked.

He refused, mumbling something sarcastic about the marriage vow really being a vow of silence, and never in her life, she knew, had she felt stronger and surer-centered than then. It allowed her to understand now—in this motel room in Monteagle, Tennessee, with her son muttering in his sleep beside her and her father-in-law fighting for his breath next door, and with an improbable train passing by outside—the sudden surge of . . . not love, but of loyalty she'd felt for him then, of something like a dedication to his cause.

They were in the kitchen of an apartment with many small

rooms, and the kitchen was the smallest. The breakfast table was stacked with things—flour and sugar and a large jar of noodles—that wouldn't fit on the shelves. The children were asleep. It was late and hot in the middle of a St. Louis summer. And she had gone up to him. His shirt was unbuttoned. Pale-chested, he gave off a feverish sort of heat. She remembered the weight of her forearms on his shoulders, the resistance in his neck as she slowly turned his head. She remembered the guarded yet complicitous closeness they came to in that moment—and she said: You hate yourself here. Go away for a year. Find something to do and some place you like better. I won't tell your secrets and you won't tell mine.

They'd gone back and forth. A year he would take—six it had been. In this smallest of six small rooms she could feel his restlessness—it reminded her of tornado weather, that anxious, electric suspension of movement and breath. She knew she could stand there when he had blown by and was gone. Where? That was up to him. He reminded her everyone wasn't lucky enough to have an Uncle Hal; no, but he had a father, maybe he could start there.

THEY came down off the mountain in a fog. It was very early. His father had woken them up when it was barely light, and he'd heard him tell his mother they were going to try to make it to Savannah by that night—but they were going very slowly now. He peered into the fog and listened to his grandfather in back, and, of course, it was like Granddad was choking on that fog while all the rest of them were breathing clear air. If he compared the difficulty he had in seeing anything in that fog to the difficulty his grandfather had in breathing, then he began to understand what dying was like, and it caused him to squirm apprehensively in his seat. His father told him to sit still, that this was very dangerous driving. With everybody so tense and concentrated he knew they wouldn't let him play his music, so he didn't even ask. The big advantage to it all, of course, was that the cops couldn't see them either. Wrapped in this fog they could go where they had to go and do what they had to undetected. The big disadvantage was that they all seemed in Granddad's shoes. He'd rather take his chances with the cops.

When he sat beside his grandfather and watched him fight for breath, it wasn't long before the feeling he had in dreams came over him, a feeling of being trapped in a world of shrinking space. He'd had dreams of being locked up in shadowy scary places like their old basement in St. Louis and the locker room at school. But he'd had the same dream of being shut up in his own room, and even outside, even of being trapped somehow out in the fields, and in these dreams the familiar objects of his day appeared to him disfigured or half destroyed, animated by a single purpose: to close off his space. When he awoke from those dreams it was as though he'd been rescued by a Higher Power; it was what he understood when people talked of believing in God. But somehow he couldn't envision that kind of rescue for his grandfather. His grandfather's disfigurement was not like bicycles bent double or houses tilted over or trees with trunks grown as thick as old stone. His grandfather wasn't going to wake up, which meant the nightmare would either continue on and on, or he would somehow escape it by going in the other direction and falling so deeply asleep that no dream could find him. Either way, it was hard for Jeff to imagine, and in those instants when he succeeded and understood what his grandfather had in store, it was almost terrifying. He preferred the cops. He wished this fog would lift so that they could see beyond the van. When his father pulled in behind a semi and said, "We'll let him lead us down," he was thankful he had "Victory Freight Company" to read, and the motto, "America Sees Us Everywhere."

The fog didn't lift. A turn in the road and suddenly they'd dropped below it. He saw a red claybank to his left, faintly misted, and out to his right an expanse of farmhouses and quilted fields, and lighting so clear and equable he could make out cows and horses and farmers on tractors at a distance of miles. Then he realized that that was not a fog they'd been in, but clouds, that they'd been up in the clouds, and said, "Wow!"

In deference to his grandfather he tried to swallow his exclamation and tone his enthusiasm down, but so much clear sight was like a reprieve for them all and he said, "You can see for miles!" When he turned around and found his grandfather looking back at him with those eyes that seemed bold and unblinking and murky and old at the same time, he went on, "You oughtta see it, Granddad, after all this fog!"

His grandfather mumbled something Jeff couldn't make out, but he saw him shut his eyes for a long blink and tuck his chin farther down into his chest as though he were trying to nod. He turned to his father.

"He said he has, son."

Then maybe his grandfather had felt that special, that providential relief that Jeff now felt, which he could only compare to being released from a claustrophobic dream—but he knew that was nothing he should talk about now. He looked from his father, who seemed to have settled from one sort of tension back into another and drove with both arms raised up onto the wheel, to his mother, who had never sat so passively still during trips. On the contrary, if she wasn't driving she was always doing things, like making sandwiches or peeling fruit, which made him wonder if her stillness now wasn't passive at all but another form of activity, even intense activity, he knew nothing about. "That wasn't fog," he told her confidingly. "We were really up in the clouds, weren't we, Mom?"

"Clouds *are* fog. They're the same thing," she said.

"Except you don't come down out of the fog, do you?"

She smiled at him, conceding the point.

"Look out the window," he challenged her. "What do you see above you?"

She didn't look, he didn't expect her to. She would have had to twist down in her seat. "Clouds," she admitted.

It was then, before he'd even had a chance to tell her, "Right, Mom," that he felt the road straighten out beneath them and looked up to see them enter a broad flat valley whose forested ridges were so safely set off on the horizons that it was barely a valley at all, closer to a great sunken plain.

He twisted around and met his grandfather's eyes. "Smooth sailing now, Granddad," he said.

His grandfather seemed to take time off from his breathing to smile, and then on a catch of breath to speak, but again Jeff couldn't understand the words.

"Dad?"

"He said 'Route 64,' that he remembers it. He doesn't realize that we're on the interstate now."

"Should I tell him?"

His father didn't answer him for a moment. Then he said to go ahead.

"It's the interstate, Granddad. Number . . ."

"Twenty-four," his father said.

"Twenty-four," Jeff repeated, and watched his grandfather tuck his chin further down in his chest and watched him slow-blink his eyes. Only this time the eyes stayed shut. Five minutes later when he hadn't opened them Jeff concluded that he'd gone to sleep. With his music now ruled out he turned back to his father and said, "I'll keep an eye out for smokeys. We're easy to spot out here."

He didn't see any for the entire length of that valley, but then as the expressway wound through the low hills flanking the Tennessee River he saw two, and more from boredom than conviction, thought, Ambush! and warned his dad. The first was cruising toward them in a spot where the east- and westbound lanes almost came together, and as he passed he swiveled his head to keep them in sight. The smokey wore dark glasses and the hat with its wide round brim obscured a large part of his face, but the mouth was visible and it looked heavy-chinned and grim. It reminded Jeff of his history teacher's mouth after the last warning had been given. As in history class, it caused him to sit with his eyes straight ahead, and then to sneak a look behind him to see who was going to get thrown out. That's when he caught a glimpse of the second cop through the two small upright windows in the back of the van, and to make sure leaned across his mother and got a long look at the whole cop car holding steady in the side-view mirror.

Then he warned his dad.

But one cop car had already driven past, and the other now pulled around them and sped on, and in place of the ambush that had never been they had a long lumpy run of forested hills. When they saw their next cop they were almost in Chattanooga and had crossed the Tennessee again. The river made a bend there and pooled out invitingly, and it was while he was daydreaming about slipping into its green water that the third cop crossed his vision and was gone before he even had a chance to get excited or to set the stage. He rebuked himself for going off guard, but he couldn't quite take that seriously either. The problem was he didn't know what law they were breaking. His best guess was they were breaking a law by refusing to take the consequences for one they had broken earlier, which meant that one of them was a fugitive. So *that* was the real problem—to figure out who. But since everything pointed to his grandfather the real real problem—really the only problem—came in figuring out a way to convince himself that that man lying back there taking little panting breaths like Mike did when he was a puppy was capable of hurting a fly.

They had swung around Chattanooga and entered Georgia now, and almost at once the terrain changed from thick hilly forests to stretches of scrub land, scored by deep red gullies and overgrown with pines. But there were ragged gaps in these pine forests and there was a general sense of raggedness about the houses and barns and the outskirts of towns that reached down to the expressway. His father said, "You missed one, Jeff," and he caught a glimpse of an orange-and-blue police car cruising by, and then minutes later, in an ingratiating, chastising, what's-wrong tone, his father told him he'd missed another. By then the gaps had begun to fill. The filling itself was gappy in spots, but the closer they got to Atlanta the denser it became, and there was a moment when the pines on both sides of the expressway were smothered in rampant green vine—kudzu, if he'd bothered to ask for the name. The vine rounded out every mean angle, covered every ramshackle wall and every dead limb, and he found himself holding his breath in hopes that a mile farther on it would cover entire houses and towns. It was as if what was dull, ugly, or dead had somehow generated out of itself its beautiful, transformative opposite—that was the reason it didn't need a name. It reminded him of what went on in his dreams, except that now the disfigurement was transfigured, it was the other way around. For as long as it lasted it was like two great waves splashing up from the trough they drove down.

As they reached the outskirts of Atlanta it began to peter out. The pine forests were knocked down and the vine had to scrabble up fence posts and mailboxes and billboards and the occasional tree. Then in the great grassy complex of expressway interchanges that belted Atlanta it disappeared altogether. He sat there stunned, strangely bereft, not quite sure if he'd seen what he'd seen or dreamed it after all. It was then—sometime after his father had turned off on the roundabout and taken them by glass-and-concrete corporate buildings that the vine could not get within a mile of—that his grandfather woke, and this time when he spoke, Jeff understood.

He said, "I wouldn't mind hearing some music now."

He didn't bother to check with his mom and dad, and before he'd even chosen the tape he flicked the switch that activated all four speakers. Of the tapes he'd played his grandfather's favorite was the Def Leppard, and that was the one he was looking through his stack for. But he found himself picking out another. This was by Duran Duran, and after putting it on he again found himself—as though his motives, his conscious intention, were of secondary concern—speeding the tape forward to a song close to the end of the first side. It was a solo. The man's voice was tender and snarly at the same time, and at its center there was an ominous emptiness or echo which seemed to be spreading all around. When he heard it coming from four speakers within the close-compassed space of this van, it was as if he were stationed at that center and that emptiness or those echoing waves spread out just so they could, with redoubled force, pour back through him. Like a black hole, he thought.

> Look down all around
> there's no sign of life,
> voices or another sound.
> Can you hear me now?
> This is planet Earth.

They were around Atlanta and heading out straight in a south-easterly direction on I-75 when Jeff smelled metal burning and saw a red light on the dash flash on. The light was flashing right under his father's nose, yet his father saw it only when it seemed he couldn't ignore it any longer. He told Jeff to shut his music off. Then he asked Jeff's mother to tell him what she smelled. She said she smelled metal burning and Jeff said he smelled it too. His father hissed, Damn! Goddam! and from in back his grandfather said even he could smell it, with his nose, and that it must be the radiator. Jeff mentioned the red light and his father had to admit that he wasn't certain what it meant, that that's what drivers' manuals were for. The driver's manual was lying on the shelf under the dash, directly in front of his mother. There was a moment's hesitation before she leaned forward and picked it up, but when she did that stillness broke around her like a shell. Jeff looked back out the window. The land was flat, sandier and drier. The kudzu he saw hung in tatters from the pines like crepe paper after a party at school. There would be certain things—baby things, he thought, like chicks and baby goats—that wouldn't survive out here as they did at home. His mother now had found a picture of the driver's dash with arrowed lines connecting names and things. His grandfather had been right. That flashing red light indicated that the radiator was boiling over.

His father took the news stoically. In fact, before his mother had spoken he had already begun to turn off. At the last instant Jeff twisted down in his seat to catch the name of the town on the green-and-white exit sign—Jonesboro. While he was down there he checked the sky. Still heavy and gray and hot—the same unbreathable clouds.

IN Jonesboro they lost the rest of the day. For half an hour they stood under the overhang of a nonservice service station pouring fresh water into their overflow tank and watching it boil back up. It was Jeff who finally noticed that during this time the radiator fan had not switched on. When spinning it with his finger failed to get it started, Larry told Connie to turn the ignition off. The heat of the day was stifling. It was gray, humid heat; more direct sunlight might have burned it off. Fifty yards down the road the jagged points of a king's crown rose into the sky, and they decided the first thing to do was check Ed into an air-conditioned room in the King's Court. After that Larry would try to nurse the van into Jonesboro's Dodge dealer, where he would throw himself into the grease pit and refuse to climb out until they had fixed his radiator fan.

A chain-link fence separated King's Court's swimming pool from the highway and another heavier chain-link fence separated the highway from the expressway, and by hurrying Jeff managed to hit the water just as his father rolled down the highway on his way into town. He was alone in the pool, which was lucky, since it wasn't much bigger than a handball court. The water, after the first welcomed impression, was warm. He swam down to the end and pulled himself up onto the diving board, where he could follow his father's four-way flash as the van crept down the right side of the road. When the van turned off at the first red light, Jeff was left with the fast traffic on the slightly elevated expressway, the stop-and-start traffic along the adjacent highway, and the drive-around traffic at the liquor store next door as customers pulled up to a service window and pulled away with big squarish sacks he knew contained beer and long slender sacks twisted at the neck he knew contained booze.

The heat lay heavy over the pool. The only real breeze was what the semis stirred up along the expressway, and it was full of diesel fumes. He swam for maybe an hour, then went back inside.

When he stuck his head through the door, Connie held a finger to her lips, and when he pantomimed a man guzzling a can of something cold she signaled that she understood. As he moved quietly up beside her she directed his eyes to his grandfather, lying on the second of the room's twin beds. Ed slept with the sheet pulled up to his chin and both pillows under his head, which titled his face up into their line of vision and gave it something of an oracular look. In fact, Connie had been waiting for him to speak for this last hour, if only brokenly in his sleep. Now she saw her son shiver, and although she knew at once it was the effect of the air conditioning on his damp skin, it aroused in her a feeling of impotence and dread. She found him two quarters in her purse, then pulling him noiselessly down to her placed a kiss beside his ear. For a moment she held him there.

After the quiet of his grandfather's room the can of Mountain Dew hit the bottom of the drink machine's chute with an exaggerated thunk. Jeff took it with him back out to the pool and alternated periods of swimming with slugs of lemony fizz until he'd drunk it all. Then he lay down on his towel. Before he dozed off he saw an orange-and-blue Georgia state patrol car cruise by, which especially caught his attention since it contained two men, and state troopers, he knew, liked to travel alone. But he went to sleep anyway. When he woke up he lay there in the drowsy heat listening to a police short-wave radio, quiet and crackling and clear, like the sound of a small gnawing animal somewhere near his head. Then he woke all the way up and went on alert. His father's van was now parked before their motel door, and that same state patrol car with the two troopers was passing slowly through the parking lot. When it came up behind the van one of the troopers appeared to jot something down. With his eyes craftily half-shut Jeff waited for the patrol car to stop—but it didn't. Then as it pulled out of the parking lot he waited for it to pass down the highway beside the fence to see if could tell something from the expressions on the troopers' faces. But he couldn't. They were wooden-faced, they looked rugged and bored. Restraining himself, he let them get a good hundred yards down the road before, a believer now, he ran in to warn his mother and father.

Ed had also just woken up, and as Jeff burst in Larry was explaining to him and Connie that the Jonesboro Dodge boys had consented to fix the van's radiator fan only after deciding that the just-expired temporary plates were Kentucky's problem, not Georgia's. When Jeff told them that the police, a minute before, had been looking at those same plates—even, he believed, jotting down the number—Larry took it as a joke, badly timed. He wondered what the police could do to them if they *were* stopped, and Ed, in a barely articulate croak, told them not to worry. After Connie had given him water to sip he regained his voice and insisted that the Dodge boys had been wrong. Kentucky temporary plates were good for two weeks. Maybe those in Georgia expired after one. Two would be enough, he added matter-of-factly, and for a moment no one, not even Jeff, said a word. Then Jeff said, "Really." The police had driven through the parking lot and driven out and had gone very slow behind their van. What he couldn't understand was why his mother and father and granddad hadn't heard that short-wave radio they had.

In the next moment's silence they heard the racket the air conditioner was making. "You're not joking are you, buddy? This is not the time to put us on. You understand that, don't you, Jeff?"

Jeff repeated that the police had been there, two of those state troopers, and they didn't look mean so much as like they didn't want to be bothered. He couldn't be sure but they might also be big.

Larry sat heavily on the bed. "That's it," he said. "Sure, it figures. We're between Atlanta and Savannah now. If Mother and Russ tipped them off, this is where they'd start looking. I knew we should have stayed off the expressways."

Sensibly Connie said, "If they were really looking for us, why'd they drive off?"

"I don't know. Maybe they just wanted to keep us under surveillance."

"That doesn't seem very reasonable."

"I never pretended to understand how cops' minds work."

"Anyway, they're not going to drive through every motel between Atlanta and Savannah. They just don't have the time."

"If they thought it was serious enough they might. If they really did believe it was a case of kidnapping . . ."

Larry looked at his father, surprised to find himself blushing. "What do you think, Dad?"

Ed shook his head on the pillow.

Jeff said, "Dad?"

"Shhh. Wait a minute, Jeff," Larry said.

They waited until Ed said, "Your mother wouldn't want any kind of scandal." Then he added, perplexingly, "Too bad."

"There wouldn't be any scandal," Larry said. "Any scandal would be two states away. What do you really think, Dad?"

Ed closed his eyes, resigned to thinking it through. For the first time Larry noticed the beginnings of a rufflike swelling around his father's neck.

"Dad?"

"What, Jeff?"

"Maybe I could go outside and be like a lookout or something?"

His son stood shivering in his swim trunks, the upper half of his body covered in goosebumps. He was still unmuscled there, which gave a girlish flare to the hips.

"If one of us was the kidnapper," Ed chose that moment to say, "she'd think it was you. No doubt about that."

"All right," Larry told his son, "go outside. But stay close. Keep an eye out."

"I'll go back up to the pool. From the diving board I can see all around."

Who was he to grant his permission or deny it to a son he barely saw once a year? Larry stood in the door and watched Jeff go, walking up on the balls of his feet, an eager and skittish gait. A woman and two little girls in bikini bottoms were already up at the pool, and in addition to the van he estimated there were now ten other cars in the lot. Then as the wall of heat broke down and began to flow in around him, he shut the door.

"Maybe you'd better call them, Larry," Ed said.

"From here?"

"It's all right."

"Will you talk to them?"

When he couldn't make out his father's reply he moved up to that narrow corridor between the beds. Connie, standing at the end of Ed's bed, gave him a guardedly imploring look. "Will you?" he asked again.

"I said I can't promise you that," Ed said.

After a moment of indecision Larry sat on the other bed, still undecided but within arm's reach of the telephone. Ed was looking at Connie now, not at his son. He was afraid she was about to leave. He could understand how a man as restless as Larry would find her particular sort of serenity baffling and irritating and even dull, but Ed also knew that what Larry had on his terms was just as incurable as what he had on his. He remembered his son striding out ahead on those watery green fairways, striking that white ball deep into the evening air, and patted the far side of the bed. When Connie sat there he didn't have to reach for her hand. "I want you to stay," he tried to whisper, but his voice failed him.

But she understood. "I thought you'd want to talk to your family alone."

Ed shook his head. He squeezed her hand. "I want you to stay," he said, this time audibly.

"Stay, for Chrissake, Connie," Larry said.

She raised her head to him, and in the light from the bedside lamp Ed could see that her freckles, after her months in the country, had risen and softened into splotches. "Are you going to call them?" she asked.

"I'm going to have to."

"Go on, Larry," Ed said. "Tell your mother . . ." He hesitated, wanting only to offer encouragement, to get his son started. "Tell her this hasn't got anything to do with her."

"She won't believe that."

"Then tell her this is something before her time."

He closed his eyes, expecting his son to ask him what the hell that was supposed to mean. But after a long pause Larry picked up the phone. It was as he was placing the call that Ed realized that these things might not be as incommunicable as they seemed, that his son might actually have understood.

Maybe he should have asked him about that day (there may have been many days) when he had walked as if on water and hit ball after ball home to the pin to see if their versions—and their visions—matched, but the phone was ringing now, Larry was holding the receiver out from his ear so that they could all hear. After the fifth ring—a long wait—they heard a click and a quickly smothered female voice as Larry clamped the receiver back to his ear.

"Hello, Nell. I didn't expect you to be there."

He heard a gasp, a sharp and angry suspension of breath, then a cold voice, bitterly informative. "Mother needs someone with her at all times now. Either I'm here or Russ or Jeannie. Since Russ has to work, I'm here a lot."

"Where is Russ?"

"I don't know. He may be out looking for you."

"But he's not?"

"I don't know."

"And Mother?"

"She's resting, Larry. Unless you've got something to say that will make her feel better, I'm not going to wake her up."

"I can't promise that."

"Is Dad still alive?"

"Yes."

"Where have you taken him?"

"I can't tell you. I wish I could—I *can* promise you that."

She held a pause. All he had to do was lift his eyes and there were Connie and his father. Even so, he felt shut away someplace with his sister, someplace chilly and bare. She said, "Asshole."

"What?"

"You don't know what the word means?"

"I know."

"That's what you are." There was a just perceptible softening to her voice. He may have imagined it. "You made me a promise."

"I know I did. But I also made another one to Dad."

Now her voice was hotter, angrier, and that softening was the onset of tears. "I was so glad you'd come back! You made a promise to *me!*"

He hoped his sister wouldn't cry. If she did he didn't see how he could keep from crying himself. But he also hoped that she would, as if with tears she could flush out that coldness and filth. He was aware of wanting two things at once and despised himself for his confused and timorous desires.

He said, "Listen, Nell. Russ and Mother wouldn't let themselves understand, I don't think they heard a word I said. But that's not the way you are—"

She cut him short. "How do you know the way I am?"

He made a blind statement of faith. "I know."

"I was a sweet little sister to you. What else do you know?"

He looked up at his father now, who in spite of his rapid panting breaths gave the impression of lying attentively still. Connie sat beside him on the bed, her hand in his, twisted around to look at Larry over her shoulder, her expression both composed and subtly alarmed, as if there were a world out there of endless, unassuageable pain that had yet to reach her door. Actually she was thinking of the feeling Larry had described to her of waking up in his father's dream, and wondering if a dying father's dream wouldn't include, in a last progenitoring sweep, all of his children, driven out to their wits' end.

Larry said, "I know that you don't despise me. And that in spite of the promise I didn't keep you might not even distrust me."

"How can you possibly think that?"

"You're no cynic, Nell."

"I don't have to be a cynic for you to be an asshole, Larry."

"That's true, that could be the case. Will you help me?"

"Help you?"

"Will you explain to Mother and Russ that what I told them and they didn't want to hear was the truth? That Dad asked me to do something for him I couldn't refuse, that it was something he'd been thinking about for some time, that it was *his* idea, not mine. And that an hour hasn't gone by that I haven't wondered and worried about you."

"You're asking me to be on your side," she stated flatly.

"No, I'm asking you to convince them that there are no sides. I told Mother I felt like I was representing all of you in this, but she won't have heard that either."

He heard Nell breathing, and breath, he understood, was what this had all been about. Hers sounded coldly restrained to him. She said, "Mother gets up early now the way Dad used to. That's because she can't sleep more than two hours at a time. By the time I get downstairs she's staring into her third or fourth cup of coffee. She wants to get me breakfast, and I let her, it gives her something to do. She's begun to talk to herself, and while she's getting breakfast she might go on about a dress she saw for me, exactly as if she were still buying me clothes in high school. And I let her do that too. She's losing a little more of her mind each day, I guess. I try to do most of the lying for her when people call or come by, which frees her to sit in front of a television she doesn't see or leaf through magazines or albums of pictures, things like that. She goes back to bed and gets up, three or four times a day. I hear her crying every so often, but it's a sort of dry whimper and she gets over it quickly, so I don't bother to go up. Anyway, she's got the door locked. At night Russ will come over and, yes, we'll talk about you and wonder where you are and why you've done what you've done, but mostly Mother tries to convince me to go back to Ron and the kids, that she's all right. How can I, Larry?"

"No . . . you really can't," Larry said.

"She's losing weight and she looks horrible, and I've been try-ing to get her to go see Dr. Spaulding. But she won't go out. She won't even go to the beauty parlor."

"I understand, Nell."

"Anyway, that's her day. If this goes on much longer I expect her to cave in."

"I don't think it will," he confided in a solemn near-whisper.

She measured him with her voice. "Larry."

"Yes."

"Trust *me*. You believe I trust you, prove it by trusting me. Tell me where you are and what you're doing and I'll try to find a way to explain it to Mother and Russ."

Was this why his father had wanted him to call from the room, so that when given the chance to betray him he would not have the guts? Because he was tempted. He could feel his father's eyes on him—they carried the pure potentiality of a curse—and he realized that if he were alone with his sister's voice in a phone booth he might very well be trusting her, might at this moment be disclosing the where and why, the whole mad scheme. For an instant he looked up, not at his father but at Connie, who must have sensed the nature of his uncertainty, for she shook her head.

He wavered, but said at last, "I can't do that."

"Yes, you can. You *can* do it. Trust me, Larry."

"I'd like to, you don't know how much . . ."

"But you won't?"

"It's hard, Nell."

She sucked up her breath angrily. "I don't think it's hard, I don't think it's hard at all. You know what I think? I think it's been pretty easy. I think you've been able to talk yourself into doing this because you never really loved us in the first place. It would have been 'hard' if you'd had a family you gave a damn about."

"No," he said.

"A family that even came close to meeting your high-and-mighty standards. That would have been 'hard.' "

"Dad . . ."

He had called to his father before covering the mouthpiece,

and now with the mouthpiece covered but the receiver bare he could hear his sister's angry accusing voice repeating his name. Then after a pause he heard her call out for her father, her voice in a higher and less certain register. "Talk to her, Dad," he pleaded in a whisper.

"Larry," Connie cautioned him.

"Tell her something, Dad. She really believes I took you away from there. You realize that, don't you? They all do."

"Larry, cover the phone," Connie said.

"That's not the way it was, Dad."

By pinching his legs together he managed to cradle the phone in a position where he could get a hand over each end. They all heard his sister's questioning wail—"Daddy!"—then little more than a squeak. Ed closed his eyes and turned his head on the pillow.

Larry remained seated on the edge of the bed, in that awkward pinched position, like a schoolboy who had to pee.

"You said you would talk to them."

Ed shook his head once, then mouthed a word that Larry neither saw nor understood.

"What?"

"The police," Connie told him.

"The police?"

Impatient now, Ed said, "Find out about the police."

"You won't talk to Nell? Not even to Nell?"

"Get her to tell you what your mother has done."

Larry opened his legs and put the receiver to his ear. "Nell . . ." he began in a tone of weary resolution.

"It's not Nell. He's there, isn't he, Larry?" his mother said.

Larry admitted that he was. His mother sounded clearheaded and unexcitable, as though she'd been drained dry.

"Put him on please, Larry."

"He won't talk, Mother."

"Are you sure?"

He didn't even bother to glance at his father. "He asked me to tell you something. He said that this didn't have anything to do with you. He said that this was something before your time."

He waited on her. Then pensively she sought him out.

"Larry?"

"Yes?"

"I pray he doesn't die a bitter man."

She'd taken him off guard, and he almost broke. "Mother . . ."

"I pray we haven't done anything to make him bitter."

But she allowed him to recuperate. She held a silence that had no will left in it, and he knew he should take advantage of it, that now was the time. "Mother, you haven't gotten the police after us, have you? Answer me that."

"The police?"

"This is still a family matter, isn't it?"

"I've quit expecting anything from the police," she said with the wannest sort of disgust, almost sweetly.

"Then you did tell them?"

"I told them that you'd disappeared. They said their hands were tied unless it was a case of kidnapping. Then I said for the time being we could call it that. But I've already explained this to you, Larry."

He hesitated. He might never have her in this stunned and quietly obliging state again. "Did you tell them where we were going, Mother? Do you know?"

"I couldn't tell them that," she said. "I imagine your father has gone looking for something from before my time—isn't that what you said?"

"Yes."

"He was almost graduated from school and gone before I met him."

"I know."

"So there was a lot of time."

He released what he discovered was a long-held breath. "Could I speak to Nell again?"

"Nell doesn't want to speak to you," she said with that nearly childlike and unmalicious frankness. "She wants to speak to her father."

"Just for a moment."

"She's shaking her head no."

"Do you know if she talked to the police, Mother?"

"Nell would have to tell you that."

He made a confused and crestfallen sound, a sort of temporizing groan, and it won from her a voice he hadn't heard in years. "Larry, we tried to help you. We tried to bring you back. We did everything we could. I can't tell you how much I wish I had you here now. It's going to be awfully hard on you, son."

"Mother, the police . . ."

"If the police haven't caught you by now I don't expect they will. I'm afraid you're on your own. That's what I meant."

He mumbled, "Yes, I see," and when his mother failed to answer did what he had to in the only clean way—by pushing down the button that disconnected the phone.

Then he said, "I don't know. She sounded like she was on tranquilizers. I couldn't tell for sure if she'd even talked to the police. We'll have to stay off the expressways is all."

He was talking to Connie and Ed, but mainly to himself, and his blue eyes had that quietly shocked and hollow look they always got when, in a crucial moment, he lost his train of thought. She still held Ed's hand, whose pressure was constant. It was how she knew he wasn't asleep. Then with a gentle start—as if he *had* been drowsing—he released her hand and opened his eyes. They were as detached as Larry's, in their state of aftershock just as unfixed, but they didn't shy back from contact as Larry's did. Out of a dreamy, unclear depth they seemed to pour out. That was the impression she got—of a want, a need, that was also a dark sort of surplus he forced you to share. He whispered, "Thank you," then reminded her that if there was anything she wanted to do . . .

She said, "I think I'd better call home too."

He asked Larry to hand her the phone.

She shook her head. "I'll go next door."

She, like everything else in Ed's life, crowded in close, then swung out to the very limit of attachment. How many times could he expect her to swing back? She went next door. She dialed the operator—they could hear that—but because of the rattly whir of the air conditioner they could not make out what she was saying. "It's none of my business and I suppose it's the only business I've got left," he told his son. "You've got to try again with Connie."

Larry gave a groan, as if he'd known all along what was coming. He stretched out on his bed. "Don't you want to hear about Nell and Mother first?" he said.

"You've got to make the effort," Ed said. "When you married her I thought she was prettier than smart. I've changed my mind about that. I've changed my mind about a lot of things. I'm not sure pretty *or* smart has much to do with it anymore. But she's the real thing, son."

"What's that, Dad, the real thing?"

"A human being," Ed said.

"Aren't we all?"

"Some of us more than others. Some of us make you happy just to be with them. And some of us make you happy to belong to the human race."

"Connie?"

"I can't get it all into words, Larry. Words take breath . . ."

"Okay, Dad," Larry mumbled apologetically.

". . . and I wouldn't know the right ones anyway."

"It's pretty simple. You're in love with her."

"If I am," Ed said, "it's only because you are."

"You're sure?"

An explanation occurred to him—caught in a glimpse—and its logic won him over. "I can feel it because you're afraid to feel it for yourself. Or maybe you're too proud. If you didn't feel anything then I wouldn't either—and I do. So there's the proof. But what happens when I die?"

"Dad, Jesus Christ."

"I mean it. What happens if I die and you haven't started feeling it for yourself?"

"I don't know."

"Don't you think I've been doing this long enough?"

"Dad, it's been a tough day. What exactly are we talking about? Doing what long enough?"

"Loving your wife for you."

It was silly and it was astonishing, but he believed it was also true. It was a son's love he'd felt for his son's wife; it was a son's love he'd kept alive while his son had been wandering the country. He'd been a caretaker. The word itself gave him a great validating relief. It meant he had to turn a son's love back over to its rightful owner, and make sure that owner took possession. He remembered that spiral of love and saw how this might be the answer to that frightened, lonely point where it all disappeared: a love to keep alive and pass on. Could he find some way to communicate that?

But now he heard his son rise up on an elbow on his bed, and something preliminary in Larry's tone told him that he was at the start of an interrogation. "Do you know why Connie is making that call from in there and not here?" Larry asked.

He decided not to fight it. "No," he said.

"Because she's talking to her girlfriend, Jan. She's telling her how much she misses her. How many lesbians you know in Welborne, Kentucky, Dad?"

"Not any that I know of, son."

"You got any feelings about that sort of thing?"

"Feelings?"

"Opinions. A political position, if nothing else. We're talking about another form of subversion of the established order. You used to have opinions on that score."

"I know I did," Ed answered. "Let's talk about Connie."

"Let's don't, Dad. I really want to know. Don't you disapprove?"

"I don't have the strength to."

"Conviction?"

"I just don't know what they do that's so bad."

"You mean the effect they have or what they do when 'their nature calls' and nobody's watching?"

"What they do."

"Ten, fifteen years ago you would have said that their nature was unnatural."

"Yes, I might have."

"But now you can no longer judge?"

If Ed was to keep going he'd need more air, and he took a chance, he broke the rhythm of his shallow panting breaths to try for a deeper breath—and didn't get it. Then when he tried to recatch his earlier rhythm he went too fast, and for a moment nothing got through. He felt a panicky flutter in his chest. It was as if his windpipe were blocked. New air couldn't get in until the old air got out, and when it finally did it came in a vehement rush. "This is *natural*, Larry! This that I've got!" He made a weary, braying sound. "I've got to sit up!"

By kicking and poking he managed to get the sheet off, but he really couldn't sit until Larry had placed a hand on his back and swiveled him stiffly around on his butt. There were five, ten new burning tributaries to his pain, and he didn't dare to straighten all the way up, but breath was getting through now. He was in his pajamas. He asked Larry to turn down the air conditioner. It went from an impure racheting high to a low hum, and in behind it Connie's voice began to get through. He raised his hand to his son and moved an imaginary switch from ten to twelve o'clock. On medium, the air conditioner emitted a low tinny whistle, and that was noise enough.

"She's like a tree," he said.

"A tree?"

"You put a blind man beside a tree and he'd know it was there. That's how I feel around Connie. You know she's there. She's solid and dependable, like a tree. She could never do anything petty and mean."

"You're sure? What if she's like a clinging vine or a fairy ring of flowers? She may be like anything . . . an attic full of butterflies."

"After all those years wandering around no one else would give you the time of day."

"Just sit out under her shade, is that it?"

"Larry, I want you to promise me something."

His son looked away, emptily amused. "I already promised you *this*."

"Something else."

"Don't you want to hear what Nell and Mother had to say?"

"Promise me you'll try again with Connie and the kids."

For perhaps ten seconds Larry looked directly at his father. He looked as if he wanted to make a plea he knew was wasted breath.

He looked as if he had learned that much at least—to treat breath with some respect. Then he said, "Dad, she divorced me. She's been living with Jan now for over a year. You think I'm still in love with her. I have no idea if you're right or wrong. She's someone else. You say you've been 'standing in' for me while I've been gone. That's sweet, I mean I understand what you're trying to say, but no one's done that with her. That's not what lawyer Jan's been doing, so if I try to get it going with Connie again I might find myself well down on the pecking order. You see what I mean?"

"Promise me you'll try."

"You know what you're saying? You're asking me to work my way back into a situation that will probably include a lesbian lover about as fundamentally opposed to me as you can get?"

"Yes."

"Why?"

"Because I trust Connie. Because I believe she'll be there when all the rest are gone."

"Like a tree," Larry sighed, and went into a slump. Eventually with his feet still on the floor he lay back on his pillow. Ed watched him shake his head and listened to him mutter until the air he sat up in seemed to thin out. A dizziness blew about him. Before lying back himself he said once more, "Promise."

When Jeff opened the door with the good news that three cop cars—and two of them state patrol—had driven right by while he'd been standing out there and hadn't so much as peeked in at their van, he found his father asleep half in and half out of the bed, and his grandfather crawled back up on top of his with the sheet on the floor. Since his mother wasn't there, he walked over to his grandfather first and got the sheet up around his neck where he'd seen it tucked before. With the police now in fact after them again Jeff had been forced back to the supposition that his grandfather was the criminal in question, but the longer he looked at this decrepit old man who panted like a puppy the crazier that seemed. His father was a more likely candidate. He slept with his mouth cracked open, which gave him a leering and unprincipled look. He'd been gone for more than a year at a time. And there'd been times when his mother had wished him in jail and Jeff had too. Still, he couldn't really bring himself to believe that it was either of them, or any of them, and suspected at bottom what was really going on was some sort of treachery that wouldn't even have a name but like so much else would turn out to be endemic to the planet Earth.

VII

HE'D been listening to the sound of early-morning truck traffic on the expressway and the dull removed roar of the day's first jets landing at Atlanta's grand new airport when, in a voice so close and clear it might have come from inside his head, his father said, "I think it's time, son."

At first he lay still. In a hynagogic leap the voice had carried him back to another moment, when Connie had woken to find her waters broken with Lisa and had made a similar announcement. He hadn't believed that either, not at first. Then his father said, "We'd better hurry," and in one involuntary motion he'd sat up in bed. In the light from the bedside lamp he noticed the overnight growth of that rufflike swelling around his father's neck, and he asked him to lie there while he woke Connie and Jeff.

He spoke to them as quietly and momentously as his father had spoken to him, stressing the rush and asking Jeff to take the keys and bring in the maps of Georgia and Alabama he would find under the dash in the van. Connie barely turned her back to him as she pulled off her pajamas and put on a pale green shift, preceded by a bra. The maps, once they'd spread them out on Jeff's unmade bed, revealed that by staying off the expressways something resembling a straight line could be made to run through Savannah, Jonesboro, and Chumleyville, Alabama.

He told Jeff to take the maps back out to the van and returned to his own room to find Ed sitting up on the side of the bed, working at the buttons of his pajamas. "Dad, what if we didn't try to make it all the way to Savannah?" he said.

At Ed's look of abandonment, Larry hastened to add, "And went straight to Chumleyville instead?"

His father had one arm extended onto the bed he'd just slept in, and as he turned aside he seemed to be examining it, running the ends of his bony fingers over it, as though it were alien and woefully inadequate, through no fault of its own. It was just a metal-framed bed, with an imitation mahogany headboard hanging on the wall. "I want my bed, son," he said.

As big as a boat—Larry remembered his father's description. He remembered Connie's observation that theirs was the first generation in this country to be hospital-born. Part of the problem was that they had no beds in their lives, not really, not where it mattered.

They went to find his father's. He realized they would probably never know if they were being pursued by the police or not until they were caught, but he crossed under I-75 anyway and drove six miles to pick up U.S. 23 at Flippen, Georgia. Today they had sun. Sharp at nine, by ten-thirty the whole sky had heated and fallen on them with broad bulling force. There was shade in the towns, along the oak-canopied streets where they began to see scraps of Spanish moss, but in the open country they were as defenseless as the cotton fields, which looked ragged and rife and utterly unapproachable in all this heat. They passed through Locust Grove, Jenkinsburg, and Flovilla, before risking an expressway roundabout at Macon to get onto U.S. 80, heading due east now to Savannah. If the heat took the piney-sour edge off the lumbermills they passed, it brought out the fetid stink of chicken farms. The riverbanks stank—the Ocmulgee, the Oconee, the Ohoope. They drove through a hog-raising area where the hogs had marsh mud to wallow in, and the odor there was fermentingly thick. By then Connie had already bought a plastic sack of crushed ice and six small cans of orange juice at a 7-Eleven and gone to sit with Ed in back. In the rearview mirror Larry watched her cooling his father's forehead with ice wrapped in a washcloth.

He had to hand it to the Dodge boys in Jonesboro—the van was cooling itself—but nothing else about this state pleased him. There was an air of phony gentility about the small towns, as if the scratched-over farmland and the palmetto swamps and the general tatteredness everywhere existed in the eye of the beholder only. The look of vicious bonhomie in the fat faces of the young men of these towns paired off nicely with the open hostility in the faces of the countryfolk, and the blacks, of course, seethed with sullen rage. He remembered that this was the state that had elected Lester Maddox governor, whose only political experience up to that time had been running niggers out of his fried chicken restaurant, and at the town of Montrose he swung three miles south and got up on the interstate, I-16 now, which would have them in Savannah in less than two hours.

"Dad," Jeff cried, "they'll nail us for sure out here! What're you doing?"

At the exit for Dudley, no more than five miles down the road, he got off and rejoined U.S. 80. "You're right," he said.

He'd momentarily forgotten the well-earned notoriety of Georgia cops. And in getting off the expressway he'd momentarily forgotten that it probably didn't matter anyway. That they weren't being chased, that the heat played tricks. That that wasn't a dying man lying behind him, his father, being comforted by a woman who had once been his wife. That this wasn't a sometimes son at his side.

He asked Jeff to get him a handful of ice, then held it against his forehead, right at the center, until a shaft of sense-restoring cold had penetrated his skull.

A bit of his U.S. history came back to him then. A penal colony this state had originally been.

"Dad, why're we going to Savannah anyway?"

He looked not at his son but through the rearview mirror at the man lying on the mattress in back. Ed's eyes were closed. He tried to remember a time when his father had permitted him a glimpse behind the regulated surfaces of things. He couldn't remember one. His childhood years had been the Eisenhower years, and though a few of their neighbors had built fallout shelters in their backyards no one had imagined having to use them. They'd soon been turned over to their children to be converted into club-houses. He'd played in one which had had its own portable gener-ator, and they'd listened to recordings of the Everly Brothers and Brenda Lee and to Elvis Presley's "Hound Dog" and "Heartbreak Hotel." Not to the postapocalyptic lyrics of the Scorpions and Mötley Crüe and Def Leppard and Duran Duran.

So why couldn't he tell his father's story to his son, a story, he in that moment realized, any one of his son's favorite rock bands might have put to music as one of its more easygoing ballads?

"We're going to get a bed, Jeff, a bed your grandfather is very attached to." Then to his shame he heard himself going on the way that psychiatrist friend of his mother's might have. "He's gotten it into his head that he's got to lie down in that bed once more, while there is still time. Do you understand what I mean?"

He did. There was something like a leap of understanding in his son's eyes, which he subdued at once, soberly bringing his voice within range of his father's. "But the bed doesn't belong to him, does it?"

"It belongs to my Aunt Emma, your grandfather's sister—she's the one who lives in Savannah. And I hope she's going to let us borrow it without any hassle."

"But we're not the only ones who want, are we? It's the bed, isn't it? What is it, some kinda priceless antique?"

"I don't understand, Jeff."

"The bed, Dad!" Jeff groaned and impatiently shook his head. "If that's what everybody wants then that's why the cops are hot on our trail! I had it turned around. No one's a criminal yet. We're getting set to commit one, aren't we?"

"A crime?"

"Yeah."

He realized he could leave it like that. It explained itself better as "Thou must not steal" than as "Thou must not die." A fought-over bed—doubly exotic for Jeff's sleeping-bag generation. So why didn't he?

"Not exactly," he said.

"Who're they after then, Dad?"

"They may not be after anybody."

"Yeah, c'mon, Dad, sure."

"What has your mother told you, Jeff?"

Jeff slid down in his seat so that he couldn't be seen from the back. "She said she didn't think Granddad was gonna make it," he mumbled.

"And that's all?"

"Like he kinda wanted us to be with him—she didn't really say that, but . . ."

"You figured it out."

"Yeah." He slid farther down, and his fair-weather face came to a frowning, pondering point right between his eyes. The eyes were the blue of mountain water that had never been roiled— Larry had seen the very lake in the Sierra Nevada. "But what's wrong with that?"

"Nothing is, but there're other people who want to be with him too." Then he added lamely, his eyes back on the road, "He can't be with everybody, can he?"

"Why not? I mean everybody could come to his house, couldn't they?"

"Because he also wants to be in another place."

"What other place?"

"The town where he was born."

"Why don't we all go *there* then?" An explanation occurred to him, and in an excited hush he ducked back in behind the seat again. "Is this someplace the police have got blocked off? Like maybe there's been a chemical spill there or a nuclear leak?"

"No, it's someplace that those other people who want to be with him might not even think of as a place at all, almost as if your granddad had made it up."

That set a cloud squarely over his face. He seemed to sense he should choose his next question carefully. Maybe it was like a riddle and his father would trifle with him until he asked the question right. Then suddenly he grinned and made a bold movement for the maps under the dash. "Alabama or Georgia?" he asked when he had them both in his hand.

When his father said Alabama he opened the map up. "Show me," he said.

From Birmingham in the center of the state Larry worked a finger up Route 231 north. "More or less there," he said. "Place called Chumleyville. It'll be small."

"I've got it! It's right here on the map. Granddad's not making it up."

"No, I know he's not, Jeff."

"So why can't we all go there?"

"Because that's not where Granddad's lived. He's lived in Welborne, Kentucky. You should remember his house. There was a park a couple of blocks away and you used to like for me to chase you through the tunnels in the playground. And there was a dog next door, a collie—"

"Dad?"

"Yes, Jeff?"

"This is all crazy, isn't it? What difference should it make to the cops if Granddad wants to be in one town or another?"

He tried one last evasive explanation. "It's just that the people in the town he doesn't choose are likely to feel hurt."

Suddenly Jeff gave his father an impatient, indignant look. "Cops don't give a shit about people's feelings, as long as they don't break the law. Everybody knows that. How old d'you think I am, Dad?"

He hesitated, although he knew. "You're twelve."

"I thought maybe you forgot. You stay away so long I thought maybe you lost track."

All he could do was abase himself a bit—and beg, beg the question. "I tried not to, buddy. I always sent you a card, and there were a couple of times there when I called, didn't I? You probably don't remember those."

"I remember them all, Dad. What's going on?"

"You mean now?"

"It's either you or Granddad the cops want. What've you done?"

In spite of himself he glanced once furtively at his father in the rearview mirror and once in the side-view mirror, as if he really

were looking for cops. Except for a rusted red flatbed truck turning onto the highway some distance back, the road was clear.
"You'd probably call it running away, and you'd probably be right.
I didn't mean to but some time ago I ran away from you and your
mother and Lisa, and now it seems I'm doing it again. The problem is, Dad's decided to run away too. If it was just me I don't
think anyone would have paid much attention." He paused, dis-
satisfied with himself, disgusted by the self-pity that seemed to
cloud into his most clearly formulated confessions. "I'm trying to
answer your question, Jeff."

Jeff wasn't so sure. "How can the cops tell?"

"What?"

"If you're running away or just roaming around?"

"They can't. They have to be told. What's happened is that
Dad waited so long to run away that somebody might convince
them he hasn't done it of his own free will."

That gave the crime a name, and naming it Jeff might have led
them off into the lurid but only semiserious world of television
melodrama. But he asked the more innocent question, the elemental one. "Why'd he wait so long to run away?"

"I don't know," his father said.

"Is it because he's dying?"

"Yes," his father said.

"It's better not to wait so long, then, isn't it?"

"If you've got to run away it's much better not to wait so
long."

"But he's really not running away at all, is he? That's just what
it looks like to them."

"That's true."

"He's going back to the town where he was born. After we get
the bed. Right?"

"Right."

"And the bed, maybe that was like the bed he was born in. . . ."

Larry watched a smile spread over his son's face. It was an
intimate smile, just between the two of them; yet it stretched the
very bounds of intimacy. It was healthy and happy and provoca-
tive of something that Larry shied back from in himself, but

something that was nonetheless there. "Granddad wants to die in the bed and the house where he was born, doesn't he?" Jeff exulted quietly with the thrill of his discovery.

"Yes, he does," Larry told him.

"I think that's neat, Dad! I really do!"

It was the word he snagged on, and unjustifiably, once he'd accepted the implications of that smile. He began to protest, "Jeff—"

But his son interrupted him. "That's not running away at all, is it, Dad?" And before Larry could answer him—and in answering agree—he realized that his foot had gone completely dead on the accelerator and that they were being passed in that moment by that flatbed truck, which pulled alongside in a clatter of unground valves and a cloud of exhaust and then, to the disproportionate delight of the three young black men sitting on its bed, surged ahead.

"I don't believe *that!*" Jeff groaned.

Larry gave him a tempering sign with his hand.

"You stay behind them and we won't get to Savannah till next week!"

Larry did as he was told—he overtook the truck carrying the still-hooting workers—and then on the momentum his son seemed to generate as he sat there they ran out the towns— Brooklet, Stilson, Blitchton, Eden, Pooler. Savannah was sweltering. Its live oaks spread like a ceiling of dense green over its broad avenues and parks, and its trailers of Spanish moss moved like underwater weeds in the air the traffic stirred up. There was no breeze. The last time he'd been here he'd been seventeen. He had a memory of a particularly charming plaza, hardly real. He found it at once. Then another just like it. Wrought-iron balconies, second-story terraces, stucco, Spanish tiles, brightly painted brick. Circling and veering out from the second he discovered in the aqueous light a third. It became clear to him that one plaza might hand him on to another indefinitely, in a sort of sonambulistic do-si-do, and he pulled over to the curb. The smell of the sea here was strong. Mixed in with it he detected the acrid fumes from a chemical processing plant. Like a fleshy film on top he smelled flowers—jasmine and honeysuckle and bougainvillea billowed up from terraces and garden walls. He thought of the clear air of the temperate zone of Mexico, the most conductive air in the world. There he'd been able to distinguish innumerable branching veins of scent, and then, once he'd become accustomed to the phenonemon, he'd been able to do it whether he'd been smoking marijuana or not. This air was gelatinous compared to that—even Jeff seemed overwhelmed. It was what the state came to, where it gelled in its southern charm and set, and he turned in it, understanding that there was a real need to keep in motion.

Could his father give him an address? He could, of course, call Emma, but he preferred showing up there; it had something to do with this feeling of being placed at successive removes from himself, something to do with this sentient, Edgar Allan Poeish air. Connie passed an address on—Aurora Street, next to a branch library. He managed to escape the closed world of these interconnected plazas long enough to consult a city map in a filling station, and when he'd plotted out a course that involved no more than five turns he started out with a clear head, a will and a way. Somewhere between the station and his aunt's house he lost it. There were two one-way streets he hadn't taken into account as he'd mapped his turns, there was a construction rerouting, and there was yet another plaza, unidentified on the map, where two of the buildings were large shadowy clapboard structures grown up into the live oaks, and where if he was interested he could probably deduce how the whole restoration process worked. It was simply a matter of letting nature do its work, simply a matter of waiting till the enshrouding Spanish moss and the sweet-and-salty air had choked off the life in the house before moving in to convert the shell. Something like that. . . .

When he heard the abbreviated wail of a police siren behind him his first reaction was of surreptitious relief. It shamed him to say it—and he didn't, the thought never made it into words—but he was ready for somebody to take it out of his hands. He sat there in the van as a young, bareheaded policeman with a ruddy round face stepped up to his window and wished him a good afternoon. The accent was as soft as the decomposing earth and overladen air they'd driven through to get here, and Larry heard himself wishing the policeman more of the same. At his side, Jeff was strangely immobile; he might have been asleep. Connie and his father had taken on a statuary stillness in the back of the van. If it was the expired temporary plates they'd been pulled over for, that would be the end of the van. If the police were going straight for Ed they'd surely have an ambulance at hand. Either way.

The fact was, these plazas of theirs were tricky, the young policeman admitted, especially for out-of-staters, and Larry had started up the wrong way on yet another one-way street. If he'd be so good as to turn around the policeman would see if he could direct him to his destination. Without even asking to see Larry's driver's license—which in that instant he realized had also probably expired—he would do it. As Larry turned the van around it occurred to him that that was the first time he'd actually spoken to a policeman since the sixties, when he and an assortment of fellow radicals, in another sort of heat, had shouted, Fuck the pigs!

SHE had the bed up in the attic, and Lord knows why she had bothered to have it set up, since no one had used it since the movers had brought it, along with some tables and chests, from Alabama when Louise passed away, but she had: a sturdy four-poster, with a simple scrolled headboard and footboard, mattress, and coiled springs. Hatboxes were piled there, and magazines and some woolen clothing, unimaginable in the attic heat. The wood was walnut, a darkening dirtied brown with dim tints of gold. The posts were fluted and the headboard gouged but uncarved. It was not as big as a boat; in fact, it seemed built for smaller, keener beings than themselves.

Aunt Emma was a pudgy-faced woman with arthritic knees and curly fine hair like transparent wood shavings; her manner was a reverent absorption in the object at hand. She explained to them that her sister, Louise, had preferred the coiled springs and mattress, but for the longest time Mama and Papa had slept on a feather mattress, and that, too, they had kept. Then she showed it to them, borne up and lying athwart two portable racks of clothes and a highboy. It looked both carelessly thrown there and, with its suggestive lumps beneath the blue-and-white ticking, crucial to some design. It was the mattress that had been on the bed when both she and Ed had been born. She could tell them that. Then they left the asphyxiating heat of the attic for the vaporous cool-ness of her sitting room, where each object gave off a precise musty odor, even the small vases and china animals, and where Ed lay on the sofa, an embroidered afghan pulled up to his chin.

And there was no convergence of outraged relatives, no stake-out of police, no team of doctors and psychiatrists discreetly on hand, just an old woman, childless and long-widowed, who lived alone and whose knees after that climb up and down the attic stairs surely ached. What did it all mean? One thing, that they would need a rack on top of the van to transport the bed, and after getting detailed instructions on how to get to the nearest shop-ping center, Larry chose that moment to go and get one. While he was gone Emma would cook them all dinner—she had to do something. But if she would show Connie where everything was, Connie would fix them something while Emma visited with Ed. But Jeff? Lord a'mercy, how he'd grown! To prove it she bustled him over to a shelf of family photos and showed him one of himself and his sister sitting in a small inflatable pool, the picture taken right down into their upturned faces. He couldn't have been more than four then. Beside that photo was a group shot of both families at Larry and Connie's wedding, with everybody in good health except Larry, who looked pale, but somehow domi-nated by the convivial presence of Connie's Uncle Hal, even though he stood off to one side.

Lacking Larry, Emma took Connie and Jeff to task. Why hadn't she gotten any snapshots since then? Didn't they under-stand that if they didn't send her snapshots she had to use her imagination, and half the time she didn't know what to think anymore. It seemed young people went out of their way to make themselves unsightly. She wondered if it was all some sort of disguise.

When Jeff told her he didn't really want to watch TV or even to have a glass of lemonade but just to go outside and study that Spanish moss, she seemed to go on a disapproving alert. She had some nice Spanish moss right out in her backyard, all he wanted. There was a big palm tree out there too if he'd like to study that.

When she had gotten Connie acquainted with the kitchen and the makings for a cold tuna casserole laid out, she came back to sit with her brother, who hadn't visited her in the longest time and who she worried in his weakened condition had lost his mind. That didn't explain Larry's mind, or Jeff's, or Connie's, but it was clear by that scrutinizing and poorly concealed alarm Ed saw in his sister's face that she thought his was gone, even though he had always been the family member she had relied on the most.

"How've you been gettin' along, Em?"

Her curls shook, the little puffed pouches of flesh that made up her face. "What am I supposed to think," she said, "you travelin' around the country in the state you're in?"

She was pleased he had come, and frightened. But forgiving. They sat for a long time in silence while with a wooden fork Connie began to beat tuna fish and mayonnaise around a bowl. He smiled at her. For a moment he seemed to catch her just right in that rhythm of filling and flowing away that had come to govern his life, and she moved inside. He whispered to her there. "Don't worry, Em."

"You say don't worry."

But she was smiling too. There was another silence while she gazed at him. Then she asked, "You hurtin' much, Ed?"

"I'm used to that, Em."

"It hurts to talk, don't it?"

"We don't get to talk much."

"I just don't want you to hurt."

She turned her eyes away, but like a curious child soon had to bring them back. "I worry, doncha know. Mama had a way of not showing it. She worried all those years when things were going so poorly and Papa didn't have work, but not so you'd know it. Some people are like that. They keep it locked up to themselves. 'Course, Papa grumbled and raged enough for the both of them. . . ."

She paused and reflected, and just that quickly he began to feel her presence draw out of him. "I'm like Papa, I guess," she went on. "I can't keep it bottled up. But you're more like Mama, Ed, bless her soul."

A thoughtful and even gentle grimness—it was as close as he ever came to understanding his mother. No, he was not like that. The full-bodied warmth of his sister, and her credibility, were about to desert him, and before they did he would have liked to have corrected her misimpression of him, because only now, he knew, would he really care if she got it right. But he had waited too long, his desire come too late, and along with so much else that had pretended to explain his life, he let her go.

As his mother might have done, it suddenly occurred to him. Was that what Emma had meant?

Gone from him, she continued to sit at his side. He lay still. A deep gravitational lethargy overtook him, and as it did, general now through the upper half of his body, he felt his pain. It was pain he could actually hear. Like a keenly pitched alarm in an empty enclosure, it warned him of the possibility that it could happen now, that the outpouring might pour out at last, leaving him with nothing with which to reverse the flow. His sister had began to talk to him again, her speech a deltaic flowing itself, moving from parents out through three generations of family, but these were different waterways, different worlds, and to die here now on the margin of her silt-filling voice would be like dying on a mud bank somewhere, far-flung, no better than that. That bed in that house in that town took on a passionate sort of urgency for him then, and a sweetness that made bitter mockery of every pleasure he'd ever known. He opened his eyes to find his sister sitting over him.

"Ed . . . Ed . . ." she whispered in that guarded hush reserved for the final mysteries.

And he managed, "S'all right, Em. I was faint, is all. It's coming back now."

"There! You're smiling again, Ed."

It was true. He discovered he was. The rueful sweetness in her voice, the anxious affection in her hand, they were little things, they were very small holdings, but they would grow for him and soon he would have his sister back. Then Connie in the kitchen, Larry somewhere nearby.

Eventually he would know the weight and reach of his own flesh again, and shaping it his pain.

"Such a sweet smile. Why are you smiling, Ed?"

He couldn't tell her. She continued to worry and coo over him, and when Larry came back with the rack on the van, they ate. For Emma's sake he sat up on the sofa and had four or five forkfuls of casserole and drank a small glass of her iced tea. She sat with him as Larry and Connie and Jeff disassembled the bed and carried it down the attic stairs. He was given his choice of mattresses, then watched them carry the feather mattress down the stairs and out onto the front porch with exaggerated care, as though they were moving the feathery remains of ancestors, the bones as brittle and hollow as birds'.

Emma held her questions until Larry had come back in to report that the bed and mattress were tied down on the rack and covered with a plastic tarp. Then she asked, Why and What and Where? She looked at her nephew as if all the madness of the times had just walked in the door and was about to leave without giving her a clue. What were they going to do with that bed? Larry glanced at his father, then delayed answering his aunt's question to ask one of his own. Had anyone from their family called since he'd talked to her last?

They had to coax it out of her. She was ashamed because she had lied. Russ had called two days ago, and she had told him she did not know where his father and brother were, although she did, she knew they were loose out there somewhere, traveling around, reminding her somehow of everything that had come loose these days from its rightful moorings, and she knew they were coming for that bed. Why? Then Ed told her, his voice filling with a benign but powerless sympathy. "To lie down in it, Em."

VIII

WHEN her Uncle Hal retired, Connie had not been sure what he'd retired from. She had never known him to hold a regular job. For as long as she'd lived with him and her Aunt Ellen he'd never talked about a time in the future when he would put by the instruments of labor and reap the benefits of retirement. In fact, until he'd taken her aside and told her to find a way to make a living in case Larry didn't, she had never heard him talk about the future at all. She knew he had made most of his money in real estate, but there were innumerable contacts and seemingly innumerable business ventures—she recalled a riverside amusement park, more than one restaurant, something to do with an independent television station, a string of groceries, promotional liaisons for Procter & Gamble, a health club—many of which fell through but which if taken together and plotted on a map would have probably given her a fairly complete overview of Cincinnati. He did Cincinnati, showed up at everything, from the Reds' baseball games, to the *Delta Queen* riverboat send-offs, to the gala opening nights of the Opera in the Zoo. He was a man about its newly restored downtown. His curly hair turned white, receded off his forehead a bit, combined with his flushed cheeks, the dimpled chin, the belly, and the bounce in his feet to stand for Cincinnati for her, the city in its prime and in the period of its rosy decline.

And it was true, he'd been a sort of

Santa Claus for her, but a Santa Claus in his elfin incarnation—
there was even a suggestion of a point in his ears. A St. Nick who
didn't mind ruffling the feathers of the long-roosting elite of the
city, and to prove it had taken a sassy and boy-crazy niece in off
the farm as a protégée. She regarded the person she'd been then
as another person, like someone else bearing her name in a dream.
Only if she carefully charted the stages of her evolution could she
make any sense of it at all. But what she wondered at now was
her Uncle Hal, and how the distribution of his interests, passions,
grievances, and pet peeves had somehow enabled him to come to
his old age uncommanded by any of them, a mercurial sort of
presence who nevertheless on contact proved to be all there.

He was the uncrankiest old man she knew. In spite of all his
financial vicissitudes (and she knew the names of partners and
fellow investors who had betrayed him), he showed no bitterness.
It was as if he'd mapped out his whole life to achieve a special
equanimity at the end, as if at any number of points there'd been
opportunities for cynicism and ruthlessness which he'd resisted,
not in the name of humanity in general but of his own particular
retirement from the world of dog eat dog. That was frequently the
impression she'd had—that he'd had to work on it, that such
open-handedness and forgiveness were not so much in his nature
as what he'd consciously cultivated in himself and finally earned.
And she admired him for it.

She was drawn to explanations of this sort because she could
not otherwise understand the role he had played in her life. She
had not been a favorite niece. Her sullenness and uncooperativeness on the farm would not have endeared her to him during the
times he and Aunt Ellen had visited. Her rebellious contempt for
any sort of authority once she'd moved in with them must have
caused a strain. To go from childlessness to having this sort of
child—and during that first year she could not credit herself with
a single act of generosity, a single selfless impulse—must have
seemed perversely cruel. Only if she viewed herself as a penance
of some sort could she make any sense of it, provided Uncle Hal
and Aunt Ellen had something they wanted to atone for. Some
family matter? Some advantage Hal had taken and her father had

been denied? She didn't know. From the beginning Aunt Ellen had seemed little more than an accessory, a convert herself to the laissez-faire tolerance her husband by practice preached, and she had frequently wondered if Uncle Hal had put up so generously with his niece and her sexual misadventures because he was secretly running around on his wife. She was aware she persisted in looking for a dark explanation for so much charitableness and light—but she wondered if he was. But if he was and if in dealing so permissively with her he imagined he was working off his guilt, that meant that in meekly following his example Aunt Ellen was also atoning for the very abuse for which her husband was indirectly begging her pardon—and it made no sense.

He was this irrepressible man, this bountiful man. He gave her a key to the house. The second year she was there he gave her the key to a Chevrolet Corvair. He never laid down the law on the rules of the house. Had she vindicated his faith in her? He knew all about her, he even knew in something less than explicit terms about Jan, and he still seemed rosily content with her. Was it a sickness he had, this willingness to believe? Or a sort of laziness? Or a screen behind which he made his secret unsparing judgments? She didn't know. There'd been times when she was ready to believe almost anything about him. Here at the end she thought he was probably blessed.

There'd even been a time when she'd thought he was coming on to her, and that, of course, would have explained everything at once. But she couldn't be sure, and it had only been late one night in the spring—and it had never happened again. As she'd stuck her key in the front door she was aware of him walking up the drive behind her, just getting in himself. She'd been with a boy named Steve Wellman that night, on a blanket beside a small lake; then off the blanket rolling around on the beer-wet sand. She assumed she still had sand sticking to her dress, and she could smell the spilled beer. But she could also smell the breezy upsurge of the spring night, and she didn't much care. She was at that stage in her sexual life when anatomical curiosity and quick local thrills were about to give way to deeper demands, and she was half drunk. Because she was she couldn't be sure if her uncle had been drinking or not. They sat down at the kitchen table and ate ham-and-cheese sandwiches from the refrigerator. They shared a last beer.

But whether eating or drinking Hal kept an enormously pleased expression on his face, so pleased he had to back off the table, it seemed, to savor his good fortune to the full. She remembered it as one of those times when her moodiness and bitchiness and his delight were at incommensurable extremes. Then he said, as though reflecting out loud for her benefit, nothing more, I hope you'll be able to tell the difference between boys and men. She'd given him a kind of worldly snort, and he said, Boys want something to talk about, that's all. A half an hour in the backseat of a car with a girl can give a boy a year's worth of things to talk about. She remembered trying to match him grin for grin, and failing. And men? she asked scornfully. Men never say a word, Uncle Hal revealed, as though passing on the best piece of news of the day. Then in avuncular high spirits he laughed. And one of the reasons she had never been able to decide if he was coming on to her in that moment or not was that she was so unsettled herself. The spring night, the beer, the raw intimacy of this tête-à-tête; the state in which Steve Wellman had left her. She supposed it was a pass; Uncle Hall kept his seat and proudly, knowingly, unprincipledly beamed. She was welcome to stay, welcome to learn the difference between men and boys. Aunt Ellen, had she been there, would have seconded everything her husband had said, making herself the third—if that's what it had been leading up to—in this improbable *ménage à trois.*

The fact was, he'd taken her in off the farm and turned her over to herself. Ungrateful and unwon, she'd done the rest. He was like a pure solution of some sort in which, at the age of fifteen, sixteen, seventeen, and eighteen, she'd found herself immersed; every speck of her had come garishly clear.

Now, as she touched the ice-cooled cloth to Ed Reece's forehead, which except for the obvious pain behind it already belonged to a corpse, she realized that what she would never be able to imagine was her Uncle Hal dead. Before he'd let himself be caught dead he'd disappear. She *could* imagine him diffusing into the night, because, she supposed, that was how Santa Claus came and went, but not lying here before her in such a concentrated and perishable state as Ed Reece on his mattress.

Not even Ed Reece as he was being driven over half the country.

Jeff kept them abreast of their progress on that score. She'd made him turn off his music early when the heat of the day and that airless electronic heat that synthesizers and distorted guitars aroused in her became too much to bear. Since then he'd acted as his father's navigator. Recrossing Georgia, he'd called off the towns: "Thomaston . . . Woodbury . . . Newman . . . Clem . . . Carrollton . . . Cedartown." He'd managed to stretch out the suspense over two hundred miles—the pitch of his voice rising in just that measure, it was remarkable, really. It was even more remarkable when he kept his smokey-sightings, as he called them, within the range established for any given town. "This is Clem, Georgia. That smokey parked beside that drive-in bank is not as sleepy as he looks. Begin to slow down now." She'd attended to Ed, and listened to her son chart for them their progress across a state which from here on she would only think of as the state of the bed, a corner of whose tarp flapped in the wind above them. Like Larry, she had no idea of what resources a man in Ed's condition could call on now. That puffiness around his neck seemed to be rising to cushion the fleshless bones, and she expected anything. He might die in that moment. When he did it would not be pretty, not the last long moo, as Larry had so sarcastically pointed out—and he'd been right. No animal that she knew would inflict such punishment on itself to shape its dying to the dictates of an idea. And he'd been wrong: for animals too dragged themselves home to die.

Curiously it had been her son's voice playing out its suspense that reminded her of that. Georgia might be the most fearful of the smokey-states, but it was also all that stood between Ed Reece and home. They were entering Alabama by the back door. Once they had—"We're across the state line now, Dad! No more Georgia cops! Piedmont, Alabama, coming up!"—her son's game-playing no longer served any purpose but its own, and she'd had enough of that. She warned him to be quiet. Larry, she knew, would want to make it all the way into Chumleyville that night, but he was driving erratically now, like a man stumbling forward to join a bloody battle, and she asked him to stop.

He didn't put up a fight.

He even sat there and let her check them into a motel. The desk clerk was a middle-aged woman whose frowsy hair and general untidiness did little to hide a suspicious nature, and after taking two adjacent ground-floor rooms Connie suggested Jeff take an evening dip in the motel pool, very much aware she was sending her son out as their emissary to the everyday world. After his swim she sent him across the street for a pizza. By the time she had gotten him into bed, Larry had fed Ed a bit of tomato soup and ice cream, and there'd been a moment when she and her ex-husband had stood beside the dying man sharing a mood of sorrow and loss, but also of relief, even of accomplishment, for the mere fact that they were in Alabama had led them to believe they would make it all the way back. Then Ed sat suddenly up in bed, made one preliminary heave, jerked to the side, and threw up what he'd just eaten, some of which Larry managed to catch in a plastic trashcan. When it was over they lowered Ed back onto the pillow. Connie sponged his forehead and washed his mouth with a damp cloth while Larry finished cleaning up. They found themselves standing there again, but less relieved now, less removed from this man's dying. Ed tried to smile at them once, but his pain hit him and made a wavy screaming pattern along one side of his face. It hit him less severely two more times before giving way to that light gravelly pant that at first would always alarm them, then give them some rest. When he seemed to have gone to sleep Connie touched Larry's hand and whispered that she was going to make a call.

She made it from a phone booth beside the highway, not wanting to disturb Jeff's rest either. For an instant Lisa hesitated before accepting the charges, explaining it wasn't because she didn't want to talk to her mother or find out about her granddad, or even about her own dad or Jeff, it was just that . . . well, she was expecting an important call herself.

Who from?

Well . . . Mike.

Who was Mike? Mike was their dog.

Funny, Mom.

Well?

Mike was Mike Kellogg. No, her mother did not know him. They'd only been there three months. She couldn't expect to know all her daughter's boyfriends yet.

Connie said, "I want you to understand me, Lisa. This is a very sad and difficult time. Your grandfather can't last much longer. Until I get back I don't want you going out at night. You're old enough to understand why."

Lisa held a tactical silence. It gave her time to put on a subdued and cooperative front. "Okay, Mom," she said. "Do you wanna speak to Jan?"

"I mean it, Lisa."

"Sure, Mom. Jan will tell you what a shit Mike is anyway."

"Does she know him?"

"She doesn't need to know him to know he's a shit, does she, Mom?"

"Put Jan on, Lisa. I'll tell your grandfather you love him and I'll tell your father you're sorry he's having a hard time."

"You don't have to say it like that! I do love Granddad and you know how I feel about Dad. If you and Jan—"

Connie cut her daughter off. "Put Jan on."

Lisa's voice went cold, then cattily insinuating. "Sure, Mom. But don't talk all night, okay? I *am* expecting a call."

Then Connie heard the phone being wrested away from her daughter. Jan asked, "Are you all right, Connie?"

"Yes, all right . . . Jeff too. We're just tired."

"Is Ed still alive?"

"Yes, but he can't go on much longer."

"Please, please listen to what I am going to say. I can't find another case like it, but if the family goes ahead and files kidnapping charges against Larry, they might make them stick if Ed dies before he gets a chance to testify to the contrary. If the charges do stick, and the family wants to, they could cite you as an accomplice. My best guess is that if a D.A. goes to work on what they'll know in that town about Larry's past history, they can get a grand jury to indict him. After that, anything can happen."

"What if we got a witness, and Ed swore he was not being kidnapped?"

"A witness from where?"

"Here . . . this town, Piedmont, Alabama."

"No one in Welborne, Kentucky, is going to believe a witness off the streets in Piedmont, Alabama, not if the D.A. knows how to work a jury. Trust me, there's only one thing you can do and it's going to cost you two dimes. Call the police and call an ambulance. Make sure the police get there first."

What was so unbelievable about Piedmont, Alabama? What made its cars and pickups, mini-marts and package stores, motels and franchise restaurants, its wrinkle of environing hills, different from anybody else's? Connie put it off on Piedmont as long as she could, then said, quietly, "I can't do that."

"Why can't you?"

"I can't do it to Ed."

"You mean Larry."

"Larry too. You'd have to be here, Jan. Once you make up your mind to go through with something like this, arguments don't make any sense. You just said you couldn't find another case like it."

Then the professional bottom seemed to fall out of Jan's voice. She sounded hushed, trapped, resourceless—it was like an agreed-upon signal: it meant she wanted to be held. "You're going to let him ruin your life, Connie. I wish you wouldn't do that. I wish you could see that every time he comes back he'll be begging for you to do something even more preposterous and sad. It's like some kind of recurring nightmare."

"He said that."

"What?"

"That he felt like he'd woken up in his father's nightmare."

"Connie?"

She imagined stroking the flesh at the small of Jan's back, then felt the phone booth's special apartness and size. "I know," she said. "I miss you too. I'd give you a nice slow massage if I was there."

"Call the police, Connie."

"I can't. I told you that."

"Call the police or I will."

"Don't do that."

"I took down the license number before you left. The police in Piedmont would just have to drive around to the motels until they found you."

"You won't do that, Jan."

"I would if I thought it would save you."

"I'm not lost. I don't need saving. I need you to be there when we come back."

"If you *come* back—if Larry doesn't get you all thrown into jail!"

In part because of the frustration she felt in not being able to comfort Jan, in part because Jan had begun to sound like her sensationalistic son, and in part because even if this came out exactly as Ed had planned it—bed, house, town, and all—it was still immeasurably sad, for whatever reason, she heard herself lash out: "Don't keep blaming things on Larry! That's enough about Larry! Okay?" Then she stopped and tried to master herself. "I'm sorry, Jan. You'd have to be here to know what we're going through. I truly am."

"I'm sorry too. I won't call the police. I just hope we don't regret it later on."

"Thank you."

"It's hard to sit here and do nothing, that's all."

"Remember to feed the goats and chickens. Do something about Lisa."

"What?"

"Whatever you can. Don't let her go out nights."

"Connie, Lisa's already gone. She went stomping out the back door when I took the phone."

"She'll come back. She's waiting for a call. Or if she doesn't, keep her in tomorrow night. Just one night would be an accomplishment."

"I'll try. I can't promise."

"I know. . . . I miss you. I love you. Have a nice bath and go to bed."

THEY left the door cracked so they could hear Ed in case he should wake and talked standing out beside the van. She described Jan's scenario for Larry, what could happen if his family did bring charges against him and Ed died before he had a chance to testify, and she wondered if they shouldn't go ahead and call the police and get a witness whose testimony would, at least, hold up in court. Of course, she couldn't really bring herself to believe that Larry's family would press charges . . . so she would leave any safety measures up to him. Then she waited while he considered their options. She thought that was what he was doing. Eventually she became aware that he simply hung there before her, in a sort of dispirited trance, and she raised a hand to his shoulder.

"Larry?"

"What?" he answered mechanically.

"If Ed could write something? Do you think he could?"

"I don't think so."

"You're not worried then?" She waited a moment, then added, "I'm bringing this up for your benefit, I really am."

He raised his eyes, not to look at her but down the row of rooms toward an illuminated soft-drink machine. In the faint glow she saw a weary but still-surprised face, disoriented but with no faith left in future turns. "All it came down to," he said, "was a case of the son kidnapping the father from the mother. That's what Mother told me."

"Criminal kidnapping is something else. Isn't it?"

"I don't know. I don't know what the courts could make of this. They might not have names for it."

"Jan looked."

"Where'd she look?"

"In her books, I guess. The state criminal library. There was nothing like it, she said."

"We're straddling two worlds," Larry replied enigmatically.

But she understood him. "When it's over we're going to have to live in one of them. Are you sure you don't want to get a witness over here?"

For a moment he looked straight at her, the blue eyes full of a fragile, fishy pallor, larger than she knew them to be. Then he said, "A peckerwood cop from Piedmont, Alabama," but without his habitual sarcasm, musing grimly in her presence.

Nevertheless, she smiled.

He said, "Dad sent me a telegram. I was eating lunch in a restaurant on the main plaza in Villajoyosa, and the deliveryman for the telegraph office knew me and put the telegram down beside my plate of enchiladas. Your father writes, 'I am dying, come home,' during your midday meal. Your brother has never really left your father's side, but your father doesn't want your brother. He waits until you have finished your lentil soup and are hungry for more before putting a telegram down beside your enchiladas. You see what I mean?"

She nodded. He was speaking in a tone of spent astonishment, numbly, no longer really aggrieved.

"Your brother is a decent man, as long as you aren't around to arouse his distrust and competitive instinct. The last thing you want is to compete with your brother. It's the last thing you ever wanted. You've made a practice of giving him what he wanted, which has only caused him to suspect that everything you've given him is simply something you haven't wanted to have. Now you take his dying father away from him and try to convince him it's nothing personal. He accuses you of being a filial necrophiliac—or something like that."

"I don't understand," she said.

"You can only love your father when he's dead."

She protested, quietly. "That's not really true, is it?"

"I don't know."

"If it hadn't been for the Vietnam War . . . or later if a whole generation had known how to make peace . . ."

"Your brother doesn't believe that, your brother—"

For an instant she thought he was talking about her brother, Sam, who had fought in Vietnam and later waged a brawling, drunken war with himself before turning to the farm. Then she realized he wasn't, but interrupted him anyway, encouraged perhaps by what Sam had done to save his life. "Larry . . ."

He paused, a puzzled and vaguely alerted expression on his face. "Your brother believes you're the bad twin back from exile—"

"Larry, honey, don't," she said.

It took her by surprise—she hadn't used that word for him in years. It caused her to look down. She heard Larry sigh. Before she looked up she'd also heard, through the crack in the door, that impure pant of Ed Reece's breath.

"I didn't want to fuck up his life for him, I really didn't," he said. He sounded older now, poorly defended, in his need to be believed perhaps not quite as truthful.

"Maybe you shouldn't have given him everything he wanted," she said cautiously. "Did you ever think of that?"

"Because it would just make him want more?"

"Or because it would only postpone the inevitable, a confrontation of some sort."

"You know, I never had a fistfight with my brother, not that I can remember."

"Well, maybe you should have."

She wasn't sure of the advice she was giving and she had never seen him in such a suggestible state. Perhaps he was finally admitting to her he had gone as far as he could go alone. He'd made it here—Piedmont, Alabama. It felt familiar to her, very familiar.

"Were you happy to see him?" she asked.

"In the beginning."

"Then?"

"The same shit . . . the same . . ." He stopped and shook his head. "There's so much I still can't take, Connie."

"Maybe that's why Ed called you back," she said.

"Except that Dad couldn't take it any longer himself. He had to get out of there too."

"I mean so that you and Russ could finally face it."

"How? By fighting over Dad? Some kind of final big showdown with your dying father in the middle?"

There was that dim crack of light to his left, and out to his right, rooms with heavy rubberized drapes, which sealed off more light and other voices, provided there were people inside. "This is crazy, Connie, you know that, don't you? If it weren't for these towns and motels and these roads and busted radiator fans you know how crazy it'd be, don't you? Look, as long as I know we've got to get from Piedmont, Alabama, to Chumleyville, Alabama, along Route 278 I'm all right. Or from Owensboro, Kentucky, to Boonville, Indiana. Or from Galesburg, Illinois, to Rockwell City, Iowa. But get rid of the hick towns and the narrow two-lane roads and all the other nuisances and you know where we'd be, don't you? It can get very savage and very abstract at three o'clock in the morning with the sound of that man dying in the bed beside you. You can't tell one town from the other then. They're all the same motel."

She saw him shudder. It was like watching a man trying to wriggle free of his own skin—and failing, of course. "You should have said something before, Larry."

"It's not easy to talk about." Then to show her how easy it wasn't, he quietly spaced out the words. "Being terrified is not an easy thing to talk about."

She'd been leaning back against the van. She stepped up to him now, and it was like stepping up to him at that coffeehouse the autumn afternoon they'd met *only* insofar as he'd been lonely and uncertain and disillusioned then and he was lonely and uncertain and disillusioned now. But the difference was enormous. That had been the result of protesting against a war which had seemed diabolically self-perpetuating, but wasn't, and would end. This was something else. Suddenly she felt it for herself too. There was that youthful illusion with which she'd gone up to him on that distant afternoon, and there was this, going up to him again now, as if widely separated periods in her life could join hands, even though one hand might be warm and the other cold.

She held him. For a moment neither of them spoke. They listened to Ed Reece's breath, and so attentive had she been to Ed these last few days, she couldn't free herself entirely of him now. She might have been embracing Ed, not his son. As Larry slumped against her, a thinner man for her extra weight, she might have been murmuring to his father that it was all right, that she was there with him. Except that as dimly into the future as it took her it also took her back, and there was still something of the boy she'd walked out into the autumn night with after watching Ingmar Bergman's poem to Midsummer Eve in the man she held—perhaps the father to that boy, it had been that long ago. So much had happened. She was used to the franker, more consolable demands of Jan. Even, she realized in that moment, to the simpler company of animals. She was not used to the sort of embrace whose clinging need of her gave rise to the very resentment that would cut it short, although she had not forgotten it. She stood there letting things from a romantic past and a deteriorating future converge in her as she held on to her ex-husband, himself evocative of both a loving boy and a dying man.

When he pulled back from her she thought he had something to say; she'd heard him draw breath. But he kissed her, and he kissed her precisely as if his greatest desire was to keep another word from escaping their lips. There was such urgency in his kiss she knew in returning it she was responding to something that had little to do with whatever attraction he may have felt for her or she for him. It left her at a distance from him, and as solicitous of him in that moment as she felt—and of his father, of all this desperate dying maleness called Reece—it kept that distance cool. She heard Jan again warning her that Larry would be her ruin. Lisa had sneaked out to squirm beneath Mike Kellog in the woods beside their house. It amused her—to be in the presence of such powerful forces without herself being overwhelmed. It reminded her . . . of course . . . it reminded her of her Uncle Hal. She saw him again that late-spring night sitting across the kitchen table from her when the meaty, drunken odors she must have been giving off would have been enough to swamp another man. But now she understood: his "pass" had been the way he'd chosen to express his amusement; men, real men, never said a word. Instead, they smiled. Sitting at the center of a sexual hurricane he had beamed like a fool. She could not match such a grin, and suddenly with a revulsion that was instantaneous and electric she knew she didn't want to. As she broke the kiss hot breath rushed out of both their mouths. She said, "We could go in the van . . ."

She followed him in and left the door open on a crack, to match the crack in the door that opened onto Ed Reece. They wanted to be able to hear him if his throat clogged or if the rhythm of his panting changed. But they didn't hear him, and making love so quietly, they didn't even attract the attention of the chance passerby, who might for once have correctly surmised what was going on behind the windowless length of that van, but who might have been disappointed had he looked in. There was more fondness in Larry's touch than passion, and more sympathy than either, and when he entered her he lay there motionless for a moment on his father's soiled mattress as though taking note of how much things had changed. She stroked the back of his neck then, and pushed up close against him. Soon she got him to move. They made love propped up on their sides, a sheltering position, each with a hand caressingly free. She was pleased to discover that they really didn't hate each other—but then, she'd never really thought they had. They nuzzled, stroked each other's hair, and smiled. Their only spoken comment was Larry's, that he was about to come—he had always been mindful in that way. She hadn't thought she would come too, so she was surprised to find a wave of warmth gathering out of nowhere in her, and then very surprised by the light it threw off and its long spending force as it broke. It left her with the side of her head against his, her lips at his ear in case she had something she wanted to whisper. She did, but it didn't come to her. Perhaps she didn't have anything after all.

PART
FOUR

IX

YOU can aim for something all your life, year after year set your sights there, but in the instant you achieve it it's as though your attention had wandered or your faith had lapsed and you'd come to your destination unawares. That was how they entered Chumleyville.

It was a town like all the rest. They would pass shopping plazas, a school with its athletic fields, that down-on-the-highway string of motels, restaurants, car dealerships, and mini-marts; the churches would be made of gray stone and weathered brick and girdled by evergreen bushes and magnolia trees. The train station would be defunct and the downtown movie house converted into a furniture store, still shadowed by its anomalous and telltale marquee. The emptiest and most evocative buildings in town would belong to those textile factories down by the tracks that had not modernized; those that had—single-storied, institutionally plain—would be located on the outskirts of town, close to the country club golf course whose long par-five fairways would stretch out along the highway. Set somewhere back from the center of things there would be a low block of buildings housing farm implements and hardware and feed supplies that in its age-dulled and profitless longevity would have achieved the status of a shrine. By comparison, the courthouse, just as old and Germanically far more imposing, would seem comical in a time when town and county records could be kept on a single computer.

They would see evidence that the town was electronically abreast—time and temperature indicators, game arcades, digital gas pumps, tellerless banks—and evidence that it preserved at its heart a stony recalcitrance to change—the red earth, the lichened trees, the glassy heat, the teeming vegetation, the people. The people would not have changed. The terms of their wealth and poverty might have, but not the way they rode out the abundance or chafed at the meanness of their lives, certainly not the color of their skins.

They had been here before. It was a town. In no instant could they declare, Now we have arrived.

Yet they'd find it on their Alabama map, going north along Route 231, a mile short of 278, five miles from Summit, seven from Bloutsville. It too had a name.

Ed said, "Help me sit up. I want to see."

They left the van idling, and between them Larry and Connie lifted Ed off his mattress and set him in the passenger seat. He would see the courthouse at midmorning, with its Confederate statue, its doughboy, with its white old-timers whittling cedar sticks on the benches and its black men standing down off the steps or squatting under the oaks, statue-still themselves. Out to his left and right, the slanting zinc roofs shadowing the sidewalks would have long since been pulled down and replaced by glassy storefronts, most of which would be cracked and tarnished now. Shopping would be sparse. In fact he'd see more lawyers, stenographers, license-seekers and minor traffic violators entering and leaving the courthouse door than shoppers in the stores. He could be excused from thinking that the town was running along on past momentum, past desire. Or that in spite of the fluttering flag, the chorusing sparrows, smells if he'd had the nose for them, and a snug four-sidedness everywhere he looked, there was still something vestigial about the scene before him. He would ask to see more.

"Drive me around," he said, but the words barely formed. He

waved a circle out before his son, then fell with his pain against Connie.

They drove him around the square, down a street of modest bungalows on oversized lots, past a brand-new post office, raw brick and mortar, then back into a residential street of deeply shaded streets and sandy yards. He would recognize some of these homes; some, the larger ones, with pillars, wraparound verandas, and enormous flower urns, would not have changed. A quality to the streets would not have changed since he'd walked them as a boy, a solacing coolness made up of dampness from their ditches, shadiness from their trees, but mostly made up of emanations from the homes themselves and the standing coolness of the lives inside. He would feel a bit of that and shiver. Connie would question him, then slip her arm around his shoulder. Soon the last local fixings of houses to people, streets to events, would fade, and his memory would offer him only a generalized familiarity, as indistinct as the glass he fogged over with his laboring breath. He would lean more heavily against Connie then, and more trustingly let his son drive. At that point the town would feel capable of the most heartless sort of treachery to him, or the most profound sort of enchantment, whatever came out of that breath-formed cloud. To see past that cloud, to restore High Street to Main, Magnolia to Maple, to connect a dailiness to a yearliness of life once again, he suspected he would have to see not through the eyes of his son, who still bore his prejudices, but through the eyes of his grandson, who had taken Ed's place on the mattress and was now kneeling to look out the back windows.

"Dad," Larry said, "isn't that the one?"

He saw a high old dilapidated house that slumped badly off to each side, as though it were made of collapsible matter and its ridgepole of cast iron. With its clapboards running in swaybacked lines down its sides and its corner posts brittly bowed, it looked more like an old bellied boat than a house.

"People are living there," Connie said.

There was a red-and-blue Big Wheel abandoned on the walk leading up to the side steps and screened porch. A line of miscellaneous wash hung in the yard, and cheap yellow curtains, fan-blown, fluttered out the first two windows down the side. They heard a child cry. The sense was of life germinating in a desiccated shell, for the white paint had flaked down to its weather-grayed wood, the screens were rusting, some shingles on the roof had blown away.

"Is it, Dad?"

"Shhh, Larry," Connie said.

He had been back to this town many times since he'd left and been able to adjust to each successive change. He would not have believed that his memory could be so brutally disputed or mocked. He closed his eyes. Somewhere inside that house lived a child, a child who stood now looking out at a frightfully old man, at another man the age of his father and a woman the age of his mother, and at a boy, a boy like himself. What were they doing parked there in a van with a bed and a mattress tied up on the top, staring at a house that nobody had bothered to turn his head toward before? He ran to ask. He ran from room to room. He came to a last, and to his parents turned heavily in toward each other in the center of their bed. Climbing up on them, futilely trying to pry them apart, he kept repeating, What are those people doing out there? What do they want?

"Yes," he said.

"It is the one?" Larry made sure.

"Yes."

In that instant he felt his grandson's breath, too long contained, explode on the back of his neck. "I think it's a great house, Granddad! I really do!"

"I haven't got any idea how I knew," he heard Larry say, sobered and amazed.

And he told him, "You'll have to talk to those people, son."

They drove him down to the Birmingham-Huntsville highway and yet another motel. They all felt the cruel and subtle mockery of it—a motel in this town. Alone, carrying what was left of their money, feeling curiously as he had on that first day when he'd gone out to buy and test-drive the van, Larry made his way back to the house his father wanted to die in. He knew he must have had this house pointed out to him as a boy; he did not remember it. He was about to enter a strange home, inhabited by strangers, which nonetheless had been a darkly intimate part of his life for almost all of his thirty-nine years, and which proved it again by drawing him to it.

This time he parked directly in front along the curbless street, out on an apron of sand, and saw at once what they'd missed before when they'd parked down at the end: that the house had been made into a duplex and that the other half was empty. He stepped up to the occupied half, banged the screened door softly twice, and waited while a woman took form out of the shadows of the porch, emerging with the tiny squares of a metallic mantilla drawn over her face. She was an unnatural blonde, sallow-complected, going to fat, dressed in jeans and a faded blue T-shirt that read, "Give Me Elbow Room—I Drink Ritter's Beer!" When she opened the door he had one of those moments of rare lucidity that he'd only experienced before on drugs. He'd known no way to explain it except to say that the drug had short-circuited, for a moment its delightful and disturbing distortions had ceased, and with nerveless calm he'd seen to the crux of some matter. This woman had a soft heart encased in a suspicious shell, for she'd suffered her share of abuse. The man she lived with was not the father of her two children. He would stay out drinking night after night until his guilt got the best of him. Then he would take her with him, and making up for a lonely week, she would get drunker than he. They'd fight and fuck then and the next morning wake up to a slightly less tolerable status quo. She especially would yearn for some sort of deliverance, but she would want it in the concrete, on the barrelhead, and for her to take part willingly in somebody else's dream, even if it could be explained to her as compellingly as it had once been to him, would be more than he could expect. Still he tried.

Standing there at the door, never taking that last step up onto the porch, he told her about their long trip and his father's dying wish. When he'd finished he looked down, calculatedly, for effect, until with unfaked disgust he had to turn away from her, turn his back on her entirely. Then he took that first step back toward the van.

Hey, where was he going?

He faced her again. She wore the angry, offended, but still intrigued expression of a woman half seduced and then stood up. She looked washed out beneath the eyes, it was yesterday's makeup on her cheeks. He said it wasn't easy.

You say you're his son?

He said he was, then noticed movement on the porch behind her. A girl, not more than five, had sat down on the glider there. She was the opposite of her mother—frail, ephemeral, soundless, with a spectral luminosity about the eyes.

Supposin' you're tellin' the truth?

As strange as it sounded he was.

Then you're askin' us—and with a cock of the hip she included her daughter—to move back into a house where a man's just died. Don't make no difference your father was a nice man.

The house seemed to ride at anchor above him, a motion so harmless and habitual he could be lulled into forgetting that at any moment it might sink or sail away. In reality it was a large, drafty, two-and-half-story wood-frame, with entrances at both sides and in the middle—not a boat. He tried—and failed—to discover in it some numinous something that would give it ascendancy over a life. The little girl had slumped back against the glider now. Her eyes shone. He said they could always move.

Could. But that'd take real money. He'd better come back when Lou got home from work, 'bout six.

But Lou wouldn't be coming home at six. By six, provided he got off work at five, Lou'd be starting on his fourth beer. Larry drove back to his father. That a still-young man, in reasonable health, even though exhausted, should return to a disease-ridden man who could barely breathe to take his charge, he knew to be absurd, but that was what he was doing. He asked Connie and Jeff, who were keeping Ed company, to leave them for a moment. He didn't sit. He would give his father a clear look at what he had to work with, at what their chances were. He said,

"Can you talk, Dad?"

"I can try," Ed whispered, summoning his strength. That swelling on his neck gave to his pallor a sickly bloom. Behind the papery lips the teeth had grown. As the flesh fell off the cheeks the eyes enlarged, and it was clear to Larry that the inside wanted out, that that was the transformation his father had in store.

"I've got you this far," Larry said. "I'll have to go back to get those people to leave. I'm not sure I can face them again."

"Why?" Ed mouthed the word.

"Because it's a cheap, mercenary, miserable scene. It's sad. It makes mockery of it. There's no end to the mockery it will make. . . ."

A grin passed over his father's lips.

"And it's the town. Nothing happened—not to me. I expected something to happen."

"What?"

Larry shook his head.

Ed repeated his question.

"Something for centuries people have been trying to put into words. A recognition, just a simple click, a greater presence, reality . . . it's because of you . . ."

His father asked him to come closer, to sit down. When Larry pulled the chair Connie had left up to the head of the bed, Ed closed his eyes, forcing his son to wait, to either touch the skeletal hand to indicate he was there, or the skeletal shoulder. He touched the shoulder.

In a fitful and slow-paced whisper, Ed said, "I told you the worst part about dying is thinking about all the living you didn't do. Comes a point when you don't think about it anymore. . . . You get old, son, and weak, very quickly, and pretty soon t'healthiest thing 'bout you s'your pain. When all that you *have* done starts to come back . . . then thinking 'bout what you haven't done takes more strength than you've got. You don't even *think* at all. . . ." He held a pause and out of a fierce and unquivering quiet declared, "I could die right now, Larry, I could. The second I decide to quit carrying this load."

His son made a protesting sound, and Ed stopped him.

"You fill up, then empty out, you do that a lot, then one day it all comes back to stay. Doesn't make any difference what you've done in your life. . . . You might never have gone 'round the block. You might have been a hermit in a cave. But when it all comes back . . . it's a real crowd. Look at me," and he raised a trembling, fleshless arm before his son. "I don't weigh anything and I'm so heavy and old I can't move. You come to that point and the only thing that matters is finding the right place to lie down. . . . There may not be a right place. I don't want to lie to you, son."

"I never thought you did. Why don't you rest now, Dad?"

"What'd you say—a click? I didn't hear a click either when we drove into town."

"But you still think this is the place?"

"I *don't* think. I can't remember the last time I had a thought of my own. Here is where whatever I'm carrying wants to lie down." Suddenly Ed twisted his head toward his son, and for an instant his voice took on a youthful, speculative tone. "D'you ever wonder what it would be like to get pregnant?" he asked.

"At one time or another . . . I guess."

"Might be like that . . . like the delivery, I mean."

"But what if it's not, Dad? What if it's not 'like' anything?"

"Everything is like something," Ed avowed.

"Yes . . . but what if it's not? What if it doesn't all come and go in waves? What if people aren't like trees?"

Ed lay perfectly still and for a moment gave the impression, just as he'd said, of entertaining rather than originating his thoughts, of letting the sum of his life think through him.

Then without answering the question he shook his head and turned away.

Larry went next door, and this time with no swimming pool to hustle Jeff off to they sent him out for Cokes. In the little time they had, he told Connie he wasn't sure he could deal with the people in his father's boyhood home again. Fifteen years ago he would have told her that the vibes there had been about as hostile as they could be; fifteen years ago they could have turned their backs on those people because there'd been no death in their lives then. There'd been outrage at countless deaths thousands of miles

away—in effect, a great enlivening force. He sat on the edge of
Connie's bed. He recited their alternatives. They could take his
father to the local hospital, but since the local hospital would be
very small they would end up having to take him to Huntsville.
They could call the police, and after gaining an exoneration for
themselves have the police arrange for an ambulance to take his
father to Huntsville. They could call his family, and by humbling
themselves, by making a clean breast of the matter, win a possible
exoneration from them, after which his family could authorize the
police to arrange for an ambulance to take Ed Reece to Huntsville
or to Welborne, Kentucky, or some other place unimpeachably on
the map. He couldn't be sure when he stuck his head out the
motel door that Chumleyville, Alabama, would be.

He lay back on the bed. But they couldn't do any of those
things, could they? At six o'clock he'd have to go back, wouldn't
he? Would she wake him at six? Until then, would she stay with
his father and keep alive in him the notion that his son was tire-
lessly at work out in the world to bring that bed into that house?
Then would she go with him? He realized he was an asshole to ask
it of her, but would she?

Then he lay all the way back, and at six she woke him. If
there'd been an alternative he'd missed she might have given it to
him then—but there wasn't. She had no choice but to leave Jeff
with his grandfather and to accompany the man who would always come waltzing in when it pleased him and make just another
indefensible demand . . . yes, yes, she knew . . . back to that house.
In an unaccommodating world she'd been given these powers of
accommodation . . . which certain chronic down-and-outers
would never fail to take advantage of, yes, yes . . . and she would
use them now. They left the motel quietly so as not to disabuse Ed
of the belief that his son had been out there all along. Larry drove
straight to that house, never doubting his turns, and she remarked
on that. A gray Ford pickup with hiked-up chassis and oversized
wheels was now parked in the unpaved drive at the side of the
house, and she noticed that it was new. A woman let them in at
the screen door. She was dressed in a pink print dress stretched
tight at every point and freshly made up with lilac eye shadow and

oily pink lipstick, Lisa's colors, in fact. A little girl, who retreated across the living room as Larry and Connie entered, hadn't been touched, however. Her hair was tangled and her face and T-shirt were smeared with what looked like strawberry jam. Curiously, her unkemptness enhanced her air of fragility, as if the dirt had given her a very delicate crust. The living room was covered in a green shag carpet; two of the walls were done in warped sheets of wood paneling and the ceiling had been dropped. There was a daybed covered in a striped spread, a china-red beanbag, an old maroon recliner, a coffee table which was bare except for three marking pencils rolled to one edge, and a small television on a stand which looked unstable on the stringy carpet.

The only other object in the room was a bolted-down kerosene stove, many years old, that the carpet had been cut around. Directly ahead, in an adjoining bedroom, more wall paneling and dirty shag were visible, but to the left in the kitchen the linoleum was so old it had almost lost its pattern. The man standing in the kitchen door was short and chunky, with a cowlick of chestnut hair angling down over a face whose fleshiness had not yet swallowed his boyish features. He had his hand in a bag of corn crisps. The woman, who called herself Melanie, introduced him as Lou. When Larry completed the introductions, referring to Connie as his wife, instead of offering to shake Lou reached behind him to the kitchen table and from a fresh six-pack of Pabst Light offered to unfasten a can for Larry and another for her. Larry hesitated—she wasn't sure why, since she knew how badly he'd want the beer—but when he did accept she declined, and then declined a can of Tab that Melanie offered as a substitute.

She and Larry took the daybed, while Lou set his recliner at its intermediate stage and Melanie brought in a straight-backed chair from the kitchen, preferring to sit stiffly there, with her legs crossed, rather than lower herself onto the beanbag. She said, "I ain't sure I got it all straight. I been tellin' Lou . . ."

Lou took over: "That's tough about your ole man. When they hang on like that it can be a lot worse. Mine got hit by a truck here five years back and that was that."

Larry said he understood what Lou meant. He spoke deliberately, almost affecting a drawl, but she could feel a fine agitation coming through the daybed.

"Like to help out," Lou went on, "but we just never thought of ourselves in the mortuary business."

He risked a grin, very much as a boy would, holding it back until he saw just how much he could get away with. In that way he reminded her, of course, of her son, but that wasn't fair, that was only something generic between boys.

Before he sipped from his beer Larry, apparently, returned the grin, for Lou now broadened his. "Not that there's anything wrong with undertakers. They get paid."

"They really do," she heard herself say, and her tone was humorless, factual, and firm.

It forced Lou to do something with his grin. He tucked it back a bit. "S'what I've heard."

"It's one of the best-paid professions in the world." She set the record straight.

They exchanged a look, and past the sunny blue eyes and the turned-up nose she knew what she was looking at. Reminding herself why she was here, she forced a smile. It broke the tension long enough to allow Lou to go to his beer.

Connie looked around for the little girl and found her peeking from inside the adjoining room, which from her angle of vision she could now see contained a child's bed and a scattering of plastic toys on the discolored green shag. Which was the room Ed Reece had brought them all this way to lie down in? She couldn't believe it was that one, and feared with a leaden premonition that it was theirs—Melanie and Lou's.

"You'd better explain all this again, Larry," she said.

"I'll tellya straight out at the start, though," Lou said, "we got a landlord that don't allow no subleasing."

"Larry . . ." she said.

He looked at her dispiritedly.

"What was that about the police?" Lou asked.

"Nothing . . . it was nothing," Larry said.

"This afternoon you said something about the police," Melanie reminded him.

"I may have said something about the little guy versus the big guy, the weak against the powerful. It's a way of talking, that's all."

"If the police are mixed up in this," Lou speculated pointedly, "you gotta figure that in the risk."

"You mean the price," Connie couldn't resist saying.

"The risk determines the price," he put to her flatly. "Always has."

"A man's dying. He wants to die in the house where he was born. Although this house is practically worthless it means everything to him. I can't believe it means anything to you."

"Sentimental value," he said.

"What?"

"That's what you call it."

"I know what you call it."

"It's like a priceless hair-loom that's really not worth that much but . . ."

"But you have to figure it in," she finished for him.

To his credit he met her mockery with a civil shake of the head. "That's the way it is," he said, and brought his recliner to an upright position. She looked at Melanie, whom in that instant she caught looking with a dubious sort of sympathy at Larry. Then Melanie looked straight at her and her expression changed. It was no longer a case of an emotionally battered woman living under the heel of a brutalizing man, not that at all, for there was fresh defiance in Melanie's face, there was a jelling of sexual possessiveness and common greed in her doughy features and undercolored eyes, and in each stringy blond curl there was something intolerant and shrill. What kept Connie from taking her aside and saying: I have no designs on your man? The money you can get I want you to have. I pray your daughter takes a big leap out of her autistic shadows. The two of us have unillustrious lives to live— why can't we be friends?

"It's sad, sure it's sad," Melanie was expostulating angrily, "but that don't give you all the right to come barging in, expecting somethin' for nothin'."

"I don't think that was what we were doing," Connie said.

At her side she heard Larry draw a long determined breath. Leaning up on the daybed, he said, "Let's talk risks, then. How do you see the risks . . ." He hesitated on the forgotten name.

"Lou," Lou said, making him wait.

"Sure . . . Lou." And he drew the breath again. "How do you see the risks?"

With Larry leaning up, Lou decided to sit back, although he did not return his chair to a reclining position. He lifted his hairy forearms to the armrests and punctuated a period of thought by popping his beer can. "Well, like I said," he started off obligingly, "we got a landlord problem, a landlord that don't allow no sublease."

"What if we went and talked to him?"

"D'rather not do that."

"All right, what if you took the risk? What d'you pay here each month?"

She could see he had a settled-upon figure ready to announce, but was holding it back a moment as though it were privileged information. "Three-fifty," he finally confided.

"I'll pay the rest of this month and all of next one."

"This month's already paid."

"I'll pay next month and the one after that."

Lou sent Melanie a straight-faced glance, but there was nothing he could do to disguise that avid leap of light in the eyes.

"What other risks?" Larry said.

"Risk of mental suffering . . . later on."

"What is that supposed to mean?"

"Coming back to a house where a man has died. You can't never tell what that's gonna do to your mind."

"One hundred dollars," Larry said.

The flat figure took Lou off guard. "Just like that?" he said. "How do you know that's a fair price?"

"I don't. It's the price I'm paying."

"There's the risk of physical suffering too. You gotta figure that in."

"I don't understand that either."

"What *if* it's a contagious disease?"

"It's not."

"But what if it is? What's he got?"

"I'd rather not say."

"How can we do business if I don't know?"

"He's got cancer and emphysema," Connie said, and she felt Larry slump momentarily beside her. Lou, who would have thought of both of the diseases, at least of the first, nevertheless underwent a sobering kind of start. It opened his eyes. She could see the boy there, the times when for all his cocksureness he'd had his bluff called. She could even experience a faint twinge of sympathy for him. This was not his game. "Neither one of them is contagious," she said.

"But they *might* be." He tried to regain lost ground.

"Fifty dollars," Larry said, "on the outside chance."

Lou made a confused, conceding sound. Melanie sat skeptical and erect, a cigarette now in her mouth.

"Anything else?" Larry said.

There was something else, but Lou appeared to have forgotten what. To bring it back and to collect himself, he took another long gulp of his beer, hanging pensively on the lip of the can. She expected him to pop it when he had his wits back in order, but he fooled her. He was quiet and concerned as he nodded into the next room. "There's Jill," he whispered. "What if she finds out?"

"Does she have to?" Larry asked.

Lou shook his head. "What if she does? It might tra-mer . . . tro-mer . . ."

And it was Lou's turn to wait, Larry's turn to let him. She did not step in. Jill's mother looked only at Larry now, a frown of disbelief screwing deep into her eyes.

"Traumatize her?" Larry finally wondered.

"Yeah," Lou said, relieved. "We gotta think of that."

"She may have already been . . . traumatized. We should think of that too. Fifty more dollars for a possibly redundant trauma."

Connie whispered, "Don't, Larry."

He swallowed his sarcasm. "Anything else?"

Clearly, Lou couldn't decide whether he was being stampeded or given a chance to write his own ticket. He glanced at Melanie,

but smoking steadily she never took her eyes off Larry. Connie
was no help, although he glanced at her too. He pushed his recliner back to its second setting and in an attempt at self-posses-
sion rested his beer can on top of his belly. "How much we got
already?" it occurred to him to ask.

"I don't know. A lot. Any 'risks' you still want to include before
we add it up?"

Pure consternation took possession of his face then as he stared
back at Larry. He was all mental motion, and no results. He was
greed running out from under itself, and if she could feel the least
bit sorry for him it was because the greed grew out of the windfall
dreams of a boy. "The police!" he said suddenly, as though he'd
come to a dizzying stop.

"What about them?"

"We never put a price on them!"

Larry gave a groan—and she knew his groans. There was the
one that deflated him, and there was this other one that blew him
up. "Forget the police! The police are out of it! I've just driven
three thousand miles and the only policeman I've seen with my
own eyes was nice enough to turn us the right way around on a
one-way street in Savannah. You wanna know the truth about the
police, you gotta know the truth about the country. It's big—and
lonely. It's so goddam lonely you can go crazy out there driving
around without a policeman or two on your tail. But *here's the
thing.* Taken by themselves the police don't exist. They're only
go-betweens. Someone's gotta love you or hate you enough to set
them on your tail, and what if no one does? You see what I
mean?"

Lou might have seen a number of things—that he'd been in-
sulted, suckered, played wildly for a fool. Or maybe, simply, that
he'd been lured into the presence of a madman and that the
money he'd all but spent had been snatched out of his hand. He
wore a wrongly wounded, righteously indignant expression. Larry
must have seen it too. He reached into his back pocket and took
out his wallet. Like a magician explaining a trick he could never
again perform, he opened the wallet and held the widened crack
full of bills up to Lou. Then he took out the bills, and Lou's

recliner shot forward into its upright position. Now she heard the other groan, as the air leaked out. "I don't know how much is here, but it's what's left. Let's just make it simple and say it's all yours. Okay?"

And before the money'd been counted, long before it would exchange hands, she'd seen the moment for what it truly was. If she hadn't seen it till then that was because these moments had never been staged quite so humbly before. Or with so much cheap ironical malice. But it wasn't ironical at all—she had to remember that. It just was. It was one of those inescapable moments that couldn't be rationalized around, justified, even explained. Ed Reece's life had come to this, and Ed wasn't even here. He was off where she really hadn't wanted to leave him, alone with her son, and if she was faithful to the logic that had brought her here she could say that this moment of base bargaining with Lou and Melanie led inescapably—perhaps even more momentously—to that one there, Jeff's, his twelve-year-old deathwatch, after all. And if she really wanted to follow her logic to the end, where either her own powers of thought failed her or an apprehensive fancifulness took over, she could say that she'd come with Ed and Ed's life had come to this just so that Lisa could be lying under Mike Kellog in the woods out beside their house, contracting an itch that could only grow. Except that they wouldn't have to escape to the woods. With Connie gone and Jan at work all day, Lisa could have her pick of the beds.

It was then that Lou surprised perhaps even himself. "You folks better hang on to a hundred of that," he advised. "You gotta eat, don't you, and, well . . . you can't tell how long your old man might linger on."

Larry folded a hundred-dollar bill into his shirt pocket, then placed the rest on the scummed and scarred coffee table. She guessed there might be more than a thousand dollars there.

"You know, I feel kinda bad about this," Lou went on.

"Don't," Larry told him.

"If it lasts longer than you think—"

"Dad may be dead by the time we get back to the motel."

On that note Lou leaned out of the recliner to pick up the

money. Before he got there Melanie said, "I wanna see him."

"See him?" Larry said. "What do you mean?"

"Don't touch that money, Lou," Melanie demanded, although she had never taken her eyes off of Larry. Her skepticism, her disbelief, had grown into something disfiguringly hard now. "First I wanna see me a dying man."

"You don't," Larry said quietly.

"You say you got him in a motel? Just open the door and let me peek inside. Otherwise we got no deal."

"We got a deal if I say we got one," Lou reminded her, blowing up a bit, but it was a face-saving opposition, a public gesture for his pride.

Which she ignored. "We'll just take that look first," she told Larry, standing before her straight-backed chair.

She meant the three of them. While Larry folded the money back into his wallet, she disappeared into the bedroom and led out the fragile and filthy little girl. They could have taken the two cars, the pickup and the van, but Larry wanted to show them the mattress where Ed slept, as if that might be proof enough. When it wasn't, he told them to get inside. Lou asked a question or two about the van, which Larry couldn't answer, and once they were all seated Connie found herself sharing the mattress with Jill, the little girl. She smelled, of her dirtied panties and of the slightly feral odor a body that young and that long-unwashed gave off, and she smelled with a cloying sweetness of that strawberry jam she had smeared on her face and shirt, which struck Connie as the most pathetic of cover-ups. It couldn't be covered up, none of it, ever—but already she was thinking about her son. He'd been born with his eyes open, and a look there that had told her he had no desire to be in this world but since he was here he'd hold the world accountable by taking it all. But the world didn't scare easily; never yet had the world been forced to settle with anybody on anything less than its own terms. She imagined him sitting beside his grandfather. She heard him talk—about music, about school, about animals, about his sister's not-so-clever tricks, about anything that could compete with that laborious and alarming activity that was his grandfather's breath . . . about his dreams. Once he got started he could go on like a filibustering senator, and she hoped he would, she wanted him to, for when he stopped and Ed took over and the world had its way, she knew she would never get that look out of his eyes . . . the look of a newborn wild thing that at one time she had had the wistful presumption to think she could domesticate, tame, turn to love. . . .

But he had stopped talking some time ago, and his grandfather had gone on breathing, except that each puppy-pant was now congested like a puppy-growl, and finally all that Jeff had been able to do was bring in a glass of water from the bathroom and have it ready for those times when his grandfather wanted to moisten his lips. The lips needed moistening—they were pursed and cracked like a shrunken apple—but except for his neck, which looked like a frog's, his whole face had a shrunken scaly look, and Jeff had returned to the bathroom and wet a cloth so that he could also moisten the forehead and stubble-gray cheeks, as he'd seen his mother do. But when he'd tried his grandfather had shaken him off with a crotchety twist of the head, the quickness of which startled him, just as those moments of soundlessness did when his grandfather stopped panting and, gathering his forces, got set to clear his throat.

He was not frightened. Once he realized that his mother and father had not just gone off to talk but had actually driven away and that he had this job to do until they got back, there were periods when he was even bored. He'd tried to watch a local news team, in the flaming oranges, greens, and blues of a cut-rate television, joke their way through some pretty horrible news. He'd cracked the curtains and cranked open the slatted window and stood there looking out at the highway that passed through town, making two smokey-sightings just to keep in form. Directly across the highway there was a drive-in restaurant of the kind that would be sure to serve chili and french-fried onion rings, and since neither he nor his grandfather had eaten he considered running across and picking up a couple of carry-out orders. He didn't because if chili and onion rings were bad for him they would be doubly or triply bad for his grandfather—his mother would not forgive him on that score. But the idea was there, it was one of the things he daydreamed about—along with the television and the smokeys—while his grandfather, within a distance Jeff could jump to from almost any point in the room, lay dying in his bed. Jeff was under no illusions about that. It didn't matter how much he talked to him and tried to cheer him up—his grandfather had never come down out of those clouds. He was going to die. It was what he was doing right now. Jeff didn't get used to it so much as used to the idea that while it went on other things did too—his boredom did and his hunger and that oppressiveness he sometimes felt at being shut up in strange rooms. His life as he'd known it up to then did, side by side with his grandfather's dying.

When his grandfather called out to him he caught Jeff looking at himself in the mirror. The mirror hung over the bureau and every trip around the room he'd passed it, but this was the only time he'd actually stopped and stood there, peering in. In one sense he was just corroborating a discovery he'd made long before. If you took the time to imagine yourself somewhere else—really took the time, for instance, to remember what it was like to be sprawled in your backyard with your dog, Mike, lapping the side of your face—and then came back here and looked hard at the face you saw in the mirror, it wasn't you. It was another boy, not very friendly, pale and unloved like an orphan. One of the songs he listened to went, "I wipe away the water from my face to look through the eyes of a stranger," and it was something like that, except that he'd made his discovery before he'd ever heard that song, and long before this moment with his grandfather in this motel room. But he had never shaken so quickly free from himself as he had today, and the boy he returned to in the mirror had never been so coldly unfamiliar to him, and in another sense, he knew that all the other times he'd amused himself at this game had been clumsy rehearsals for this time, when he'd performed it so well it almost took his breath away too. The boy stood before him cut off at the waist, with bright estranged eyes, as empty as ice. That's when his grandfather had called him.

He managed to leave that other boy in the mirror, but not, on such abrupt notice, to completely regain contact with the first boy, himself, whom he'd left at a safe distance from this room. He went to his grandfather trembling then, very much as if he'd gotten up out of a sickbed himself. He said, "What is it, Granddad? I'm here," and listened intently to those pants as if just behind them at any second a stream of words might make itself clear. Then the pants ceased. The silence which followed was suddenly his, intimately his; it was like the stilled waters of that mirror in which he had seen the reflection of that orphaned boy; he understood that whatever it was his grandfather wanted to tell him would now have to pass through that silence, that silence was not something that came and went at the mercy of other noise, but something—a mysterious presence—that stayed. His grandfather said, "The Reeces are all children. Later you'll understand. Don't hold it against your father."

He'd heard every word. He didn't want his grandfather to have to repeat himself, costing him what it did. Still, he said, "What?"

"It's not his fault." His grandfather stopped and for a moment panted furiously, as though he were storing up breath. But all he added was, "Yes, it is."

Then the eyes half closed, that strenuous and anxious and inwardly alert look came over his face, and his grandfather went back to the race he was gradually losing between the breath that propelled him along and the wind that was blowing up from behind.

This time Jeff did not leave his side. He was sitting there, still waiting to hear what he could about the children the Reeces had been, when the door to the room opened and he saw first a little girl, then a strange man and woman, then another woman who resembled his mother and a weary-eyed man who resembled his father, looking in. But he couldn't be sure. Until they convinced him otherwise, he knew he'd be smart to treat this as a vision of some sort left over from the game he'd played with himself in the mirror and to keep his eyes on the little girl. She had bare feet and skinny legs and stringy hair and discolorations all over her body that at first he thought were bruises but then realized were smears and stains. She was looking at him. Her eyes were as large and round as some nocturnal animal's—that shivery and still. Then it occurred to him that she was looking at him and not at his grandfather for the same reason that he was looking only at her, and he smiled.

He heard the strange man say, "What about it, that satisfy ya?"

And the strange woman replied, "All right, mister, you got a deal."

NO one slept much that night. Larry and Connie alternated sitting up with Ed, and Jeff's dreams were too close to consciousness to be called dreams at all. Shortly after dawn, before the heat of the day descended, while the morning was still like a translucent vessel of some sort, they drove Ed across town. The room he wanted the bed set up in wasn't Melanie and Lou's bedroom after all, but a much smaller room just off the kitchen, used for storage now. It had two windows, one giving onto the screened porch and a larger one looking out to the street, both of whose shades had been permanently drawn. Because the shades were so old, the light in the room was a drab parchment orange.

Passing directly back through the kitchen and into the rear half of the house, Larry and Connie discovered a staircase, semi-exposed to the outside, leading upstairs. The door at the top of the stairs was nailed shut, so they brought the clutter they found in the front room—some odd pieces of furniture, no bed, mostly cardboard boxes full of old shoes, kitchen utensils, magazines, and a few books—out to a damp narrow corridor that ran alongside the staircase and piled it there. At the end of that corridor they had a reduced view of the backyard—the branches of a pecan tree, sand, and scraggly tufts of grass. They could also see the corner of a rotten, yet-to-be-demolished garage. The rest of the house was more meager than they'd expected, not the duplex they'd assumed they'd rented, but only half of that: the room where Melanie and Lou slept, with a couple of shiny beer signs and an Alabama Crimson Tide pennant on the walls, a box spring and mattress on the floor; Jill's room, where dirty clothes and plastic toys seemed to sprout out of the green shag; the bathroom, tiny and old, like the stone of a soured fruit.

They went back outside and while Jeff stayed with his grandfather brought in the bed. Before setting it up they tried to sweep out the room with a broom they found propped beside the stove, but the tips of the bristles were clotted with grease. Larry couldn't budge the two windows, although he did manage to raise the shade on the front one perhaps a third of the way before its spring failed. That gave them a view into the spirea bushes grown up along the house. An overhead light whose bulb surprisingly worked gave them a better look at the sepia-tinted wallpaper, which was coming off in flakes the size of the flowers figured there. The mustiness from that disintegrating paper was astringently sharp, but in a house of such transient odors somehow permanent and pure, and they set the bed up in it, positioning the head beside the kitchen door. Then they fluffed the feather mattress out over the slats, pausing a moment to note what would have struck anyone entering the room at that moment: a sudden sense of fertility there, as though the mattress were a just-turned plot in a field otherwise barren as a bone.

They had no clean sheets. Before resigning themselves to using those in the van they took another quick tour through the house, searching through a towel closet outside the bathroom, then a chest, and finally along the top shelf of the closet in the master bedroom. There, in addition to a softball glove and a wide-brimmed leather hat and a wadded house robe and a cracked case of electric hair rollers, they found sheets, all colored, a couple with blue flowers the size of cabbages, depersonalized but unmistakably theirs, Melanie and Lou's. They were clumsily folded and marginally clean. Connie put them back. She brought Ed's sheets in from the van, and before Larry lowered his father onto the feather mattress had covered it with the sheet that had covered him for the last few days.

It was barely eight o'clock in the morning then. None of them knew the exact date. For ten more minutes Ed didn't open his eyes, working on his breathing instead. Then that look of concentration in his forehead relaxed and for a moment his features settled into a state of repose. His eyelids seemed to float open. The eyes were so badly scummed Larry and Connie couldn't be sure they were focusing on anything; but gradually an expression began to tighten around them, and continued to tighten until it threatened to signal a state of outright rejection. It didn't, they believed, get that far. At the point when it might have, everything in him seemed to relent, and it was only then that they realized that his whole body had performed that drama of imperfect recognition they had followed in his eyes. He fell back now into the mattress.

Larry remained at his side, seated in one of the kitchen chairs whose vinyl covering was slit down to its foam-rubber padding, while Connie went to familiarize herself with Melanie's kitchen. Not a single one of the pots and pans was really clean, but she did find a Teflon electric skillet that was and enough plates and silverware and coffee mugs to go around. Except for half a saucepan of macaroni and cheese, a nearly empty jar of mayonnaise, another of dill pickle solution, and a bit of a quart of milk, Melanie and Lou had taken the refrigerator's store with them. She left Jeff sitting on the glider on the screened porch, took the keys to the van and the hundred-dollar bill Lou had returned, and drove to a 7-Eleven close to the motel where they had stayed. On the way she passed a Kroger's, where she might have bought more cheaply and for days, but she continued on to the highway and from a limited selection picked up breakfast supplies, tomato soup and strawberry ice cream for Ed, hesitated a moment and added a package of six frozen veal cutlets, a sack of frozen potatoes, another of peas, beer for Larry and herself, Mountain Dew for Jeff, and then as an afterthought salami and mustard for sandwiches, unwilling to calculate meals and days.

The sun was hot and glaring now. By the time she got back Jeff had wandered off the porch out into the side yard, then down along a hedge and into the ramshackle garage with its cool dirt

floor and its smells of a cave. When she had breakfast made she
walked out back to call him in. She called twice, quietly, standing
at the top of the wooden stairs, while blue jays cawed in the pecan
trees above her. Directly below, to her left, she saw the nearly-
horizontal doors that opened onto the cellar, and she stood in the
coolness of this house's age and damp rot while she waited for her
son to cross the sunlight separating her from the garage. He came
with an old mule collar draped around his neck, which she identified for him and then asked him to leave with the other clutter
they'd piled along the stairs. But when he said he wanted to show
it to his father, she let him bring it into the kitchen, where its salty
reek of old mule sweat was lost anyway among the more powerful
odors of coffee, bacon, and eggs.

When his parents changed places and Connie went in to sit
with Ed, Larry told Jeff that he remembered seeing mule-drawn
wagons on the streets of this town many times, but that was all he
said. He ate mechanically, then fell into a daze over his coffee. Jeff
went into the room where they had set up the bed to look at his
grandfather. He didn't see him at once, but that was because Ed
had sunk down deep into that fluffy feather mattress. For a moment Jeff envied him that mattress, then he felt the heat that had
already begun to build in that small closed room and heard the
fluttering fastness of his grandfather's breath. He went back out
to the screened porch, whose glider had a loud rusty creak that if
you caught just right you could almost make toll, like a bell.

Shortly before noon the phone started to ring. It hung on the
kitchen wall, and Connie, Jeff, and Larry converged on it from the
bathroom, the screened porch, and Ed's room, respectively. But
none of them picked it up. They watched it ring—the plastic
yellow casing visibly vibrated—and listened to it stop. Then they
returned to what they'd been doing before the phone had rung,
Connie to the washing out of underwear, socks, pajamas, clothes
the four of them had worn, in the tub. As she was hanging them
on the line in the side yard three people walked by. Two were
high-school-aged boys, dressed for baseball, but the third was an
old woman laboring through the heat with a shopping bag, who
stopped in the sun to observe Connie closely. The next moment

she had Larry alone she asked him if he thought there wasn't someone from the town his father would want to see, someone who had been there all along, and Larry said he'd wondered the same thing. Actually, he'd wondered why there hadn't been because he knew that his father had never had anything like that in mind. But, yes, he understood, someone . . . an emissary from the town. Then she'd gone to sit with Ed and he'd gone to lie down, not back in Melanie and Lou's room, but there on the daybed, and on a pillow he'd brought in from the van.

He didn't sleep. For perhaps half an hour he lay just under the surface of the heat, in a fast-moving stream of images and sensations that gave him no rest and eventually became an assault. To stop it he stood, and remained there minutes more beside the bed; then took four steps and placed his hand on the cool grilled top of the kerosene heater, clearly the oldest object in the room. He saw a large window fan set beside the beanbag on the floor, and he walked over there. When he tried the fan it blew the curtains breezily and whited out the sound of his father's breath, but also gave the impression of a wind which might at any moment intensify and raze this room, a room which gave the impression of having been razed and carelessly rebuilt many times before. He turned the fan off. Out on the porch he found his son slumped on the glider where he had first seen Melanie and Lou's little girl, Jill. Behind the glider was the window to his father's room he hadn't been able to open, and whose shade he hadn't been able to adjust, and the sounds that came from behind it now—all Ed's—might have belonged to that poor unfortunate family who lived next door. There was always a poor unfortunate family who lived next door.

Then Connie lay down and Larry sat with his father. Jeff went into Jill's room and stretched out on her bed. The heat in Ed's room had hit its peak and held, and after failing to raise the front window again Larry brought the fan in from the living room and set it up on the kitchen chair, intending to blow the hot air out. His father asked him to turn the fan off. He would eat a little strawberry ice cream, which Larry held to his thin, twitching lips. Water he asked to sip constantly—they badly needed a straw. It had gone past the point of helping him into the bathroom, and when it came to that Larry brought a pitcher in from the kitchen, and by rolling his father over on his side and laying the penis well within the green plastic lip, he helped his father to pee. When he had to shit—for it came to that too—it was in a yellow pail Larry found under the sink. A single harmless squirt left very little to clean, but he did that too, aware that almost the only flesh left on his father's body was to be found in these flaccid white cheeks. They never knew exactly when the heat began to abate. By then—almost six—both Larry and his father had fallen asleep. But when a clatter of the screen door woke him, followed by an exasperated female voice demanding to know if Melanie was there or wasn't, he sensed that the heat of the day had let off, that they had gone over the top, and a cooling that would continue on until the early morning had begun. By the time he came fully awake, Connie had gotten up from the daybed and intercepted their visitor in the living room.

"What's going on here?"—he heard that, then Connie's explanation that they were old friends, not of Melanie's but of Lou's, who had just gotten in town and were staying here while Lou, Melanie, and Jill were away. "Melanie didn't tell me she was going anywhere!" The woman's voice had a querulous and overbearing whine to it, and he heard Connie playing to it, telling her she should know how Melanie was. Sure, she knew. "G'dam that girl!" And Connie didn't know when she'd be back? Connie said about a week. He heard them go back and forth, and came close to dozing again before their steps sounded on the front porch. There, their visitor leveled on Connie as if she were Melanie's stand-in. "You tell her that Marie came by, and you tell her to get her act together if she wants to bust up ole ten. She'll know what you mean."

He waited for Connie to come get him, then stepped out into the kitchen to learn that the woman, Marie, may not have believed a word Connie had said. Connie worried what would happen if Marie went to the police, and Larry replied that it didn't concern him, that he'd quit worrying about the police—what could they do to them now? Connie had wanted an emissary from town, hadn't she? "Bust up ole ten"—emissaries sometimes spoke in code. Wearily, he went to stand on the screened porch, where a light breeze had all but removed the last chemical trace of Marie's perfume. He stood in the breeze, watching supper-bound motorists parade past in their cars, their speeds dreamy and sedate. He heard Jeff step into his grandfather's room and say something unintelligible, but questioning and kind. Then he heard him step out. Either his father's panting breaths had become too weak to make themselves heard on the porch or they'd entered the background noises of his life now, like the sound of his own breath.

He stood there until Connie called him in to a supper of cutlets, potatoes, and peas. The kitchen table was close to Ed's door, and they were up and down as they ate, without establishing an order each taking a turn, including Jeff. After supper they continued to take turns, then to pair up. The heat in Ed's room had diminished, but the terrible painful closeness hadn't, and sooner or later they sought relief on the porch. Mosquitoes had found their way in through a ripped corner of the screen, but still they sat there. The night was far more resonant than the day. Past the immediate noises the house made cooling, or that insects made trilling in the bushes or ticking against the screen, they could hear an airiness that was liquid and vast, within which every other sound the town made, even the four-stage acceleration of teenagers racing their cars, was quickly submerged. They felt the presence of Melanie, Lou, and Jill then less and less.

But crowded into Ed's room they got no farther than his enfeebled fight for breath. Since the only electrical socket in the room didn't work and they couldn't find an extension to run a lamp in from the kitchen, they were forced to use the overhead light. In it Ed lay in a dust-grimed pallor, his pale blue pajamas still damp from sweating out the day's heat. They couldn't tell if he was content. He lay on a bed he'd once thought as big as a boat, and on a feather mattress that might have cradled him close or borne him aloft as on a wave, but his breath came so rapidly now it was as though he had to race to keep up, and they couldn't imagine he had the time to feel content. He did return the pressure of their hands. But only when they weren't expecting it would he open his eyes, and then they couldn't tell what he saw. It was a steady gaze, but groggy, or else imbued with a gravity of purpose they simply knew nothing about. The only time they knew exactly what the eyes said was when the phone rang again, and then they saw alarm there, followed by an irritation so profound that by the time the rings reached six it had hardened to a curse. They let the phone ring out, but unlike that first occasion when they'd met to watch it finish, this time no one moved. They moved and met on other occasions.

As the night wore on they took full, if shadowy, possession of Melanie and Lou's house. At the kitchen sink, at the refrigerator, stepping out into the front yard, onto the back steps, beside the bathroom door—even, as though sleepwalking, although none of them really slept, back in Melanie and Lou's room, under signs, like glossy escutcheons, heralding Miller Lite and Budweiser Beer. Jeff had been given permission to watch television, and for a brief while he tried, but he really couldn't sit still either. Except that he must have, they all sat with Ed for seemingly every minute of the night, in a night then, which they could only explain as affording them double-time, for they also made these long and aimless tours through the house. Except that on occasion they met, it came to that. In the early morning Larry stood in the door to Jill's room, which gave access to either the bathroom or the master bedroom in back, and said,

"When he dies I haven't got anything else. They'll hate me, you know that, don't you?"

"Maybe they won't."

"I've got to have someone, Connie. I can't live like this."

"Don't make me promise something I can't keep."

He either turned to wander back into Melanie and Lou's room, with its Indian spread thrown over barely made sheets, or he returned to his father and a room made ghostly still by his laboring breath. Connie either went into the bathroom or passed through a small, pantry-sized door to that open-ended corridor in back. From there she could return to the kitchen and a beer she'd been cooling her throat with most of the night. Jeff might be standing before the open door of the refrigerator, caught in its watery glow like some foraging animal in the headlights of a car. He would head off in another direction—across the teeming shag of the living room to the bare boards of the porch. For their coolness and firmness he would search out spots of sand in the front yard to stand on—until he'd have to move again. Then he would either step out toward the street and a light which burned there, swarming with gnats, or he would circle the house, picking his way through the darkness, which smelled of honeysuckle and souring apples and an untended boxwood bush, and touching off the barks of the dogs next door. His father might meet him on the back steps, or his mother might. If they weren't there the only thing he'd recognize in the deeper darkness in the backyard would be the mule collar, but only because he'd remember where he'd left it when he'd finally done as he'd been asked and taken it outside. He'd use it to steer himself back in.

Although none of them had really left. They'd sat there on the kitchen chairs and the side of the bed or angled in against the windowsill, and although they talked among themselves and noted peculiarities about the room—the dark preserved rectangles on the walls, for instance, where pictures once had hung, or the crumbling oval-shaped molding in the ceiling out which the light cord dangled—it was as if they had never taken their eyes off of that man's face or listened to anything but his breathing and singsong moans. By dawn, each of them, even Jeff, was of two minds. They knew that measured in minutes and hours Ed's life was almost over, and they also knew that minutes and hours were like islands in a sea of time that could suddenly be washed over, that time, if it chose, could overflow itself. They knew and knew better. The room got hot again. Each of them ate, although Ed wouldn't. He peed in his pitcher, coaxed to it by his son. The phone rang again, twice, in quick succession. The clothes outside dried, were folded, placed back in suitcases. Ed's Samsonite was readied for yet another trip. In a pocket of the blue check pants they discovered a yellow golf tee that had survived the washing and drying, the trek around the country, the motels, Ed's operations, his months of convalescence, all the time since he had stood before it and it had offered him a ball to be driven—so much time that they passed it around silently, marveling over it as they would a talisman. They were and were not prepared. It was after seven, the heat in the room had begun to cool, there was a moment of merciful suspension, and that two-mindedness of theirs had drifted toward a truce. It surprised them, as the never-doubted and long-awaited always does. Ed said, in a voice that above all sounded well rested, "Call them now, son."

Larry leaned into his father. "Call them and tell them what, Dad?"

"Tell them to come."

"Are you sure? They'll take you back."

Hardly a motion, Ed shook his head.

The phone would not reach—that was the first thing he had to explain to his mother when she asked to speak to Ed. The second thing he phrased as a question: Did she remember the house in which Ed had been born? He had to repeat the question and rephrase it—that abandonment he heard in his mother's voice had reached into her memory too. Chumleyville, Alabama. There was a large white house with green shutters down in one corner of which her husband Ed had been born. Did she remember it? Angry, suppressed voices surged around her, but at their center she held a pensive pause. Ed had pointed a house like that out when he'd asked her to marry him. Actually he'd staged a little show. Just so she could make him the happiest man on earth, he'd been born in that house, in a corner room, she believed she recalled. Was that the one?

"We have him here now. He wanted to come back to this same house to die."

For a moment she didn't respond. He had to imagine her stunned, then soon, too quickly, disconsolate, overcome. But when she spoke her voice, though quiet and contained, was mostly miffed. "Who is this 'we'?"

"Connie and Jeff are with me, mother. He wanted it that way. It's all been what he wanted from the start."

"You know I've always thought Connie was a sweet girl, but what does she know about taking care of Ed? He can be the biggest baby sometimes."

"Mother, we've all been taking care of him."

Someone, in a tense whisper, was trying to relieve her of the phone. She hurried to get in, "You can't baby him, Larry. All he wants to do is lie in bed."

And he said, "Mother, you don't understand. He asked me to call you. It's time. He wants you to come."

In an aside, his mother made a brief protest; then she was gone and a hand had covered the phone. When it had been removed he heard her at a distance, her presence, her at one time incalculable presence in his life, reduced to a futile whine.

"Put him on, Larry."

"I can't."

"Put him on, Larry."

"The phone won't reach, and there isn't another. We're lucky to have this one."

"What's his condition?"

"He's dying, Russ."

"You're in Chumleyville, Alabama, if mother hasn't gone completely mad. Will he last until we get there?"

"I don't think so. Be prepared."

"Will you?"

"Will I what?"

"Last. Be there when we get there. Or will you run the second he's gone?"

"I'll be here, Russ."

It was Nell comforting their mother, he thought. He held fire a moment to see if the sound of her voice might reach him too. Then he said, "Russ, this is the way he wanted it. He didn't choose this house to be born in, but he's chosen it for his death. You won't think much of it. It's falling apart. In the part that's still habitable someone's thrown down some K Mart carpeting and that's about it. But it's what he wanted. Don't come in here brandishing a sword."

"I don't have a sword. What's the address, Larry?"

"I don't know. You'll have to find it the same way I did."

"In the dark? You know what time it'll be when we get there?"

"I'll leave the porch light burning. Outside you'll see our green van. But you'll find it, Russ. You've known where it is all your life, if you can believe such a thing."

He went back in with the others. His father's eyes were open, and for a moment he stood there looking into them, in the absence of almost everything else offering loyalty, at least. Then he sat back down. Almost at once he stood to offer his father water. This time their eyes did not meet. Half lidded now, Ed's gaze was trained on the front-window shade, where the light had gathered to a dusky orange, and it held steady, even though his breathing was giving him a bumpy ride. Just perceptibly, he shook his head. When Larry sat back down he didn't get up again until the evening light had grown so weak it could no longer penetrate the shade, only illumine it; then, instead of subjecting his father to that overhead light, he went into the kitchen and turned on both the ceiling light there and a small glass lamp on the table. When he switched the porch light on he'd promised Russ, its glow fell onto the bed through the smaller of the room's two windows, and if he'd removed the shade and cleaned the panes he could have gotten more. But he stopped there. It was a small miracle as many bulbs worked as did. The streetlight in front, which when night fell cast shadows of the spirea bushes along the bare floor, they took as a bonus. And then there were cars, the penumbral reach of their lights. Later there might be a moon—but they had enough. They sat still in it, and quiet, even Jeff, listening to Ed's breath, which had also grown quieter and less strenuous, until without warning it caught, made a confused, gargling sound, and for a last time Larry got to his feet.

"We're here, Dad," he said. "We're right beside you."

He couldn't be sure, his father might have nodded, and for an instant when he reached for his hand to hold he couldn't find it in the suddenly insufficient light. But he saw that the eyes had closed, and they all heard a sound that they hadn't heard before, an idle and airy clacking in the throat, much slower-paced.

IT wasn't a boat, although it bore him up like a boat and sailed out of this house and town with him on its deck like one. It was just

motion. There was no way to measure it because there was no way
to measure how far planet Earth had sailed on into uncharted
space since the moment of his birth, but he knew one thing: he
had never been here before. He'd been moving too. He'd given
numerous names to his movement, and each name a likeness—he
understood that too. But this movement was pure, and incompa-
rable. It did not loop or circle back on itself. It did not conform to
a map. He couldn't even be sure it wasn't going in multiple directions at once, so it did no good to talk of a true or false bottom to
his life, or a shape of any sort. Things moved. They did not stop.
Moving, they broke up into smaller and still smaller things. He
parted ways with the heat, with his thirst and his pain, with the
people who had accompanied him this far. Whole chunks of his
life disappeared like juts of land to a fast-rushing stream. Like
nothing. Eventually, he saw that a man might part with all that he
was, might, if he persisted in thinking of himself as out on an
ever-accelerating cruise, jettison everything he carried on board
until he was down to the unjettisonable, the indivisible. That
would be his fear, which was none other than his fascination. He
saw that. Then he woke up.

Except he had not been asleep. It had not been like that. He
had drifted into a state of double awareness, so that while he lay
here with his son and grandson and ex-daughter-in-law he had
simultaneously been approaching a moment of abstractest motion, situated on the edge of abstractest space. He had never
stopped feeling the pain which clawed up into his throat now—
except that it hadn't pained him. His misgivings about having
dragged Connie and Jeff along on this, or about Larry, his older
son's powerlessness and the extravagant amount of energy it took
to accomplish a single man's death—he had suffered those misgivings and he hadn't. He'd come to Chumleyville, Alabama, and
had found it and he hadn't. Sylvia, when she arrived, would find
perhaps just so much of the town as she would of the girl she'd
outgrown to marry Ed. And about that, about that bride he'd
somehow schooled to a matronly correctness while secretly hoping she would outrage them all, he'd been contrite, sorrowful,
indifferent, and amused. About his weightless flesh that would

and would not move, about the breath that trickled in and out of his lungs, about this tiny tattered room where he'd begged to be brought and where he'd received a child's first impression of the world—he'd been all-involved and entirely removed. Then he'd woken up. Except that he hadn't. A part of him had remained behind, fast approaching in fast-disembodying motion a sealike space of unlikenesses, while the rest of him had returned to a lifetime of moments like this one and memories of them all.

But with a phrase on his lips. Our fear and our fascination are the same. We fear only what fascinates us, and we never know why.

Was it death? He was reminded of his spiral of love; fear of our loneliness at the funneled-down point caused us to extend our spiral far and wide. But why did we fear our loneliness so? What so fascinated us about our naked selves that we converted our loneliness to fear and in the name of love spent a lifetime looking the other way? Was it death? Was that all it was? The sight of ourselves huddled down in our lonely holes, as if that were the black be-all and end-all of creation, as if all motion stopped there?

This small enclosed room had cooled but the feather mattress retained the day's heat. He lay in it as though half submerged in a pool of warm water, in contact with each of the slats that held the mattress up, but somehow unconvinced by them. He knew where Larry sat, Connie and Jeff. They whispered occasionally, brief observations, as though *they* were conserving their strength, but he didn't need the sound of their voices to locate them in the room—Larry, close, at the head of the bed to his right, then Jeff, sitting farther back, then Connie, at the level of his feet but within reach of his hand—because he had a special sense for their weight, the density they brought the air to around them. He remembered running into this room as a small child to wake his father, who always lay with the dead weight of some hibernating animal that might at any moment wake up and crush him if he shook and prodded too long. Compared to his father's his mother's weight had been tentative, ancillary, and his sense of it now uncertain. Why they'd had their bedroom here and not in one of the larger rooms upstairs or in back, he didn't know, but since his own room had been upstairs it meant that when he woke frightened at night he had to search through the whole dark house before he found them. He must have found them and his mother must have comforted him, although that was not what he remembered now. He remembered his father's weight, half buried in this mattress, miraculously held up by these slats.

Although he no longer believed in it.

He believed that crouched down in his dark hole he had dreamed it into being, and then as a measure of his loneliness and fright had managed to hoist every gravity-rich pound of it out onto the first whorl of that spiral. After that, the rest had been easy. The others he could blow into place with the loving force of his breath. And once he'd started there was no reason to stop. It could go on, like Jack's beanstalk, like a lovingly broadcast SOS. Why would anybody want to unwind that spiral and take it all back to the moment a child awakes in the night, that is not just a night but a nothingness of night, and which forces him, for lack of anything anywhere else, to lay hands on himself, a self that is also lacking, that as he clings to it in terror begins to vanish within his grip?

Is that how it had been?

He didn't know. Something now was pushing him along. Something, impatient with his speculations, with his monotonous pain and rattling breath, wanted to put that part of him into motion that had remained faithful to this place, this room. There was a veiled and ominous quality to this impatience; terror would be here soon, it seemed to be warning him, and if he didn't want to get caught in it he'd be wise to move. But there was something else, so faint at first he knew to disregard it, but growing, as the merest trace of a scent grew to become an outpouring: something was impatiently pushing him along, but just as impatiently, if he could trust his senses, something was calling him forth. But he couldn't trust his senses—not at once. Suddenly he was privy to all the wishful machinations of the human heart, and he had his share. If like a coward he abandoned this room he'd find terror all along his path. It was terror that was calling him forth, disguising the stench of his rot with the breath of a rose. Better to face it here. He had no illusions. This bed was not a boat—it was a bed. This room was not an impregnable bunker—it was the room in which he'd been born. He had always moved, traveled, cast out, walked his eighteen holes. Now he would lie still.

But he couldn't. There was a yearning *for* something, he could doubt it no longer, there was a moving *toward,* and it made itself felt in him as a small pleasurable ache, even though his whole body was wracked by the iron-cold obduracy of his pain. In the midst of this misery he'd become, he felt for the first time in he didn't know how long like a man with prospects. There was a joy yet left in his life, and as he took the first steps out towards what waited him there—it was movement, self-transporting, it had no name—that crowding from behind he'd attributed to his fear ceased. If he hesitated he understood it would begin again, but he had no desire to hesitate: his desire was to continue. His sense of direction failed him in the same instant he willingly gave it up. Up, down, forward, back—they no longer mattered. That small pleasurable ache of anticipation was like a homing signal, and as it responded to another signal outside, as it attuned itself there, inside and outside no longer mattered. He was moving toward a mating—that was all he understood; his fear had ceased the instant he'd admitted to his fascination—that too. The rest was no more than the outdated trappings of his life, explanations for himself he'd once entertained, like clothes he'd once worn. They caused him no embarrassment; on the contrary, as more and more of them fluttered into view they actually added to his pleasure.

How rich was the imagination of even the most ordinary man! How agile and youthful and wonderful to watch were its productions, and how dull, by comparison, ungainly and old was the pain that thought it could drive them offstage. They would not go! Stage dark, they would illumine themselves like will-o'-the-wisps. What difference did it make if they were not true? Like the tides, he would empty out and flow full. He would blow a great loving spiral into the sky, then unblow it as his breath came home. This load he carried and could unload when he wished—it was a juggler's trick, a he-man's stunt, it was music whistling past the hollow stops of his bones. Truth? Death moving with the iron-dark weight of a glacier was truth, while all along—yes, he understood it now—he had preferred truth's lies.

So at last it was a lie he had subscribed to and given a shape: they had driven the country, *re*driven it; emptying out, spiraling back, stepping free of that load, they had traced the lineaments of his long-lasting youth, they had come for the bed and they had come here. Only here was now there, in his unmapped movement place was every place at once, and he saw the vast undulant cornfields of Indiana, Illinois, and Iowa again, the ear of corn clasped to its stalk, the leaves peeling back in a fountain spray of green and gold. Dirt roads ran back to the islanded farmhouses. The trees there were towering and old, ever-green, sculpted from the permanence of summer. Lines of wash caught the sun. There were no flowers, but there was always a child, a small girl standing in the dappled front yard. She would not run from a stranger, although the dog beside her would bark itself hoarse. Suspended as though by a Plymouth Savoy, he would raise his hand and wave and she would wave back, hesitant and a bit grave as if she knew in such an interminableness of corn and wheat and soybeans and beef-fattening pasture they would never see each other again. But she would be wrong. He saw her in the towns he now passed, coming out of church and school, a small shadowy house that would belong to an aunt, a store her mother had remained behind in. She was always gazing at the road, always a bit grave when she raised her hand, apparently never remembering that he was the man she had said goodbye to countless times before. He smiled at her. She rode before him in the bed of a pickup, in the last seat in a school bus, in the baggage area of the family station wagon, with her chin propped on her hands staring out the back window of the family car. And he smiled at her—she would see, she would see. Old men wore harmless old masks, and they frequently drove these roads alone, and it was true, sometimes they even scared themselves, but that wasn't the end of it, she would see.

This motion took him everywhere and nowhere at once, permitted wave after wave after wave after wave. Skirting the cities, ignoring the expressways, he stuck to the country roads and towns where there was no business to be done. Twisty and close-quartered, Kentucky appeared, then Tennessee, the ragged cotton fields and palmetto swamps of Georgia. He knew he was coming closer, that every turn he made from here on out would be a shortcut home, but that small pleasurable ache that had guided him up to now had undergone a change. He felt it as something airier yet solider, as though it had swollen to its true dimensions and prepared him for a feat of some sort. He felt . . . gifted. Gradually, an activity made itself known to him, then the particulars of time and place.

It was early evening, always summer, and he had traded the suspension system of a Plymouth Savoy for the springily cut grass of a golf course's first tee. As he stepped up to his ball his feet never touched the ground. His drive was long and straight, rising off his clubhead in a rhythmic extension of a swing he'd been born with and had never known until now. His short iron was as delicate and deft as a surgical incision. His putt curved into the center of the cup. He drove himself far into the second fairway, then the third. By the time he'd birdied his way out onto the fourth and stood with an esplanade's view of the green below, that swelling sense of prowess that had carried him this far had begun to subside, as the light had: pale gold turned to pale purple, his great golfing gift to a quiet expectant pleasure, and he said to the little girl who stood beside him, You see? You see? Two holes out ahead of them now his son played alone. Look there! He saw the white of his son's ball as it hung against the deepening sky, spinning like a planet, and he saw the arcing shaft of the club that had put it there; his son's hair was blond, his body lean and unencumbered, and his swing . . . his swing too had been a gift. You see, don't you? he said. The little girl looked at him, expressionless, then out to where he saw his son walking on the great watery breast of the fairway and where she saw the corn that had always grown out beside the barn, or the road that if she stood on the curb in front of her house always ran out of town. Gravely, she raised her hand—but he wouldn't let her. You will! he promised her. You will! smiling fervently, he swore. Then—motion in a vacuum now, windless and pure—he ran out to join his son.

He was no longer there. The light had failed. The fairway

where he had stood looking out onto the next green was no longer a fairway, but, yes, was an esplanade, looking out onto . . . space, a sealike space of unlikenesses. He was back. Here is where he'd stood when he'd thought he'd gone away, his pleasure a quiet consummation at discovering himself whole. All motion had halted now. It was understood that he could go no farther, that when motion resumed he would simply be gone. And it was getting cold. That space before him was the color of colorlessness. It was the breadth and width and height of dimensionlessness. To his ears its soundlessness was absolute. Its single property—its coldness—he knew in truth he had to attribute to himself, and it, he, was getting colder. All he could say was that there was a point where this ended and that began, and even that he realized was a convenience he allowed himself, just one more of those trappings with which he had tried to cover the imponderable facts of his life. There was another, fading so quickly the images he saw there when he opened his eyes were barely distinguishable from the dirty sepia-colored walls—there was a room. Connie was in it, and Jeff, and Larry, and even though he confessed to the game he was playing with himself, he tried to fix them there. They helped—he blessed them for it; they were leaning in close. Connie, whom he deeply admired and in his son's stead loved. Jeff, whom no one could protect from stories such as these. And Larry, whose territory, however far he traveled, extended no farther than this. Truth's lies, he thought, the three of them. In an instant I'm going to be asked to choose between them and that featureless space—and I'll choose them. Fear cut through him then like a blade of ice from top to bottom, and he said it again, I'll choose them.

Choosing them, he closed his eyes and discovered that that space which had stood at an esplanade's remove before him had now spread inside. It was like nothing he had ever known in his life. Yet inside . . . it bloomed. Inside it reached out in him like the branches of a frozen tree. Inside it filled him with a gelid smoke. But inside it also made a hippy, swaggering movement the way Cochise did when he wanted to knock one a mile down the fairway, and then it snuggled a bit, too, like Sylvia when she got into bed with her cold feet and behind. He understood there was no end to the things it might do. Inside it might turn itself outside and hold him suspended, warm once more, as his mother's womb had done. He smiled at the likelihood, however remote, and died.

THE instant Ed's breath ceased, the room filled with a palpable silence, a presence as strong and restful as any of them had ever known. For Jeff it grew around them with the transformative wonder of the kudzu. For Connie it evoked the world of animals, the way they uncomplainingly accomplished all of nature's demands. Larry submitted to it as a disbeliever might to proof of a god. Something was in the room. Death did not supplant life by proxy. The instant Ed died it was as if two great processes had met to oversee the passing of command, and processes had to have names. For a long moment, the three of them could not look at Ed, the presence of that which had transcended him was so strong. They sat dry-eyed, stunned, uplifted and humiliated at the same time. Then Larry said,

"He looked at each of us. Just before he closed his eyes he went from one to the other."

Connie said, "He wanted to thank us, I think. I'm sorry the rest of your family couldn't have been here. I feel bad about that."

Larry thought for a moment. He understood that nothing would be quite so easy and inconsequential as it had seemed before. Just speech, how hard it was to get truth into each word. "It wouldn't have been the same," he finally said. "They wouldn't have brought him to this room, Connie. Dad was right about that."

They looked at it then, the peeling walls, the crumbling ceiling, the sun-faded shades. Like the gouged headboard of the bed and the splintered flutes of the posts, it was already numinous and healed. She said, quietly thrilled, "It's strange how he knew we would."

In all his dreams of small close rooms none had seemed quite as small and close to Jeff as this. Yet somewhere in it there must have been an opening through which fresh possibilities flowed, for it did not oppress him. On the contrary, it soon restored his sense of adventure to him, and at last in the uncertain light allowed him to stand. Then he looked down on his grandfather. "He's smiling. Isn't he smiling?" he said.

It was the smile a man offers himself in private, made public now—amused, ironic, self-deprecating, but stubborn and boyishly still unreformed, really a determined little grin.

"Yes, he's smiling," Larry said.

XI

HE said, "Look at him, Russ. Is that the face of an embittered man? Do you know what it means to die with a smile on your lips?"

Russ had turned the overhead light on. In its dusty uniform glow Ed's smile seemed even more amused and determined, and there was something like a questing thrust to his chin. "Did he suffer much at the end?" Russ wanted to know.

"He was in pain, but he also seemed out beyond it."

"What is that supposed to mean?"

"Look at him, Russ."

There was no trace of pain, or if there was it was only the pain of exertion that had gone to fix the muscles of that out-thrust smile. It was Russ's face that was in pain, congested with so much grief and anger and, unmistakably to someone who had seen it as often as his brother, the sulkiness of having been cheated of his due.

Russ turned off the overhead light. "It's over, Mother," he called into the kitchen. "It's all right, Nell. Let her come in."

Perhaps Larry should have turned the entire room over to them as Connie and Jeff had done, but he couldn't. It was not so much fear that they would malign him as that they would misrepresent his father, whose spokesman he understood he'd become. What he did do was stand away from the bed, facing the front window, the bush-shadows there on the shade unfocused now since a moon had risen to compete with the streetlight, as his mother and sister entered. He heard his mother make whimpering, fussing sounds and he assumed she was already touching, perhaps tidying, her husband. On entering his sister sang once "Daddy!" in a high childish wail, then immediately turned her attention to her mother, most likely caressing her face, busying herself about her hair, never ceasing to warble that Ed was at rest now, that they should be thankful it was over for him, that if there was a heaven that's where he was. His mother, when she began to make sense, asked Ed just where he thought he was going and how far he expected to get without her at his side. Her voice had a dazed forgiving lilt to it, but she really wanted to know. "Where were you going, Ed? Here? This room?"

Larry turned when he heard his brother come back in. "You'll have to ask Larry that, Mother," Russ reminded her, and when she turned to him, and then Nell did, and he saw all that turbulent emotion in their faces and shoulders and unstill hands, he said, "Please, not here," and asked them to follow him out of the room.

He led them into the living room, where Jeff had fallen asleep on the daybed and Connie sat on the beanbag, slumped over on her knees. When he reached the kerosene stove he turned and said he would try to answer their questions now. For some time no one asked him anything, nor did they sit. The light in the room came from a weak-bulbed lamp beside Lou's recliner, and in it they all appeared shadowy and stunned. Finally Russ said, "Mother?" and Sylvia responded more sensibly and equitably than any of them had the right to expect.

"If this was what he wanted to do, why didn't he tell us, Larry? Do you know that?"

"Yes." He paused, not because he wanted to make them wait, although Russ might have interpreted it that way. But he had to be mindful of their position, and of his father's, and of the truth. "He himself believed that he was doing something crazy, and since he had put up with what he considered was so much craziness of mine he thought I owed him something in return. He didn't think that you should have to indulge him in this . . ." and here the pause was unintentional, ". . . or that you would. He did not hold it against you at all. As I said, he himself considered it an *idée fixe.*"

"A what, Larry?" Russ said.

"An obsession, a monomania, like I said, craziness he thought I would understand. I didn't at the start."

"Larry," his mother objected, "Ed wasn't crazy. You won't find anybody who knew him who will say that."

His mother's mind was so clear now, so composed, he became aware of its fragility. Gently, he said, "I gradually discovered that Dad was a very private man, or had a very private side to his personality. It was like a dream he kept dreaming and finally had to act out."

"Ed had sweet dreams, Larry. He used to tell me his dreams."

"Mother, we each know different people. I'm a different person for you than I am for Nell, or than I am for . . ." He hesitated before pronouncing his brother's name.

"And what if it wasn't what he wanted, Larry?" Russ said.

"What if *this* wasn't what he wanted?" Larry signaled the house they stood in a corner of.

"What if *this* was the way *you* knew him, but not the way he knew himself at all? What if this was craziness *you* picked up wandering around the country? You never could stay in one place long. What are your dreams like, brother? You see what I mean?"

"I see your version of me, that's all."

"Just answer my question, Larry."

"What if we went outside and duked it out first?"

He made the offer with no sarcasm in his tone, only in his choice of words, and he saw his brother's head snap out of its habitual tilt.

"I want you to answer my question," Russ repeated, fighting a tremor in his voice.

"Straightforward stuff outside, Russ. No way to get confused."

He almost whispered this, with an intimacy he didn't fake, and for an instant no one was around him, his father did not lie dead in the next room, he was offering himself up for a kind of ritual cleansing free of all ill will.

"Answer my question, Larry," Russ said.

"The answer is yes."

"Yes?"

"Yes, it turned out my dreams were very close to his. They were *his* dreams, I insist on that, although you won't believe me. It may be that he learned them from me, if you can ever 'learn' dreams, if such a thing is possible. But I don't think so. When he told me he wanted to come here to die, that only by stopping where he started could he make any sense of it, I tried to talk him out of it, but I won't deny that it struck a chord. I felt it was unfair of him to ask me to do it, and tremendously unfair to all of you, but it also seemed right, unarguable, in ways that might not make much sense to you, since your dreams are *not* like his. Be glad they're not," he added as a consoling but not very convincing after-thought.

"Maybe they are. Maybe Nell's are. Did you ever think of that?"

"Dad didn't think you'd understand. I had to agree with him."

"Where'd you get the right to make that assumption?"

Larry began to say something about their lives together, about the knowledge any brother may claim to have of another, but ended up saying simply, "From him."

"What do you really know about dreams, huh? I bet you think I go home at night and dream eight more hours of working in that store. I won't speak for Nell, but she may have dreams about something other than driving her kids around town all day. You didn't bother to ask."

Russ stood before him now in an offended slump, that might also have been an embattled crouch. The light was bad and he was tired. He said, "I know I didn't. I won't blame it on Dad. I'm sorry."

"That's when you made it *your* dream," Russ explained to him with a bitter and aggrieved sort of logic. "You didn't want to share it with us, just like you've never wanted to share any of the things that really counted. All the rest you couldn't give away fast enough. But not Dad! You kidnapped him, Larry."

"Good Christ, Russ!" he groaned.

Suddenly he had stepped up to his brother and taken the low, thick, slightly tilted shoulders in his hands. "I want to ask you one question," he said, shaking the shoulders, insistently, three times, before dropping his hands. "Does the smile on that man's face look like it belonged to a kidnap victim?"

When his brother wouldn't answer, when that face before him, so like his mother's, full of puckers and lumps, began to lose the look of sentience and harden like clay, he raised his hands to the shoulders and shook again. "The police are going to take one look at that man in there," he said, "and who're they going to believe, Russ? Answer me that."

He shook until his strength deserted him, or until the utter pointlessness of it was apparent, then stood there with his hands on Russ's shoulders as his sister stepped up beside him and took one, then the other hand down. She had done this, in one way or the other, so many times it seemed the most natural thing in the world. "We never called the police, Larry," she told him. "Once we understood what had happened none of us could do that, not even Russ."

He turned to her now. In this light the hollows under her eyes were the listless color of meal.

"I don't think I ever really believed that you had," he said.

"Except for Dr. Matthews no one knew he left home, not even his closest friends. You see," and she said this confidingly *and* compassionately, as though she were talking about some poor acquaintance of theirs who deserved their help, "we really hadn't had time to believe you had come back peacefully, of your own accord, so we all expected something, we just didn't know what." It was her hand on his shoulder now, gently shaking, coaxing him, in this difficult time, to her point of view. "But that was only because you hadn't given us a chance to believe."

"He wired. He wired he was dying and had something he wanted me to do."

"You told me."

"He was not an easy man to understand. I think he had more

lives inside of him than any of us could imagine. So many that it hurt him to have to choose one. It *scared* him to have to choose one."

"Poor Daddy," Nell said.

"He was like a child that someone had come up to and said, 'Be this, and forget all the rest!' "

"But at least he did that, didn't he?" Nell pleaded patiently.

"What?"

"Became what he had to *be*. A good father and husband and friend. A good citizen in his town."

He looked at his sister disconsolately, in a moment so quiet that he believed he could hear his father drawing breaths again, going to the bottom of his lungs for each of them. But that was the sound of his own son, deeply asleep on the daybed. "I don't know," he confessed in a whisper. "I never gave him the chance."

Then he was crying in his sister's arms, for the first time in his life sobbing uncontrollably, and not just for his father and what he'd missed there. But because he suddenly felt his father's life and death and his own tardy sonship as a pattern, and that no matter how hard he tried to prevent it nothing in this life of deep grievous insufficiency could ever finally be made good. His sister was crying with him. Then his mother broke in between them and pulled him down into her arms. She had no voice, he could feel her sobs trapped in her chest, but she held him anyway, his head pulled down against hers, until he'd gone to the end of his crying and stood there limp before her with a weak smile. Then she said, "He never did anyone harm. Did he?"

They all said, No, he never had.

By then Connie had gotten off the beanbag and gone to hold his sister, then his mother. She paused before Russ, waiting for some sign that she should come closer. The sign was an ugly gashing downward of the mouth, followed by the collapse of the lower half of his face, as finally Russ's tears overflowed. The moment Connie stood back from him, Larry placed his hand again on his brother's shoulder, but now at arm's length and with the fingers still. He made no attempt to go closer; nor did Russ invite him to. He said he was sorry, and wearily, Russ nodded his head.

None of them slept, except Jeff, who never woke up. By dawn Russ had roused a funeral-home director out of his bed and arranged for Ed's body to be driven that morning to Welborne, Kentucky, and it was only then that Larry realized his father had never said a word to him about where he wanted to be buried. For an instant he considered what it would take to oppose his family once more and insist on a burial here, in Chumleyville, and knew that whatever it was he didn't have it in him. All he could do was keep calling until he got one of the three transport companies listed in the yellow pages to answer. By then it was almost eight. The transport company would send men to pick up Aunt Emma's bed and ship it back to Savannah after the funeral-home people had gone. That left Aunt Emma herself, and he described for her, lovingly and commemoratively, as though it were a photograph she could place beside the others on her shelf, the details of Ed's death and his smile. He promised he would get the movers to agree to set the bed back up in her attic; yes, she could always visit Ed there. Then he turned the phone over to Connie, assuring her that with all the money Melanie and Lou had made on this short-term subletting they could absorb the cost of a few long-distance calls. He left her talking not to Lisa, who like her brother was asleep, but to Jan.

Two hours later, when everyone was ready to go, he left the motor running in the van and walked back inside. It was a habit he had; in the past it had borne fruit. As though they were already ten miles down the road, he would take a tour through the house in search of the one thing they were sure to discover they had left behind. He discovered they were not leaving something behind but something undone. On top of the cold kerosene stove he placed a note—because he was sure Connie hadn't—informing Melanie on Marie's behalf that she'd better get her act together if she wanted to bust up old ten. He had promised to lock the door when he left, and although he could not imagine why anyone other than his father would ever want to enter this house, he kept his promise. But by failing to leave the key under a pot of withered geraniums beside the door, he also broke it. He slipped the key into his pocket instead, almost startled and then vaguely depressed to discover that it was the only one there.

FOR the entire next day Ed's casket lay open at the Pauley and Son Funeral Home in Welborne so that his many friends and admirers might have a chance to pay their last respects. At least two members of the family remained with the body at all hours until after ten, when Russ drove his mother home. Nell's husband, Ron, who had come down from Lexington, took his children over to Russ and Jeannie's to sleep, while Nell stayed at her mother's side. Larry badly wanted to look for another motel, but because he had no money left nor the stomach to ask for it had been forced to take what he'd been offered—his old room. Connie, it was assumed, would stay with him, and an extra cot had been found for Jeff out at Russ and Jeannie's with cousins he barely knew. Ed's casket was kept open until approximately ten o'clock the next morning, when it was closed and taken to the First Presbyterian Church for the eleven-o'clock service. By twelve-thirty it had been driven down State Street, along the bypass, and out the Millersville Road to the Woodland Cemetery, where, after a brief prayer, it waited on its straps to be lowered into the ground.

But from the first mourner to pass by until the last prayer it had been Ed Reece's day in Welborne.

For a man not born and brought up in the town it was a remarkable outpouring. Businessmen Ed had had dealings with, fellow members of various civic organizations, people close to him in both his country club and his church, his many golfing buddies—they all came. Town luminaries, who had discovered in Ed Reece's decency and industry qualities the town could not long do without, stopped by the funeral home to offer their condolences to the family, and it was true, many did remember Larry: Dr. McManus did, and Lawyer Bridges did, and Police Chief Bradley asked to be remembered to him when Larry was not there to greet him in person. The mayor came, for purely apolitical reasons, although Ed had contributed to his campaign. The vice-president of the local college, who had once had the pleasure to present Ed with a civic-service award, told Sylvia that the real pleasure had come in discovering that people such as her husband still existed, people who sought neither glory nor immoderate wealth for themselves, but simply the chance to do good. He regretted that the president of the college, who four years earlier had been recruited out of Texas, had not had the chance to know Ed himself, otherwise he would have been there too.

Sylvia had been deeply impressed by this speech, and others like it. And finally because everyone who could possibly be expected to come did, and because there were so many of them, Larry had stopped listening through the words. There was something like a genuine if generalized admiration for his father at large in the town—and then it got particular. Men and women, more humbly dressed and less tastefully groomed, began to come by, who had to introduce themselves since no one in the family had any idea who they were. Herb Counts. Alma Raynor. An enormously fat man named Sid. Odel Jenkins. A woman who called herself Lilly Whitehead, which for some unaccountable reason Larry thought might have been a pseudonym for the woman his father had known in Iowa. They all told a version of the same story. Either Ed had personally driven out an after-hours case of cups or towels or bags to a Dairy Creme or beauty parlor or a grocery in the sticks, or he'd let a bill ride until it no longer existed, or when he'd suspected they'd been in dire straits had made them a gift, calling the case of whatever it was they needed the extra he'd happened to have in the truck. These people just wanted the family to know that although their businesses all had failed they had never forgotten Ed Reece.

A philanthropist? Not if you listened to the men he played golf with. He could squeeze a nickel until he'd bled the American buffalo dry. Wouldn't change a ball until he'd cut a smile in it for every day of the week. No one knew how he'd managed to glue that putter of his together. He had a soft heart, ole Tuffie, but don't ever make the mistake of thinking you could breeze by him in a game of skins. He could scramble for his par from anywhere on the course. You could hit every green in regulation, never three-putt a one, and here he'd come, blasting out of a water hazard or a sand trap or knee-high rough and then sink a forty-foot putt just as you were putting his scat-money into your pocket. He'd claim just once in his life he'd like to go around a course and hit every green and take his two putts the way the game was supposed to be played, and he'd get a kinda dreamy sound in his voice when he said it, but you'd have to be a fool with something left over to believe him. He liked the look of his money after you'd already gone ahead and spent it. It was sweeter when it came home, he used to say, and that was probably because it had some of yours stuck to it. A philanthropist? Sure, Scotland's full of them. You'd better ask the Rabbi and Hawk Larkin and Jimmy Paul Willard and Cochise how much money Ed Reece gave away.

Standing there to receive Ed's friends and admirers, Larry had to wear one of his father's suits. Connie had packed her own, plus a pair of brown slacks and checked shirt for Jeff, which she now had only to iron, but Larry had to enter that long closet again, where he'd last gone to look at an old Samsonite, and select a suit from those hanging there. His father's pants were tight on him and the coat slightly short in the sleeves, but Connie was pushing at the limit of her suit now too, and she helped him choose a charcoal gray of summer weight. He might have found a shirt of his own to match, but he put on a short-sleeved shirt of his father's instead, and then a tie of Ed's of dark stripes. It was a moment when Connie thought he might try to go too far, do too much, or just give too much of himself up, and she moved in beside him as he stood before the full-length mirror on the closet door. It wouldn't take long, and certainly no trick of the eyes, for her to see Ed in Larry; after what they'd been through the trick would be to keep the face of anyone she cared about from wasting down to bone in her sight. Except for his blond hair, which was thinning rapidly, and those bird-shell-blue eyes, when the time came he and his father were going to look about the same. She didn't know who she was going to look like, not her mother or father, she hoped, with the long gray stoniness of their faces once they'd stopped arguing. The standing answer to them all, of course, was her Uncle Hal. The standing answer to everything, she knew, which was no answer at all but the thing itself, rosy and undiminished in his decline, enigmatic through and through. Perhaps she was going to look like no one she knew, which might mean that rushing herself twenty years into the future she had the thrill of one discovery left her, just as twenty years earlier, as a girl aspiring to the very pinnacle of an actress's romantic dream, she had been rushed here. To discover what? That she would be a woman who took care of animals? Were animals—except at the pinnacle of an animal lover's own innocent dream—ever enough? "I can't promise anything," she told that man before her in his father's suit. "I do love Jan, Larry. Do you understand?"

Like Connie, Ed wore navy-blue. His shirt was white, his tie was blacker than blue. On his lapel were pins of some of the organizations he belonged to: Rotary, Chamber of Commerce, the Salvation Army, and United Givers' Fund boards. After bleeding him dry, Pauley and Son had combed his hair and put the color back into his cheeks and discreetly plugged the nostrils through which so much painful breath had been drawn. But they hadn't been able to do anything with his grin. Ed gave the impression of having been caught in the act of slipping out of sight down inside the broad shoulders of his coat, but if anything the grin seemed tougher now, a mocking taunt to the skilled fingers that might have wanted something more serene. It hinted at resources that most dead men were not privileged to call on, and more than one mourner instead of quietly weeping at the death of a good man performed an indelicate double take before standing there for a long moment as a grin of his own began to form.

When Jeff saw his grandfather laid out he surmised at once the little story this new grin told. Number one, they were all the victims of nothing so malicious as a hoax, but, yes, of a mischievous game; they were not to look for Ed Reece here. Number two, the grin, which seemed about to break up into a rollicking laugh, was really a clue. It told them to look for Ed Reece somewhere where they wouldn't find big ornate boxes to lie down in or little satin pillows to lay your head on, and where no one wore dark blue suits and ties. Jeff got number three by adding number two to a clue that his grandfather had given him—and no one else: the Reeces were all children. That wasn't *just* a clue, it was the key. It was also where they would find his grandfather when they got tired of looking for him here.

No one really wept, not uncontrollably. There was no keening or banging on the coffin. Pauley and Sons' Green Room, separated from its Blue Room by a collapsible partition, with banks of flowers along the walls and all-weather carpeting on the floor, seemed to inhibit raw displays of emotion. Sylvia, the many times she got up to stand beside the coffin, merely gazed at her husband. Frequently Nell was with her. "If he could only see how much the people love him here," Sylvia mused for her daughter. "I'd give the rest of my days if Ed could wake up for just one minute. . . ." And as she trailed off Nell would reassure her, "He knew, Mama. I know he knew. No one ever hid their affection from Daddy." They were standing there when Ed's oldest friend, Gil Conners, came up from behind and put his arms around their shoulders. "Ed always did like to play that last hole in a rush," Conners grumbled fondly, then directed their eyes to the position of honor just beyond the casket where instead of a floral display the members of Ed's last foursome had set up a miniature of the eighteenth green, lovingly landscaped, complete with bushes, trees, sand traps, little hillocks and swales, a brook and a bridge. There was a tiny white ball, presumably Ed's, under the bright red flag, on the flawlessly glued-down green.

It was outside, taking a breather from the smell of flower-scented water, that Russ said to his brother, "Admit you're surprised, Larry. You never believed Dad was this well thought of in the town."

"I'm surprised," Larry said.

"I'm not," Russ declared quietly.

A moment later Larry changed his mind. "I'm not either, not really. There're good people here, Russ, but there's an awful lot of bluff and a lot of that weekend swagger, and Dad was never very good at playing that game. I don't think the majority of these people realized it until now, but he must have been a kind of touchstone for them."

"A touchstone for what?"

"He was realer than they are."

"The people here aren't that bad," Russ said.

"No, they aren't, they really aren't, it's just that Dad could never really swing with them—could he?—and that made him something special."

Russ got that cautious, confused look on his face, and quietly backed off. "Dad was like a lot of good men in town, but you'd have to live here to see what I mean."

"I'm not saying there're not good men here, remember, I'm not saying that."

The Reverend Weldon Curtis was a reformed roughneck from the Oklahoma oil fields, who after thirty-five years of service to the ministry had lost all trace of his rowdy beginnings in his manner, movement, and speech, although during the time Larry, Russ, and Nell were growing up he referred to them constantly in his sermons. They were proof that a man could overhaul himself from top to bottom. He had learned the language of profanity, and then with a great deal of labor and humility but finally also delight, he had learned the language of God. He was a year away from retirement now—although still sturdy-seeming under his robe, his round bald head like a muscle flexed with thought—but in delivering Ed Reece's eulogy he referred to those adverse beginnings again. He only realized how much he'd had to overcome when he reflected on Ed Reece who'd had to overcome so little. There wasn't a man on this earth who didn't have to overcome something, but from what he could judge Ed Reece's life had flowed by like a beautiful stream, only slightly muddy at the start (his own had been a cattle crossing in comparison) and crystal-clear at the end. Flowing into that stream were smaller ones, and rivulets, and these were his good deeds, his service to his family, church, and community, which Curtis went into at length. But a man's nature was to be found in that main channel, and in Ed Reece's case that was water sweet enough to drink. In a manner of speaking—a manner that would not have occurred to him when he only knew how to boast and profane—that was what all the friends and loved ones of Ed Reece had been doing these too few years they had had him among them: dipping their hands into the main channel of Ed's sweet nature to drink.

Curtis's voice in it quavering depth seemed the equivalent of the stream he was describing, and as it flowed over the heads of those who had filled the pews it provoked a number of sobs and tear-laden sighs. The scene at the cemetery was less intense. Not everyone at the church service came, and Curtis, after spending himself on the eulogy, offered little more than a benediction for the concluding prayer. At one time well out into the country, the Woodland Cemetery had now been overtaken by the expansion of the town so that wherever you raised your gaze you were sure to see the rooftops and television antennas and sloping lawns of a subdevelopment. Ed and Sylvia were lucky to have plots there; for some time now the cemetery had been rumored to be full. But perhaps that was the real measure of the love and respect which the town bore the man. Space had been made. The general feeling now, with the coffin suspended on its bands, was one of relief: Ed Reece was home.

And it was a nice day, bright and unhumid and pleasantly cool, and the green awning that mourners might have had to crowd under in case of rain or a punishing sun had been unnecessary. As soon as the prayer was over and it became clear that Ed's coffin was not going to be lowered anytime soon, those present spread out a bit and began to socialize. Russ and Jeannie's Eddie, Glorie, and Sue, Nell and Ron's Alan and Shelley, and Connie and Larry's Jeff, who during the prayer had all stood in an obediently straight line before the coffin, made their way to the open area out past the cars. Jeff's position with his cousins was unclear. They were polite to him, and technically speaking had been generous with their things, but a certain perfunctoriness can get into the best behavior of children, and when Jeff sensed it in his cousins he felt a strange pang of loss for his grandfather. If it had been up to him he would have stayed there with the grown-ups, and waited for the coffin to be lowered into its lead-lined shell, but somehow it wasn't up to him, and he accompanied his cousins back to the grassy area behind the cars, where they soon discovered there wasn't much they could do if they didn't want to stain their clothes. They avoided talking about their grandfather, but eventually got around to music and cars, and sometime after that he wasn't sure why but he was volunteering to show them the van. Although he couldn't see it at first among all the other cars, he walked straight to it. Again he wasn't sure why, or why it mattered as much as it did, but he hoped it was locked. When he discovered the back door was open and that there was room for all six, ten, or twenty of them if that's how many wanted to climb inside, he said they couldn't go in. He said his dad would get mad. He hinted that weird things had been going on inside that van, but he refused to say what. His cousins didn't force the issue. They could have stormed past him if they'd wanted to, but with only an old gray mattress and a couple of stereo speakers to look at they probably decided they'd already seen enough. When they drifted off back in the direction of that field where there was nothing to do, Jeff stayed with the van.

He had a wait before his father and mother found him there. There were well-wishers that Larry had to respond to, more stories about his father's generosity, sweetness, cussedness, or cunning he had to listen to, a few questions about what he'd been up to since the last time anybody'd had news of him, and then a few embarrassed clearings of the throat when that last news had had something to do with his protest activities. He'd stood beside his mother and sister awhile and entered conversations with friends of theirs. He'd also stood beside the Reverend Mr. Curtis until the minister had begun to eulogize his father again. He'd resumed his acquaintance with Nell's husband, Ron, aware that Ron was making an effort to respect the occasion and not to sound mad as hell for what Larry had done. When he'd happened to catch sight of Russ standing all alone, seemingly abandoned by the many well-dressed and mindful people that made up his town, he stepped up to his side and did not take him around the shoulder—the older brother to the younger, the taller to the shorter, the stronger to the weaker—as he might have done, but simply whispered in his ear, "Later, when things have had time to settle, I hope we can put an end to this feud of ours, I really do," and raised in return a tentative smile, which he left at that, not wanting to pursue it any further, not then.

He moved away. His mother approached him, remarking in a wan doubtful voice that the family would all have to get together to decide on a monument for Ed, wondering without saying as much if Larry would still be there. When he nodded, not very reassuringly, she went back to Nell. Nell chatted with everybody who came within her range, pleasantly, almost tunefully, and he wondered about what this day would do to her. Under the awning, beside the suspended coffin, a big ostentatious silver-handled box, he found Connie. He saw in her face the same thwarted desire he felt in trying to get beyond all that had been staged here these last two days to his father. He also saw uncertainty, indecision, which combined with that unfulfilled desire to give to her face a look of momentousness, even a youthfulness, as if she stood on the brink of something, stood there for the first time.

"One of life's inescapable moments—wasn't that how you put it?" he said.

"Lisa's boyfriend's name is Mike Kellog, by the way. How does it sound?"

"I want to take you and Jeff back to Missouri, Connie. I barely got a chance to say hello to Lisa, much less to Mike Kellog."

"I haven't said hello to him either."

"D'you have any money?"

"Very little."

"It's funny. There isn't a person out there today who wouldn't lend me a hundred dollars on the spot. But I can't ask for it."

"Jan gave me a credit card we can use."

"I'd rather not."

"I know you'd rather not. I'd rather not mix you two together either, Larry. You know what Ed said?"

"No."

"That you and Jan were alike. The reason I was attracted to you both was that you were willing to fight for what you believed in."

"It's not the same, Connie. You know it's not. I can't fall on Jan like a comrade-in-arms."

"No, but you might find some things about her you can like."

"And what about her? What's she going to find in me to like? The only thing I've liked in myself these last few years is the fact that I never completely fell out of love with you. That's the rock-bottom truth."

She found his hand. She was close to tears—it was that thwarted desire, that momentousness, that sense of yet another youthful start all come to bear in her face. "Please don't ask me how," she said, "but we're going to have to learn to share ourselves more. I don't know how."

He smiled. He leaned in to kiss her cheek while with his free hand he reached into his pants pocket—his father's pants pocket—and brought out the keys to the van. He said, "It's all I've got but I'm glad to share it. Thank God, Dad had me put it in my name."

Besides the three van keys on a chain and a medallion-like tag advertising Cushman's Dodge, there was another key of tarnished copper lying on his palm. Seeing it took the smile off his face. For a moment a hugely disproportionate sense of shame welled up in him, and he hid the keys in a fist. Then he opened his fist and laughed hollowly. "It's the key to that house in Chumleyville," he said. "I meant for it to be buried with Dad. It would have been a nice gesture, don't you think?"

They both looked then at the coffin, with its battened-down hatch as leakproof as a submarine, and as remote. "Why don't you put it with the keys to the van?" she said.

"In case we want to go back?"

"Somebody might," she said mysteriously, and that too took the smile off his face.

He fastened the Chumleyville key onto the chain.

They worked through the diminishing crowd of family and friends—their family, their friends, his, in fact, on this day he had inherited from his father whose day it had originally been. No, they were not leaving yet. They were going, he discovered then, for a ride. They would not be gone long. When they were in the open and almost to the cars they each felt an arm come down on their shoulders, which instead of bringing them together forced them apart so that Gil Conners could step in. Conners shared his weight between them, as befitted Ed's oldest friend. With all the emotion of the last two days the dollops at his cheeks, nose and chin had grown ruddier. In a punchline-promising drawl he said, "Reverend Curtis had some nice things to say about your father, son, and I won't deny a one of them. But there's something he left out. When you come to write the epitaph on his tombstone, I'd like to see you give it some thought."

For Conners's benefit and pleasure Larry played it out all the way to the parked cars, half dragging the man his father called Cochise along. "It'll have to fit," he said.

"Sure it'll fit," Conners drawled even more slowly. "That stream Reverend Curtis spoke about flowed on and on, but you can carve this right under your Dad's dates. You write, 'Here lies a man who could sure hit that ball,' and your Dad'll rest easy, son."

Golf—how his father had loved the game, and how blandly contemptuous and affluently arrogant it had come to seem to his son. Larry assured Gil Conners that that was the best epitaph they had so far, number one, in fact, and then they half-hugged, half-slapped each other on the back. Behind his glasses, Conner's puffed eyes were wet. "God bless you, son. God bless, you, dear," he said, and then when they would have been glad to hold him up a moment longer, he shambled off to his car.

At the van they found Jeff lying half on the mattress with his feet hanging out the back door. He wondered what had taken them so long, but was not about to bring it up, a funeral being something you simply did not rush. When they told him they were going to take a ride, he pulled his feet in and closed the door. Out on the narrow highway running into the hills east of town, he had the feeling that it might now be all over, the funeral, that is. If he got the wording right and asked in a polite manner he thought they might very well say yes. So he gave it some thought. He wrote the sentence out in his head three or four different ways. But he kept snagging on the word "disrespect," which he was determined to work in. Finally, he gave up and said it as simply as he could.

"D'you think Granddad would mind if I played some of my music now?"

He addressed the question to his father, but when his father didn't answer he looked at his mother. She was looking at his father too. Then Jeff looked back and saw that his father was crying, and cursed himself for his selfishness, for his childishness, for his . . . disrespect, for disrespectful was what he'd been.